HELL HATH NO FURY

MICHELLE MORGAN

www.bloodhoundbooks.com

Print ISBN 978-1-914614-27-9

ALSO BY MICHELLE MORGAN

The Webs We Weave

This book is dedicated to Charlotte and Leslie –
For all the 'banana spider' laughs.

Heav'n has no Rage, like Love to Hatred turn'd,
Nor Hell a Fury, like a Woman scorn'd.
– **William Congreve, 1697**

1

It was April. The day was grey, bitter and damp, which fitted my foul mood, and made everything seem even worse than it already was. I was in Simon's car, and despite the rain, he insisted on driving with the window down by three or four centimetres. 'The windscreen will steam up if I don't,' he said, and I didn't have the energy to argue. Simon explained about condensation or steam or something equally as unappealing, but I wasn't interested and didn't understand a word he was saying. Who wanted to know about condensation anyway? Who could think about something so trivial, on a day like this?

The rain splashed onto the window, and sprayed me with that fine mist that seems to soak you from the inside out.

'Simon, please could you put the window up now? My face is getting wet.'

My married lover grunted and pressed the button. My window lurched towards the top of the door, and then the rain splattered against it.

'If we steam up, I'll have to put it down again.'

'Can't you just put the fan on,' I asked, but Simon ignored

me. I wiped the drizzle from my forehead, and tried to straighten my damp fringe.

'Is it much further?' I asked, and Simon shook his head.

'About two miles. I'll drop you off in the short-stay car park, and then you can text me when you're ready to be collected. But if it's after three, you'll need to get a taxi, because I'll be in a meeting.' Simon gave a swift glance at me and shrugged. 'It's with a big client and I can't get out of it. Sorry.'

My breath caught in my chest, and I realised that tears were close to streaming down my face. I held them in because I didn't want Simon to see them. I didn't want him to think I was weak, or childish, or both. We stopped at a traffic light, and I turned my head and gazed out at a young couple, holding hands in the rain, and swinging their arms as they laughed at some private joke. They looked around the same age as me, and yet they could saunter down the road together, happy in each other's company. No seedy hotel rooms for them. No instructions not to call at home or God forbid – go visit. Not that I ever knew his address, to be honest.

Nineteen years old! I was just nineteen years old!

I felt like I was fifty-five.

How had I gone from a happy, innocent acting student, to carrying the baby of my married, thirty-five-year-old lover? It had all happened so quickly that I was still trying to catch up. As the lights turned green, memories of the last three months streamed into my mind. Simon Travis was the marketing consultant drafted in to organise a campaign for my acting school's performance of *Oliver Twist*. The play had been done so often that I wondered how anyone but our parents could ever be interested in seeing it. But credit where it's due – Simon had come in, seen the performance with fresh eyes, and was somehow able to get the public excited about it.

During the first day he was on set, Simon wandered over as I

2

was sipping warm water from a paper cup. I had a toothache and it took all my energy to give him a smile. He was tall, with thick black hair and broad shoulders, but his legs were a little thin, and didn't really match the rest of his body. He wore a pale-blue shirt that was unbuttoned at the collar, and untucked from his black jeans. Simon's nose had a small bump in the middle, and he had a brown freckle below his left eye. I couldn't take my eyes off it as he spoke to me.

'So, who are you playing?' he asked. He smoothed his hair, and I noticed his perfect nails and a gold wedding band, glinting under the lights.

'I've only got a small part,' I answered. 'I'm playing a servant in the posh guy's house.' My sore tooth throbbed against my gum and it took me all my time not to wince.

'A servant? I'd have thought for sure that you'd be that girl who's in love with the evil bloke. What's her name?'

'Nancy?'

'Yes, that's her. I could see you playing her.'

I didn't know how to react to that. Was he saying I was talented enough to play such a big role, or was he implying that I looked like a life-worn prostitute? Either way, I shook my head and got back to swooshing the warm water around my irritated mouth.

A week later, Simon was back in the rehearsal room again. This time clutching a bunch of files and photographs that he showed off to the director. The two of them bundled themselves into a corner and yet every time I let my eyes wander over there, Simon would stare back. At one point I could have sworn he even winked at me, though at the time, I put that down to a flicker from the stage lights.

That evening, we both happened to leave the building at the same time, and Simon offered to give me a lift home. I should have said no, but it was cold and late and I was desperate to get to bed. Besides that, in our conversations between scenes, he had proved to be rather fun with his quick wit and jokes. Despite the age gap, I was growing to like him.

A lot.

I slipped into the car and ten minutes later we were parked in a lay-by in a country lane. As Coldplay rang out from Simon's CD player, he slumped in his seat, and complained that he hadn't slept with his wife in two years. I wasn't sure how that had anything to do with me, but I smiled and responded in all the right places, and concentrated on listening to the music.

'I plan on speaking to a solicitor soon,' he said. 'My wife and I haven't been a real couple in years. It's time to let go, but I'm just worried about the kids, that's all.'

I knew where the conversation was going, but it didn't make me feel uncomfortable. In normal circumstances, I'd have wished I had taken the bus home after rehearsal, or maybe even phoned my dad. But instead, I felt special that this older man had turned his head in my direction, though I also knew that I was entering dangerous territory.

I may have been flattered, but I wasn't stupid.

Or at least I didn't think I was.

'You've got kids?' I was surprised because I had never thought of him as a dad, but why would I? In all the times I'd seen him at rehearsals, I'd never thought of his private life at all. Why would I?

Simon smiled and turned on the interior light.

'Yeah, two of them. My son is thirteen and my daughter is ten.' He reached into his pocket and sprung open his wallet. I couldn't help but notice the shape of a condom, stuffed into one of the pockets. 'Here they are. Great kids. Must take after my side of the family.'

I didn't know if he was serious or joking, so I didn't laugh, just in case.

'They're very nice,' I said, and then regretted saying something so trite.

'Thanks. I'm going to check out an apartment next week, so that I can make the break from the wife. We'll see how it goes. It would be nice to move forward at last.'

He turned off the interior light, and stuffed the wallet back into his pocket. Then he twisted his body round to face mine, and brushed my knee with his hand.

'How old are you, Lottie?'

'My name is Charlotte.'

He laughed, and bit his lip.

'Okay... How old are you, Charlotte?'

I'd like to think that I was grown-up enough not to fall for his patter, but the way he said my name stirred something inside of me. I knew that whatever was about to happen in that car, I had no resistance or strength to stop it.

'I'm nineteen.'

He whistled through his teeth.

'Nineteen! Wow! I'm thirty-five, but it doesn't seem two minutes since I was your age. I'm still wondering how I got so old.'

'You're not old.'

'I'm not?'

I shook my head, and two seconds later, Simon's lips were pressed down on mine, and his hand had left my knee and was heading up my thigh and under my panties. I felt his fingers enter me and I gasped. I had never been touched this way by an older man, much less a married one, and while I knew I had not given direct consent for this to happen, it didn't feel as though he was taking advantage of me. Nobody had forced me to get into the car, and I hadn't protested when he pulled over in the country lane. I wasn't a virgin, and as his tongue entered my mouth and his hand pushed up inside my bra, it didn't feel wrong at all. In fact, it felt nothing but good.

At the time.

Over the coming months, Simon and I met in a variety of different hotel rooms around town. He was much more experienced than any man I had ever been with, and he taught me everything I wanted to know about my body and his. Most of the time Simon wore a condom, but sometimes he 'forgot' to put one on. After the first time it happened, he told me not to worry; that he was free of disease, and his children were born via IVF because he had a low sperm count.

'I've been told that I'm unlikely to father any children naturally,' he told me, with a shrug of regret. 'Slow swimmers. Had to use a sperm donor for the kids, which was fine, because they're still my kids, despite the biology.'

I didn't care to hear about his struggles with fertility, but I listened because I wanted to be the girl who empathised with his failures and celebrated his successes. I'm ashamed to say that I never felt sorry for his wife, because Simon told me that they were together in name only. As far as I was concerned, he wanted more than anything to leave, but found it hard because of his children. I found it endearing how much he loved them, and how despite everything, he never wanted them to be hurt.

Simon made his wife sound like the ultimate bitch: a cold narcissist; frigid and incapable of loving anyone but herself. I decided I would be the woman he left her for, and while I knew I had not been raised to treat another human being so badly, at that moment I didn't care, because she didn't love him, and I wanted him more than I'd wanted any other man in my life.

I told Simon that I loved him, about a month into our affair, and he smiled and kissed me on the forehead, and told me that he was fond of me too. Fond of me! The words rang in my ears for weeks, until one afternoon when we were lying in yet another hotel bed. My lover's hands traced their way up and down the curve of my waist, and he looked me dead in the eye and smiled.

'I love you, Lottie,' he said. 'I've never felt this way about anyone in my entire life.'

I believed every single word he said, because I needed to. If he'd told me he was a rocket scientist who flew to Mars in his spare time, I'd have believed that too.

After that, whenever we spent any time together, I'd smile and thank God that Simon was mine now. It had been so long since he'd had sex at home, that I felt as though I was doing him a favour. I was compliant with every sexual idea he had, and I was convinced that we'd be together for the rest of our lives. Just as soon as his unloving wife could let go, we'd be able to settle down, have our own family, and buy a home... One of those big houses with the long driveway and the fancy cars parked outside. We'd have dinner parties for his colleagues, and they'd congratulate Simon on his amazing taste, and ask how he managed to win over such a perfect, young woman...

It makes me cringe when I think about what a bloody fool I was. I'm ashamed of the person I became while I was with my married lover, but at the time I couldn't help myself. It was as though he had control of everything in my head. He just had to push a button, and I ran to him, ready to do anything he asked me to.

Because I thought I loved him.

And I believed he loved me, too.

Maybe he did. In his own way.

After a while, we started to alternate the hotels we went to, because Simon said that way nobody would know what we were up to. I may have been a besotted teenager, but even I knew that was ridiculous. Everyone knew what we were doing. The cast and crew of the play would give each other sly looks every time we 'discreetly' left the theatre together, and even the director raised his eyebrows whenever Simon arrived at rehearsals.

At first, I wondered how anyone could have known about our affair, but then it struck me – no businessman in history had been that committed to a crummy student play. Didn't he have other work to do? Other marketing projects to organise? Probably, and yet every day he'd find some reason to visit the rehearsal room, even if it was a poster to drop off, or a form to sign. Documents that could be delivered via email, were handed over in person, and a quick text became a long, face-to-face conversation. Afterwards, we would leave separately, and then I'd hop into his car when nobody was there to notice.

But they did notice, and my friend, Sophie, was the first to comment on it.

'You know some of the other students are calling you the college whore, right?'

I swung my head and gave her the dirtiest look I could manage. Sophie threw her hands in the air.

'Hey, it's not me who's saying it. I told them to cut it out, but you know what they're like. Everybody loves a good gossip.'

'Tell them to mind their own business,' I said. 'Simon and I are friends, that's all.'

Sophie didn't believe me, and neither did anyone else in the cast. They continued to talk, but I was too blinded by Simon to care. As far as I was concerned, soon we'd be together full-time. We would rule the world!

Things changed two months later, when I saw two pink dots appear on a pregnancy test. I sat alone in the bathroom of my parents' house, and my heels bounced off the floor as I studied the results. Pregnant! I was pregnant! But how could I be? Simon had been so sure that he was infertile – or at least that is what he'd convinced me of – that it had never crossed my mind that we could make a baby together.

As I headed to meet Simon for a date in yet another hotel, I couldn't help but allow a little bit of excitement to creep into my heart. Okay, so it wasn't something that was planned, but we were in love, weren't we? We'd have wanted a family sooner or later anyway, and this might just be the push he needed to break free from the shackles of his loveless marriage. I had to keep telling myself that.

But things didn't quite work out the way I thought they would. When I told Simon that I had a surprise for him, his first thought was that I'd bought some slinky underwear or kinky sex-related toys. He waggled his eyebrows and laughed, but his excitement soon disappeared when I held the test out to him. Instead of being happy, or even accepting of the fact that we had created a child, the first thing Simon did was snatch the test from my hand, and stuff it into his pocket.

'We can't risk anyone seeing this,' he said. 'I'll get rid of it later.'

A ripple of sadness engulfed my heart. When my married older cousin found out she was pregnant, she kept her test in a fancy box, along with the baby's first booties, lock of hair and other items of memorabilia. I had hoped to do the same, but now my pregnancy test was destined for the trash. Simon paced around the room; straightened pictures, adjusted curtains and played with those little sugar sachets that come on the tea tray. But not once did he look at me.

'I know the number of a clinic – it's a good one and they'll take care of you, but we'll have to move quickly...'

'What do you mean, a clinic? You mean to confirm the pregnancy? I can do that with my own doctor.'

Looking back, I must have been the most stupid nineteen-year-old who ever existed, but you've got to understand that I was inexperienced and besotted with this person.

This person who had cried on my shoulder about how much his wife hated him, but wouldn't let him leave…

This person who told me I was the only woman he had ever loved…

This person who disappeared before my very eyes.

Simon slumped onto the bed beside me, and grabbed my hand. His palm was cold and sweaty, and the complete opposite to how it felt every time he ran it up my thigh or over my breasts.

'Lottie…'

'Charlotte!'

'Charlotte, you're not seriously thinking that we can keep this baby, are you? It's impossible under the circumstances. You know it is.'

I didn't hear his words in my ears alone. Instead, they travelled down to the depths of my stomach, where the tiny new life was just beginning. I had been hurt by men before, but Simon's reaction had to be the worst I'd ever experienced. My lungs felt as though they were collapsing, and I wondered if I'd ever breathe again. This must be a joke. Cruel and senseless, yes, but a joke nonetheless.

Except it wasn't.

I snatched my hand from under his, and rubbed it on the duvet; ridding myself of his touch and scent; trying to delete this conversation from my mind.

'I don't understand,' I said. 'You told me that once you'd left your wife, we would get our own place and settle down. I know it's earlier than we thought it would be, but it's still okay. Maybe if she knows about the baby, your wife will let you go and you can get on with your life.'

His mobile rang, and he sprang up to decline the call.

'That was her, wasn't it? Why didn't you just answer it and tell her what's happened? You could have all of this sorted by lunchtime!'

Simon curled his arms over his head, and groaned.

'For God's sake, Charlotte, will you grow up? I can't tell my wife about this! She would use it against me when we do get divorced!'

'But...'

'No!'

I threw my hands to my face and burst into tears, right there in that dingy little hotel room, with the UHT milk on the dresser, and the fake flowers on the table. Everything was fake in that room. Every little thing. The tears didn't stop, and it was several minutes before I heard Simon sigh and sit down beside me. He nestled my head onto his shoulder and rocked me like a child... Rocked me like the child he didn't want.

'You know we can't have this baby, don't you, Charlotte? It's too complicated. It's not the way I imagined it to be.'

I pulled myself away from his grasp, and wiped my eyes on the back of my sleeve.

'What do you mean, not the way you imagined it to be? According to you, you couldn't even have children naturally, so surely you didn't imagine anything at all.'

Simon touched the base of his neck, and swallowed so deeply that I could see his muscles contract.

'I... I just thought that if a miracle happened and we were ever blessed with a child, it would be when all of this business with my marriage was over. We'd have our own place, and she – or he – would come racing into the bedroom in the morning, and throw themselves in the middle of us, demanding to watch *Peppa Pig*, or *Mr Tumble*, or whatever they watch nowadays...'

He laughed as though he could actually imagine such a thing, and for a moment I felt certain that I could change his mind. I reached out and touched Simon's shoulders. They were so tight they felt like granite.

'If you leave her now, we can still have those things! We

could get a house long before the baby is due! It doesn't even need to be in Northamptonshire. We could go anywhere we like! We've got at least another seven or eight months...'

Simon tightened his fists and lowered his voice.

'No, Charlotte. It can't happen like this. With a bit of luck, maybe we can have a baby in a few years, but we can't have this one. Not now. Not this way. Besides, I've got my career to think about. I'm in line for a promotion, but this scandal could halt the whole thing. Do you understand?'

I nodded, though in reality I didn't understand a thing. Just months ago, I was a budding actress, content only when rehearsing a part or standing under the theatre lights. All I had ever wanted was to become a professional actress, but this man had entered my life and sent everything spiralling out of control. I'd have done anything for him, but the only thing he wanted from me now was to visit a clinic and rid him of the 'problem'.

And so, two days later, I sat at the traffic lights on a damp April day, and wished that the line of cars would never move. Or I hoped that if it did, we'd get to the clinic, and they would be closed... Forever. Or even better – I wished that Simon would realise what a terrible mistake he was making, and he'd scoop me into his arms like in this romantic comedy I had once watched with my mum.

But as we pulled into the hospital car park, there was no sign of regret from him at all, and no change of plan. Instead, he pulled the car into a waiting spot, left the engine running and let out a sigh.

'Don't forget, if you're ready after three, you'll have to get a taxi. Just keep the receipt and I'll pay you back.' He put his hand on my shoulder, and I tried to shrug it off, but he was too strong. 'If you're out before three, give me a call and I'll try to get out of work to pick you up. I can't promise anything, but I'll try.'

He gave me a quick kiss on the top of my head.

'Good luck, Charlotte,' he said. 'I'll be thinking of you.'

My hands shook so much that I wondered if I'd get the door open, but a few seconds later, the cold, wet wind hit my face and I slid out of the car. I walked two steps and then turned to ask my lover if he was sure this was the right thing to do.

But he had already closed the door and was driving across the car park.

And I never saw him again...

Until now...

Ten years later.

2

Simon Travis. Simon Travis. His name whirrs around inside my head until I feel nauseous. What is he doing here? I can't let him see me, and yet I'm not sure how I can escape without him bumping into me.

I'm on the top floor of Waterstones bookshop in Northampton. I only popped in to see if they had the new Stephen King novel, but now I'm hiding in the horror section, book clutched to my chest and hoping that this won't turn into my own version of a thriller. Simon stands in the sports section, looking at a book about Ian Botham. His hair is greyer now – salt and pepper my mum would call it – but he still looks the same. A little bigger perhaps, but aren't we all, ten years later? He must be forty-five by now. Middle-aged, heading towards fifty, but still holding on to his looks.

Blood rushes to my head, and I feel as though my arms are hanging by threads. My heart thumps so loudly that I half expect someone to tell me to be quiet. Twenty minutes ago, I was drinking coffee in the café next door, but now I feel dehydrated, as though I haven't ingested any fluids in a week. I need to get out of here, but how? How can I escape this man I have avoided for the past decade?

There is one route from the top floor to the bottom, and that is through a door right next to where Simon is standing. I can't risk going past him, so instead, I continue to loiter in my section, half-hidden by a stack of new Dean Koontz books. I open up my Stephen King novel, and pretend to read, though in reality, my eyes are poking over the top, like in one of those bad 1930s spy films my gran loves so much. Simon is enthralled by his book, and next to him a woman crouches down, examining a book that I can't make out. It isn't until she stands up and talks to Simon that I realise who she must be.

His wife.

So much for their marriage being over, ten years ago! If it was, they seem to have recovered rather nicely, I must say. What a fool I was to believe his lies, but at least I had an excuse – I was just nineteen years old. What's his excuse for being a lying, manipulating bastard? I watch the couple cosy up amongst the sports biographies, and memories of that awful day come flooding back to me. Standing on the pavement outside the clinic; distressed and alone. Needing the father of my child to give me some kind of support, as I prepared to go through such a traumatising event, and yet receiving nothing but a view of the back end of his car. As I seethe at the obscenity of his behaviour, I lower the book from my face, and it is at that point that Simon looks up and sees me.

Shit.

His face is inquisitive at first. His eyebrows knit together and he tilts his head to one side, as if trying to figure out where he knows me from, and who I am. His wife recognises his curiosity and seconds later she, too, stares over in my direction. I lift the book once again but it's too late. I can hear the woman ask who I am, and then they're both next to me, close enough that I can smell her perfume and feel his aura wafting around my head.

'Hey! Lottie, isn't it?'

I lower the book and there he is; eyes burrowing into my face. Still trying to infuriate me by calling me by the wrong name.

'It's Charlotte, actually. Hello.'

'Right! Yeah! I thought it was you! How've you been?'

'I've been fine, thank you.'

Simon reaches over and grabs my hand, pumping it as though I'm some kind of long-lost business associate. I guess in a way, I am. Meanwhile, the woman stares at me, and I have no option but to meet her eyes and smile. She looks to be in her early forties: sleek, black bob, impeccable make-up, white jacket, high-heels and pencil skirt. She's every inch the wife of a successful businessman, and the complete opposite of me, in my scruffy jeans, old winter coat and trainers.

Simon drops my hand and I reach for his wife's. It's cold and clammy, and when she lets go, I have to resist the urge to reach into my bag for my antibacterial gel.

'I'm Charlotte,' I say. 'I used to work with your husband. Kind of.'

Her head flinches, and she scrunches her mouth into a ball.

'I'm Monica. And you kind of worked with my husband? That sounds ominous.'

There's a chuckle, though it doesn't reach her eyes. Simon recognises her confusion, and runs his hand through his hair. His wedding ring laughs at me; laughs at the way I let him walk all over me, back in the day.

'Charlotte was in one of the plays I helped to publicise when I worked at my old place. *A Christmas Carol*, wasn't it? 2010?'

He's such a bullshitter.

'*Oliver Twist.* 2011.'

'Right! I knew it was some Charles Dickens thing. I see you've moved on from the classics now though.'

'Pardon?'

Simon pulls the book away from my chest, and taps the cover.

'Stephen King. I've just finished reading that one. It's pretty good. Not as good as *The Stand*, but then again, what is?'

Monica smirks.

'Well, *Misery* is more my cup of tea, but it's all subjective.' She grabs Simon's wrist and studies his watch. 'Darling, we need to get a move on, if we're going to pick up Betty.'

'Oh right, yes. We need to shoot off, but it was nice to see you again, Charlotte.'

I nod, and then without a goodbye, Simon and Monica head across the sales floor and disappear through the archway that leads to the staircase. As they round the bend, my former lover takes one last look, and then gives a brazen wave.

I don't respond.

I can't stop shaking as I drive away from the shopping centre and head back to Bromfield-on-the-water, the village where I have lived my whole life. What is he doing in Northampton? The last thing I heard about Simon fucking Travis was that he had moved to London to start his own marketing business, and I knew that because I looked him up on LinkedIn about six months after he did a runner. I breathed a sigh of relief, and tried not to think of him again. As far as I was concerned, he had gone and I hoped he'd never return. But now here he is in my nearest branch of Waterstones, and I don't like it. I don't like it at all.

I pull into the Bromfield Primary car park and turn the radio up. The 1980s station blasts Wham! into the car, and I feel comforted. Not that I was around in the eighties, but my mum was, and she played those tunes all the time when I was a kid. And beyond. The man in the car next to me winds his window up. I crank the volume even more, and then I close my eyes and hum along to 'Freedom', trying to rid myself of the vision of Simon and his awful, understanding wife. Does she know what a lying creep he is? She can't, otherwise she'd have divorced him by now. Just like he told me he was going to do, a decade ago.

The passenger door flies open, and my almost-ten-year-old son, Tom, throws himself into the passenger seat. His strawberry-blond hair flops down into his eyes as he heaves his backpack onto the seat behind us.

'Hi, Mum,' he says.

'Hey, baby,' I reply, and give him a kiss on the top of his head.

'Eww! Don't do that here! Somebody might see!'

Tom rubs at the top of his head, and I laugh.

'Had a good day?'

He leans over and turns down the radio.

'Why are you always listening to granny music?' he asks. 'Charlie's mum listens to rap. Can we listen to rap?'

'No, we can't. Now pop your seat belt on. It's Friday, and you know what that means!'

'Lasagne!' he shouts, and then licks his lips.

I laugh, and ruffle his hair, and his little hand flies up to straighten it again. My beautiful boy. The same beautiful boy who wouldn't even be here, if Simon Travis had had his way.

3

As I watched the red lights on Simon's Audi head out of the clinic car park, the enormity of what I was about to do struck me right in the centre of my stomach. I knew I was still a teenager, but I had been grown up enough to get myself into this situation in the first place. I also felt that given the chance, I was more than capable of caring for my own baby. My mother's four siblings were all younger than her, meaning that I had always been surrounded by cousins of various ages, so I knew the score.

Every Sunday our families would get together, and me being the oldest, I would be put forward as an unpaid babysitter or children's entertainer. I had lost count of the number of times I'd read them my mum's old copies of *The Magic Faraway Tree* or *The Naughtiest Girl in the School.* I even changed more than my fair share of nappies, and was always eager to give a bottle to a hungry baby cousin. It was good training for the future, even if I hadn't realised that the future would start so soon.

I shuffled towards the clinic doors, and they slid open with a screeching, unwelcoming sound. I went inside, but not enough to ensure that the doors closed behind me. Instead, they made a juddering movement, as if they couldn't decide if they were open, closed or somewhere in-between.

A middle-aged woman with a 1950s hairdo and horn-rimmed glasses, looked up from the reception desk.

'Can I help you?'

Her smile was warm and comforting, and her voice managed to calm the beating in my chest, even for a moment.

'I... I...'

I turned to take one last look into the car park, and saw Simon heading out of the exit. His wheels made a squealing sound on the tarmac as he turned onto the road. He couldn't get away quick enough.

'Do you mind if I just sit here for a moment?' I asked the lady with the warm smile.

'Of course,' she said. 'Take all the time you need. When you're ready, just let me know and we'll get you booked in.'

I nodded and sat down on one of the blue plastic chairs, lined up against the wall. Across from me, a young woman with flame-red hair filled in a form; her hand flying across the page as though her life depended on it. She sat with her boyfriend; his knees shaking up and down as he watched her write. His face was ashen, and every so often he rubbed his mouth with the back of his hand, and took a deep breath. He was nervous – terrified even – but at least he was there. At least he had come into the clinic with his partner, instead of dropping her at the door with barely a goodbye.

I gazed at my surroundings in an attempt to calm myself, but it was a losing battle. I'd never been in a private clinic, and it was certainly more attractive than my local doctor's surgery, but that said, I'd have rather been anywhere else than in that room. There was a wall-mounted television, showing a muted episode of *This Morning*, and a round, three-legged coffee table with a pile of old, ragged magazines on the top. Next to me, a table hosted a machine that offered free coffee in white paper cups, but my stomach gurgled to even think about drinking coffee at that moment in time.

Across from me, the flame-haired girl finished filling in the form, and handed it to the receptionist. She caught my eye on the way back to her chair, but neither of us smiled, as though we thought maybe it was inappropriate under such circumstances. Her boyfriend picked up a copy of *Vanity Fair* magazine from the table, and offered it to her, but she shook her head, and he threw it back onto the pile. As they waited their turn to be called, I held no judgement towards them or anyone else who might find themselves in that room. But as I stared at a painting of a dense, foggy forest, I knew that I'd never be ready to book myself in. I couldn't give up my baby just because Simon Travis told me to, and at that moment I realised just how controlling and domineering he had been, over the months I had known him. I had gone along with it all without question, but that was about to change.

As soon as the realisation hit me, I sprung up from my chair. The kind lady at the desk smiled, and expected me to approach her, but instead, I turned and bolted for the door. It swished open and I threw myself out so quickly that I almost bumped into a passing woman. I mumbled an apology, and then threw up in a nearby flower bed.

While I worried about how I would break the news to Simon, in the end I didn't have to, because he never came back to the theatre. The director made an announcement that he was leaving our marketing work to a client, while he pursued other projects. Simon said he was sorry that he wouldn't be able to see us shine in our future productions, but – just like in a failed job interview – he wished us the best in our future endeavours.

As the director read Simon's prepared statement, several people gawped at me. I knew what they were thinking. We must have had some kind of lovers' tiff, and he'd gone back to his wife. I never commented on it. Instead, I just wondered how pretentious you had to be to prepare a leaving statement for a student theatre production. I had been so wrapped up in Simon that I hadn't seen how egotistical he was, but now it all made sense.

What a wanker.

I wondered for several weeks if I should tell my lover what I had done, but then decided it was best not to. After all, he had arranged the termination, dumped me at the clinic, and then disappeared from my life. What possible good could come of him knowing that I was going to raise his child? Besides, I realised that in spite of the 'love' we held for each other, he had never shared his home address with me, and his phone was a pay-as-you-go, which was switched off the moment he left the show. There was a method in his madness, my mum said, as I cried on her shoulder and explained – with minor details – what had been going on with an unnamed, older man.

'You're not the first, and you won't be the last,' Mum said. 'But you'll be fine, and so will my grandchild.'

My dad paced the room and seethed.

'If I get my hands on him, I'll end up in prison,' he snapped. I couldn't help but smile at that remark. God bless my five-foot-six-inches, skinny dad. He wouldn't stand a chance against Simon Travis, but it made him happy to imagine that he did.

∾

That was over ten years ago, and now here I am, with a beautiful boy, who I have never regretted keeping. Not even when he was teething, or throwing himself on the floor in the middle of Tesco, aged two. No, not ever have I regretted having Tom. He's my everything, and even though I gave up my acting aspirations as soon as that production of *Oliver Twist* was over, I couldn't care less. Acting has given way for a part-time job as a school receptionist, dreams of living in a mansion in Beverly Hills have turned into the reality of a tiny rented cottage in Bromfield-on-the-water, and the idea of a fulfilling love life is just that – an idea.

But in spite of the sacrifices I have made over the years, I can honestly say that I am happy and I am content. If I have any regrets, they're few and too small to talk about, but I do know this – I have never regretted declining to tell Simon about his son.

Not once.

Not ever.

But now, in one trip to Waterstones, the life I've created for my son and I over the past ten years seems fragile. What if Simon knows about Tom? What if that's why he's back in Northamptonshire? No, I don't think that's possible. I never named him on the birth certificate, I never discuss Tom's father with anyone at all, and the one time my son asked about him, was when he was five. I explained that his dad was somebody who chose not to be in our lives, but assured him that it didn't matter; that me and his grandparents loved him more than anything. He has never asked about him since, though I'm sure one day that will change.

My mind whirrs, trying to think of other ways Simon could have found out. Not from social media. I don't have Twitter or Instagram, I don't use my full name on Facebook, and I limit my posts to real friends and family. There are no photographs of

Tom on my account, and my parents know not to tag me in any posts they may put up, so that my page remains anonymous to the outside world, as far as I'm aware.

If I think about it, there is no reason for Simon to know about Tom, and the chances of him returning to Northamptonshire for that reason, are miniscule. He was last seen speeding away from me, and if he had the slightest inkling about Tom, I'm sure he'd continue to head in the opposite direction.

At least I hope he would.

'Mum, is dinner ready?'

My thoughts are interrupted by Tom, leaning on the door frame, holding a book about Al Capone, with his school uniform awry. I shake myself back to reality, and smile.

'Not yet, I was just about to make it,' I say.

Tom licks his lips.

'Don't forget to put on extra cheese, please,' he says, before darting out of the door and sprinting up the stairs.

'Change out of your uniform, and stick it in the wash,' I shout, as his bedroom door slams closed behind him.

I go into our tiny galley kitchen and gather together everything I need to make a lasagne good enough for my son. Cheese, pasta sheets, white sauce, tomato sauce... What else do I need? Mince. You can't cook lasagne without mince. I stoop down to take the meat out of the fridge, and as I do so, there's a terrific crash from outside. I jerk and the packet jumps out of my fingers and back into the fridge. Good catch.

I shut the fridge and then open the back door. It's beginning to get dark, and the familiar feel of autumn is in the air. Damp twigs, and the heavy smell of burnt leaves, makes me want to reach for a dish and make pumpkin pie. If I knew how to. Baking has never been my strong point.

Over the fence, I can hear the voice of my neighbour and friend, Zach.

'For God's sake, Trevor,' he mutters. 'What the hell have you done?'

'Are you okay?' I pop my head over the rickety old fence that separates us, and see Zach standing in the middle of what looks like the remains of a tornado. He's wearing a T-shirt with rock band Kiss emblazoned across the front, and his black hair sticks up in all directions. His jeans are torn at the knees, and for reasons unknown to me, they are tucked into his electric-blue socks. He's a mess, but a friendly, welcoming mess.

'Hi!' He flashes a smile, and then grimaces. 'I thought I'd do good and shove all the remains of the old shed into a bonfire, but Trevor had other ideas.'

Trevor is Zach's crazy Labrador, and – it would seem – creator of the tornado. The dog stares at me from the patio, a plank of wood in his mouth, and his tail wagging as though about to take off.

'I'd watch him if I were you,' I say, gesturing towards Trevor. 'If there are any sharp bits on that wood, you'll be worrying about more than an abandoned bonfire.'

Zach takes a step towards the dog, and it swerves him and heads off to the bottom of the garden, slowing only to manoeuvre his way around the old apple tree.

'I'll have to get it when he's calmed down,' Zach says. 'He's worse than having a kid sometimes.'

'Ha, wait until you have one of those, and then come back to me.' I smile and wonder what it must be like to be in your mid-twenties with just the responsibility of a dog instead of a child. But in all honesty, I can say that while Tom has had his moments over the years, he's never ran through an unlit bonfire, and sprinted off with a plank of wood in his mouth. Thank goodness.

Trevor bounds up to Zach, and the two embark on a tug of war with the timber. I watch for a moment, before a voice catches up with me from the upstairs window.

'Mum!' Tom shouts. 'When's the lasagne gonna be ready? Hi, Zach!'

Zach looks up and waves, while Trevor sees an opportunity to make a run for it.

'I've got to go,' I say. 'But you can come over later if you like? There's something I want to talk to you about.'

Zach stoops down to gather up the bonfire wood again.

'Sure. I'll bring some wine.'

I guess at this point I should explain something about my neighbour. Zach has lived next door for a couple of years, and we've been friends ever since Trevor came charging through the fence and joined the picnic that Tom and I were enjoying in the garden. Once we'd got over the shock, Zach joined us for the afternoon and we've been friends ever since.

Some people may wonder if we've ever been a couple, or have even come close to getting together. The answer is no. Kind of. Sometimes. It's a bit complicated, as they say. We're both single, and we have got 'together' a few times over the years – normally after a drunken evening in front of Netflix. I guess that's what they call friends with benefits, or something. Anyway, we don't give it a label, or even talk about it. If we end up in bed together, we just pretend like it never happened, and then get on with our friendship. Is that healthy? Probably not in the long run, but it works for us. For now.

I bid my neighbour goodbye, and leave behind the damp air and smell of conkers and pine cones, as I head back into the warmth of the kitchen. As I go to close the door, there is a rustle in the bushes at the bottom of the garden. My heart leaps into my mouth, and then the ginger cat from down the road launches itself onto the bird table.

'Shit!' I throw my hand up to my chest, and grab onto the sink. Damn Simon Travis. He's got me scared of a cat now. I slam the door before the feline finds its way into my kitchen, and then I lock and bolt it. Just in case.

~

'So, what did you do when you saw him there? I bet you almost shit yourself!'

Zach throws his feet onto my little green stool, and takes a large glug of rosé wine. He's heard little bits about Tom's dad over the past two years, and to hear that he's back in Northamptonshire has got my friend intrigued to say the least.

'Shush! I don't want Tom to hear our conversation.'

My friend gestures towards the ceiling.

'His music is on full blast. He can't hear his own voice, never mind ours! What is that anyway? It's just a noise to me.'

I laugh, and reach for the bowl of chilli crisps on the coffee table.

'You sound like an old man. It's some kind of rap thing. I think his friend told him about it.'

Zach grimaces and holds his hands to his ears.

'Awful,' he says. 'I hope it's just a phase, or you may not see me for a while. Anyway, back to what happened earlier. How did it feel to be in his company? It must have been a shock at the very least.'

'To be honest, it was terrifying. I'd got more than used to not having Simon in my life, but then there he was, standing right in front of me with his wife of all people. The one he was supposed to be leaving when we were involved with each other. I tried not to show any kind of emotion, but I'm sure he was well aware of my discomfort.'

'Ooh, what was she like?'

I untie my hair, and it flops down to my shoulders. I need to get it cut, but Tom needs new shoes this month, so it'll have to wait.

'Slim, bobbed hair, forties... Dressed like someone you'd see on one of those old eighties programmes, like *Dallas* or *Dynasty*.'

'Have no clue what they dress like, but wow anyway.'

Zach crosses his arms, and his nose wrinkles.

'I wonder why Simon left London. If you like, I can see what I can find out about him. Do some digging in the databases.'

My friend is a reporter, who sees everything as a potential story. His research skills come in useful for things like advance concert ticket sales, or finding out who is turning on the Christmas lights, but I'm not sure how he could help in this scenario. I shake my head.

'Thanks for the offer, but no, it's okay.'

'You sure?'

'Yeah. To be honest, I was hoping he was just here for a visit, but then Monica mentioned picking up someone called Betty, who I think must be their daughter – so maybe it's more than a visit. Who knows? Either way, I wish he'd never shown up in Northampton. It's far too close for my liking, and I've been anxious ever since.'

Zach leans over and pats my shoulder, as though I'm a little puppy on the way to the vets.

'Don't worry about it,' he says. 'Everything between you is ancient history by now.'

'Not everything.' I gesture upwards, where Tom's music is still thudding through the ceiling. Zach waves my comment away.

'Listen, you have no reason to worry about Tom. As far as Simon Travis knows, Tom doesn't even exist.'

'But is that true though? Maybe he's found out, and that's why he's back.'

My voice cracks, and I bite down on my lip in an effort not to cry. I'm too emotional sometimes. It's my biggest flaw, according to my mother.

'Hey!' Zach says, 'Simon does not know about Tom, and if he did, don't you think that Northamptonshire would be the last place he'd be? He doesn't sound like the sort who would step up to his responsibilities.'

'I did think about that earlier, but then I don't know if I'm kidding myself.'

Zach grabs my glass of wine from the table, and hands it to me.

'You're not kidding yourself, and you know it. That guy has no reason to be back in your life. Today was just bad timing, that's all.'

I lean back into the cushions, and feel comforted as they swallow me up. Zach's right.

He is right.

Isn't he?

4

The weekend passes with the usual routine – Saturday morning I stand on the sidelines and cheer Tom in his under elevens football match, and then lunch is a pizza from Asda. Pepperoni and pineapple for me, and double cheese for Tom. Then Sunday we head to my parents' house – the same house in Bromfield, where I was born and raised.

After dinner I help my dad with the dishes.

'Are you okay, love?' he asks, as I dry a never-ending stream of pots. I look down the hall towards the living room, and hear Tom and my mum laughing over a game of Scrabble. Should I tell my dad that Tom's father is back in the county? My dad's getting no younger, and I'm not sure how he'll react to the news. I decide not to risk it, and instead, I opt to tell him about my mundane village life.

'I'm fine,' I say. 'I didn't get much sleep last night. I woke up at 1am and Tom was watching television in his bedroom. He had woken up and couldn't get back to sleep, so he decided to watch *Gardener's World* on some random DIY channel. *Gardener's World*! Who would watch that at 1am?'

'Your mother!' Dad laughs, and then reaches into the sink

and wrenches out the plug. The water gurgles down the hole, and leaves a trail of dinner bits behind. Dad blasts the water into the sink and waggles his finger into the plughole until they're all gone. He has the hands of an old man now. The hands I used to see on my granddad, have now jumped onto my dad, and it makes me nervous. My mum and dad tried for years to conceive me, and finally did when my mother was thirty-eight and my dad forty. But while it was a miracle for them, it is now a constant worry for me, because I can't cope with the idea of them becoming old... and the alternative is even worse.

While my dad puts the last of the pots away, I can't help but gaze at him. His grey, thinning hair that sticks up at odd angles, the wrinkles beneath his eyes, and the jowls at the sides of his mouth, that disappear when he smiles. But in spite of their age, my parents are still active, happy and – apart from my mum's high blood pressure – in relatively good health.

'So, who do you think is going to be on *I'm a Celeb* this year? Your mum reckons they'll snap up that woman who chaired that parish council meeting, but I'm not so sure.'

I laugh and shake my head. While I'm here worrying about my parents getting older, they're more concerned with what semi-famous folk will be going into the jungle – or the castle – or wherever they choose to hold the show this year.

This discussion is all so normal for a Sunday afternoon, and yet everything seems different, after the events of Friday. What if Simon is thinking about me right now, while I'm yapping to my dad about silly reality shows? What if he's wondering how to approach me about our former relationship... or our son... or both?

My paranoia is disturbed by Tom, who sprints into the kitchen, arms flying around his head.

'Mum! Granddad! I beat Grandma at Scrabble!'

I turn and give him the biggest smile I can manage.

'You did? Well done!'

My dad gives my son a high-five and a cheer.

'I spelled out zebra for a triple word score!' Tom shouts. 'Z... E... B... R... A... zebra!'

'Fabulous,' I say. 'And how many points did you get?'

Tom shrugs.

'I dunno, but it was enough to beat Grandma!'

He rushes back into the living room and I can hear him demanding another game from my already tired mum. My dad chuckles.

'What a great age. No worries, except beating his grandmother at board games!'

I nod. No worries, indeed. I just hope it stays that way.

I've only been sitting in the school reception for twenty minutes, and already I've had a rabid parent on the phone, a child throwing up in my wastepaper basket, and a teacher complaining that her register is covered with cake crumbs. I turn the parent over to the principal, send the child home with his mother, and deny all knowledge of the crumbs, before I sit down and tally up the cash that's come in for a trip to see a local pantomime. The rest of the world may now be run by online payments, but here at Bromfield Primary School, we still like our cash in envelopes, thank you very much.

As I go through the never-ending supply of twenty-pence pieces and other shrapnel, Tom appears in front of my counter. Most of the time my son avoids me when I'm in my role of part-time receptionist, but when he needs something, I'm the in thing. His friend, Charlie, loiters behind, hands in pockets, pretending he can't see me.

'And what can I do for you, young man?'

Tom grimaces at my fake, old-school secretary voice.

'Year Four are doing a cake sale after assembly, and I don't have any money.'

'What happened to the two-pound coin I put in your pocket on Friday?'

'I spent it on a Year Three sweet sale. They were selling gigantic marshmallows.' Tom's arms shoot outwards, to demonstrate (or exaggerate) just how big these sweets were.

I grab my bag from under the desk, and retrieve my purse. Just as I'm rummaging for a couple of pound coins, the security system notifies me that there is a person coming through the double gates. They've been stuck open ever since we had a delivery of toilet supplies first thing this morning, though I'm assured that they will be fixed by the time I leave at one. I squint at the monitor to see who the visitor is, and my breath catches in my throat.

It can't be.

But it is.

Simon Travis saunters up the middle of the driveway as though he owns the place. My muscles stiffen and my mouth falls open at the sight of him on the screen. What the hell is he doing here? I have no idea, but I thank God (or the security firm) that we have an electronic lock on the door. There's no way he's coming in here.

Just as I'm preparing to dive under the desk and ignore the inevitable buzz of the doorbell, one of the cleaners comes out of the toilets and heads straight for the front door. Before I can stop her, she releases the lock just as Simon reaches the entrance. He smiles and stands back to allow her to pass.

'Mum! Please can I have the money? The Year Four teacher says that everything will be sold out by lunchtime, and we're about to go into assembly!'

Shit, for a split second I had forgotten that my son was

standing in front of me. He needs to be gone. He needs to be gone now!! I grab a five-pound note from my purse and stuff it into his hand.

'Take this, okay? Buy Charlie something as well.'

Tom squeals, and he stares at the note as though it's made of gold.

'Wow, thank you! I can get the biggest cream cake with this!' He grabs his friend and the two of them sprint from the reception and head down the corridor, muttering about how many cupcakes they could buy for five whole pounds.

They have just left when Simon appears in the foyer, held captive between two electronic doors; one leading to the outside, and the other to the inside. Although the cleaner should never have let him in, he can't enter the main school without my consent. However, from where he stands, he does have a clear view of me, sitting just feet away behind a sheet of glass.

I try to keep the fear from my face, as I stare up at the father of my child. He smiles, points at the mechanism that opens the window, and then waggles his finger in an effort to get me to release it. Instead, I speak to him through the security panel in the glass.

'Can I help you?'

Simon laughs.

'Is that an invitation?'

He winks, and bile leaps into my throat. He always was a dirty bastard. My knees knock against the bottom of my counter, and I push down on them with as much force as I can muster. Still they move, but at least from the waist up I seem calm.

'Are you here on some kind of official business? If not, I'm afraid I'll have to ask you to leave.'

'Well, I'm not here to pick up a child, if that's what you mean. My days of being old enough to have primary school kids are long over.'

My stomach lurches, and I think if only he knew... If only he knew.

Does he know?

'Please can you leave. I can't have you in my workplace.' The sternness of my voice shocks me, but by the look on Simon's face, he's amused by it. I need this man to leave. I need him to get out of here before Tom runs back to my desk with his cupcake or whatever he needed the money for.

'Simon!! You found us okay, then?' The voice of our principal, Margaret Holmes, comes booming down the corridor. Margaret likes to think she is in the 1960s, with her long, golden (though going grey) hair, and her never-ending supply of kaftans and flared trousers. Firmly in the Generation X category, Margaret is a flower-power hippie on the outside, and hard as nails on the inside.

My ex-lover waves at her through the glass door, and two seconds later, the principal pushes the interior button and he's inside.

'Hey, Margaret! How's your day going?'

Simon beams at the principal. They must have met before. But where?

'I'm very well, thank you. Thanks again for agreeing to come in for our careers week. The children are used to having talks from doctors or hairdressers, so it'll make a nice change to hear about marketing.'

'You're very welcome. No problem at all.'

Margaret points to the visitors' book.

'Just pop your signature into the book, and Charlotte will give you a badge.'

Simon flashes me a smile, but it's more of a sneer. He leans over and signs the book, and I hand him a badge. His hand lingers a little too long, and he manages to brush his thumb against mine as he backs away.

'Thank you, Charlotte,' he says. He unzips his jacket and pins the badge to his shirt pocket. I feel a lump in my throat, but I swallow it down. I must not let him see that I'm bothered by him. I must not.

I watch as Margaret and Simon Travis saunter off down the corridor, towards the hall. In the distance I can hear the familiar sound of children chattering as they pile into assembly. We've been doing these career talks for several weeks now, and I knew they had all manner of people – parents mainly – booked in, but never did I think one of the speakers would be the father of my child.

Wait!

The blood drains from my face and pools around my shoulders, as I realise that my son – our son – will be one of those eager little humans, waiting for Simon to tell them about his career. I swallow hard. What if Simon sees him? What if he recognises him somehow? I'm told all the time that Tom looks just like me, but there are moments when he'll smile and I'll think of Simon. That lopsided grin that he has, was shared with his son.

I hang around reception long enough to hear the last chain of children trundle towards the hall, and then the familiar cries of 'Shush!' as they enter and take their places on the floor or gym benches. When the hall door clunks shut, I turn the reception phone onto silent mode, and then dart out of my little booth.

I walk about ten feet, before I'm met by Annie Wells, carrying her class register.

'Here's the register, Charlotte,' she says, and then thrusts the folder towards me.

'Thank you, Annie,' I reply. 'Now, hurry to the hall, or you'll be late for assembly.'

'It's okay,' she says. 'My teacher told me I had plenty of time.'

I clutch the register to my chest, and follow Annie as she skips towards the hall. She pushes against the heavy door, and four hundred kids look up at her as she makes her entrance. When the door closes again, I move forward and gaze through the little window at the top, staying at an angle so that I have a direct view of the stage, but nobody else should be able to see me.

Simon Travis is being introduced by Margaret, and from my place behind the door, I can just about hear what she's saying.

'I'd like you all to give a big Bromfield welcome to our special guest. Today we have Mr Simon Travis, who has come to talk to us about his job in something called marketing. Does anyone know what that is?'

A hundred tiny hands shoot up, and Margaret points to one.

'Is it someone who works on the market?' asks a boy from Year One. The older children snigger, while everyone else stays silent and waits for the answer.

'No,' says Margaret, 'it's not someone who works on a market. But that was a terrific answer, Jacob, so well done. I won't bore you with my explanation of what someone in marketing does, because I'm sure Mr Travis can explain it much better. So please clap loud and proud for our special guest. Mr Travis, over to you!'

Margaret steps back, as the hall breaks into applause. Simon thanks the principal and then dives into an inane talk about his work. Some of the children gawp at him with their mouths open, while others whisper to their friends, and teachers tell them to be quiet. At the back of the hall, my son, Tom, sits on the gym benches with his classmates. It's their turn to feel important and grown-up in the 'big kids' area, instead of sitting on the floor with the younger kids. He stares at the stranger in front of him, and seems to soak in everything he says.

Tears sting my eyes when I think of how the speaker is his

father... His father who didn't want him, and cannot ever know about him. Will Tom remember this encounter years down the line? Will he be aware of the man who came to talk to them about his career in marketing? Will this talk sow a seed and Tom will follow his father into that line of work? Will he hold it against me that I never introduced them today? Or any day?

So many questions.

With no immediate answers.

'Excuse me, are you waiting to go in?'

I swing round and see Linda Turner, a permanently offended teacher from Year Two, standing behind me with her arms crossed. Linda looks like a matron from a Carry On film, though I'm told she was a local beauty queen back in the day. Her clothes are always earth tones of brown and green, and mainly woollen and musty-smelling. But the weird thing about Linda is that although her fashion sense is drab and meaningless, her hair is always adorned with a colourful slide in the shape of a flower. She wears a different one every day, and today's specimen is a scarlet rose, with electric-blue tips. Where does she buy these things? Rumour is that she makes them all on the weekend, but I don't dare ask her if that's true.

Linda has been here since 1983, but although she thinks she is senior to everyone in the building, in reality she's never been promoted. She's coming up for retirement, but despite the fact that I've worked here for five years myself, she always talks to me as though I'm a newcomer. I guess if you haven't been here for thirty-odd years, you just don't count.

'No, I'm not waiting,' I say, and I step away from the door so that she can enter.

'I noticed there was someone waiting for you at reception,' she says, poking her grey shoulder-length hair behind her ear. 'Maybe you should go and see what she wants.'

The door whooshes shut behind Linda, and I hurry back to

my desk. There I deal with a little girl with a poorly knee, and then I leave a rambling message on Zach's answer machine. Three minutes later he calls me back.

'Hey! Are you okay? What do you mean Simon is in the school?'

I sigh and hold my hand to my forehead. It feels hot and clammy. Am I coming down with something? I have no idea.

'I mean just that,' I say. 'He came in as an assembly speaker. He's talking to the kids right now! What if Tom recognises him? What then?'

Zach rustles some papers on the other end of the line, and I can almost hear him rolling his eyes.

'Will you calm down? Tom is not going to recognise Simon. He has no idea who he is, other than some old guy coming to talk about jobs. It's all fine. Just breathe, and for goodness' sake, don't let Tom see that you're freaking out. Okay?'

I hold my head in my hand, and try to steady my breathing.

'I'll try,' I say, and then I bid my friend goodbye.

5

It's 1pm and I've just handed over my job to Amy, the afternoon receptionist.

'Did I miss anything important this morning?' she asks.

'No, not a thing,' I lie.

'Nothing at all?'

'What's that they say? Same crap, different day? Yeah, that's what you missed.'

Amy grabs a tube of bright-red lipstick out of her handbag and runs it over her lips, from side to side.

'Sounds fabulous,' she says, and then snaps the lid back onto the lipstick. 'Have a great afternoon. At least it's not raining.'

'You too.' I grab my handbag from under the desk and take one last look up the corridor. The last I saw Simon Travis, he and Margaret were having a working lunch with three other teachers, in the meeting room. I had to carry in a tray of sandwiches and treats supplied from the local bakery, and could feel Simon's eyes trailing me from one end of the room to the other. I never looked at him, and I'm proud of myself for that.

I sling my handbag over my shoulder and press the interior

button. The door swooshes open, and just as I'm about to step through, a familiar voice comes at me from down the hall.

'Hold the door,' Simon shouts, and for a second, I wonder what would happen if I just let it close onto him. Would he be mushed up like one of those cartoon characters that Tom still laughs at? It would be nothing less than he deserves.

I hold my hand on the door, and the sensor beeps at me in disgust.

'Thanks!' Simon piles through, and adds a hasty scribble to the visitors' book. 'You want this?' He flashes his visitors' badge at me, and I shake my head.

'I'm on my way out,' I say. 'You can leave it on the ledge there.'

Simon throws the badge onto the wooden windowsill, but Amy is too busy examining her eyebrows to notice. It's none of my business, so I keep on walking. The low sun hits me as I exit the school, but the crisp autumn air means it holds no warmth whatsoever. I hold my coat around me and hurry up the drive, trying to get away from the sound of Simon's footsteps, right behind me.

'Wait! Hold up! It would be nice to catch up with you. It must be like what? Eleven years since we saw each other? Twelve?'

'It's ten and a half,' I say. How could he forget that?

'If you want to be pedantic, you could always say it's been a matter of days, since we bumped into each other in Waterstones on Friday.'

I look up at him and he flashes that awful smile of his. Too confident, too self-assured... He's a legend in his own lunchtime.

'Funny how we haven't seen each other in a decade, and we bump into each other twice in the space of three days, don't you think?'

'Yeah, it's hilarious.'

He trots beside me in an effort to keep up, but I'm going so quickly it looks like I'm training for a marathon.

'Hey, don't walk so fast. It would be great to catch up with you for a while. Where are you parked? I'm in the car park next to the post office. If you're there too, we could walk together.'

I turn to tell him that I don't need him to walk me to my car, that my car is in the garage of my house, just a mile or so away, but I manage to stop myself at the last moment. I don't need him to know where I live. That's the last thing in the world I need.

'How have you been? You look terrific by the way.'

I ignore Simon's attempts at flattery and instead, point down towards the row of shops, at the end of the street.

'I'm going to the post office,' I say. 'And then I have a dentist appointment, so I need to rush off.'

By now we have left the school premises, and as I head towards the shops, Simon comes too. What am I going to do if he follows me into the post office? Post an imaginary parcel? Enquire about postal orders?

Stamps! I'll buy my Christmas stamps early. Anything to get rid of this idiot.

'So, how long have you worked at the school?' he asks.

I swing round and look him straight in the eye.

'Look, I know you're the master of small talk, and it might have worked with me ten years ago, but it's not going to work on me now. I'm not that nineteen-year-old that you manipulated all those years ago. I'm my own person now.'

Simon jerks back and screws up his eyebrows.

'Manipulated? What are you talking about? We both entered into that relationship if I remember rightly, and I didn't hear you complain at the time.'

He is so out of touch that he doesn't know that I'm referring to him cajoling me into having a termination! Has he forgotten?

Did it mean that little to him? We reach the car park and Simon uses his beeper to open his flash, black BMW.

'Hey,' he says, 'maybe we got off on the wrong foot. Let me buy you lunch. For old times' sake.'

'No thank you. I've told you; I'm going to the post office and then on to the dentist.'

I carry on walking; my hands shaking in my pockets out of rage, or fear or both.

'Another time then?' he shouts, but I don't reply.

'Did you enjoy the careers talk today?' I ask Tom as we're eating dinner. I don't know why I ask, except that I need to know his reaction. I need to know that there was nothing about Simon that seemed familiar or strange... He bites into a piece of chicken, and scowls.

'Oh, the man who talked about his market job? It was okay, I guess. Not as good as when Lily's mum came and talked about being a hairdresser. She brought some wigs, and Mrs Holmes tried one on. She looked like Grandma!'

'Grandma doesn't wear a wig.' I help myself to more roast potatoes, and Tom laughs.

'I bet she would if she had one,' he replies. 'Maybe we should buy her one for Christmas!'

'Oh, I'm sure that would go down well,' I say. 'So, you liked Lily's mum better than the marketing man then?'

'Yes. Lily's mum gave us stickers that had scissors with googly eyes on them. The market man didn't give us anything at all.'

Tom pokes at some green beans with his fork, and I breathe a sigh of relief.

'A bit boring then,' I say, and my son nods.

'Yes, a lot boring!' he replies, and then sticks the beans into his mouth.

It bothers me that Margaret Holmes somehow knows Simon Travis, and I scour my mind for everything I know about her private life. Our head teacher isn't one for sharing personal details, and perhaps the only thing I know about her is that she's not married. One of the teachers got into a fight with her a year or so ago, and caused a magnificent scandal when she remarked that Margaret might loosen up a bit if she found a man. It went all around the school in hours, and it wasn't long until the teacher in question left quietly. Until that remark I just assumed that Margaret was married, but what do I know? I'm not one to go poking into anyone's business.

Until now.

After Tom has gone to bed, I check Margaret out on Facebook. I'm not sad enough to have the principal as my friend, but I'm sure Linda Turner is. I search for Linda's profile, bring up her friends list and sure enough, there is a listing for Margaret Holmes. I click onto her profile, but find that everything is locked down tighter than a high-security prison. There is one photograph – of a sunflower – and her friends list is non-existent. I should have expected it to be like that, since she's the principal of a school, but still, I lived in hope.

I don't know any other way of finding out how Margaret knows my married ex-lover, so I log out of Facebook and turn on the television. Seconds later my phone rings. An unknown number. Expecting it to be a call about my 'recent accident' or some old PPI claim, I sigh and swipe to answer.

'Hello?'

The line is silent, except for a slight buzzing at the other end.

'Hello?'

There is a click, and then a recording tells me that the other person has rung off. I look at the clock. It's 9.23pm. I know that telemarketers don't ring so late, but it must have been one of those. Or a wrong number. I remember one time my dad got a call from some woman waiting for a guy called Tony to pick her up from the pub. She argued for ages that my dad was Tony, until he switched off his phone.

I decide to follow my dad's lead. I hold down the button until it asks if I'd like to switch off, and then I pop it onto the table. After my people-pleasing teenage years, I have now learned to be a woman who can stick up for herself. I have lived on my own with my son since we moved out of my parents' house five years ago, and I'm doing pretty well, thank you very much. However, the past few days have caused a strange sensation in my gut, and having a stranger hang up on me isn't what I had in mind for this evening.

I get up from the chair, and pull the curtains together, so that there are no gaps in the fabric. Then I check the doors for the seventh time, not because I'm paranoid, but because my mother always told me it was better to be safe than sorry.

6

Tuesday morning, and I'm back at my reception desk. Tom has already found a reason to visit me (to show me his new school photograph) and I've had the usual array of phone calls and emails to contend with. But now it's five past eleven and all is quiet. Not long now and I'll be able to hand everything over to Amy, and go home to sort out the washing, before I pick Tom up at 3.30pm.

'Charlotte,' Margaret says, as she marches out of her office, with her oversized handbag dangling from her arm. 'If anyone asks where I am, please tell them I've gone to a meeting at St Brendon's. I should be finished by 12.30pm, so ask them to leave any urgent messages with you. Non-urgent queries can be left in their heads until further notice.'

Margaret stares at me over half-rimmed, silver spectacles. There's a deep crease between her eyes, and despite being in her mid-forties, she seems far older. I count the numbers on my fingers, and realise (not for the first time), that she's just sixteen years older than me. Much younger than my parents, and yet she could be an old woman. All these years of taking care of other people's kids has taken its toll, and I can't help but wonder how she would look if only she'd lighten up a little.

I nod and smile and tell her to have a good meeting, but instead of smiling back, she grimaces.

'I don't go to these meetings to have a good time,' she says. 'They're a vital and necessary part of my job.'

And with that, she waltzes out of the door; her electric-blue kaftan swinging as she goes. What a bitch. I've never known anyone to be offended because someone wished them a happy time, but there you go. Someone must have ruffled her feathers this morning, and I'm just glad that by the time she gets back, I'll be almost ready to leave.

Two minutes later, Linda Turner storms down the corridor, as though she's on some kind of SAS mission.

'Charlotte, do you know where Margaret has gone? I have something I need to discuss with her.'

As I tell Linda that the principal will be out for the rest of the morning, she lets out a disgruntled sigh. Her already wrinkled forehead knits together even more than usual, and today's flower slide – a bright-yellow daffodil with pink leaves – shudders under the strain.

She straightens her brown, woollen skirt and crosses her arms.

It is then that a thought occurs to me.

'I'll be more than happy to tell Margaret that you are looking for her,' I say. 'I might be gone by the time she gets back, but I'll be sure to leave a note on her desk.'

Linda's lips disappear into a thin, orange line.

'That would be helpful,' she says, and then disappears back down the hallway.

'No need to thank me,' I mutter under my breath, and then I give her the middle finger from the safety of under the counter.

As soon as she's gone, I scrawl a note to Margaret, turn the switchboard to silent, and then head to her office.

Margaret always says that she has a duty to provide the children with comfort and familiarity. In that regard, her room is more like a living room than an office space. At the entrance, there is a flowered sofa, complete with several stuffed toys: a teddy bear, a frog and what looks like a blue-spotted armadillo. The filing cabinets are covered in flowery stickers, and there is a small bookcase filled with colourful children's books. In the five years I've been here, I've never once seen a kid go into Margaret's office to read a book, but maybe they're just there for show – a way of putting the kids at ease before they get a rollicking for punching someone in the playground, or dancing on the tables instead of doing maths.

The room smells like old coffee, and also something I can't quite put my finger on. Something funky that hits the back of my nose in an unexpected way. I look around and see a bunch of forgotten, wilted flowers on a shelf. The water is rife with mould and leaves, which surely is the answer to the smell. How can Margaret not notice it? I don't know, but I'm surprised that some quick-mouthed kid hasn't told her that she has flowers rotting away on the shelf.

At the far end of the room, underneath a large window, is the desk. It is loaded with colourful files, papers and documents of every description, but that doesn't bother me. I know exactly what I'm looking for: the principal's appointment diary, and the entry for yesterday.

I pretend to deliver the note from Linda, and just happen to place it right next to the brown leather diary. It's one of those old-fashioned diaries that is just a folder with loose pages held inside with a ferocious clasp. Margaret has had it so long that the leather is flaking from the cover, and the once gold-embossed letters are now blank. It must have some kind of sentimental feeling attached to it, though, because she never used the new one she received in the Secret Santa draw a few years ago. I remember when she unwrapped the flower-covered diary, and watched as her mouth tried to smile, but ended up as a strange, squiggly line.

'Oh, how very kind,' she squeaked, before poking the gift back inside the wrapping paper. Now it is stuck on a shelf beside her desk, out-of-date and never to be looked at again.

My hands feel sweaty as I turn the cover of the vintage appointment book, and then I flip through the pages until I get to Monday, October 11th. I stare at the different names, notes and numbers scrawled onto the page, until one stands out above all others: 'Simon Travis. Assembly speaker for careers' week'. His phone number and email are written underneath his name. Margaret is a stickler for recording those kinds of details under every name in her diary, but there's nothing else that gives me a clue as to how her and Simon know each other.

Did I expect to find more?

No, but there was always a chance.

I pick up a pen, reach for a yellow Post-it and then write Simon's number and email onto the paper. At this moment I don't have any intention of using either of them, but to have them in my possession gives me some kind of power at least. Should I need any.

'Charlotte, do you know where Mrs Holmes is, please?'

I swing around and see Marie, a blonde-haired girl from Year One, staring up at me. Her voice seems far too loud for such a little person.

'Gosh, you gave me a fright,' I say, but Marie doesn't crack a smile.

'I need to give her a note.' She hands me an envelope with 'Magrett Homes the head', scrawled onto the front. I'm sure the principal will be thrilled to see herself described that way.

'Thank you, Marie,' I say, and I pop the note onto the desk. 'I'll just leave it here for her, and then she'll see it when she gets back.'

The little girl nods and skips off down the corridor, her black patent shoes squeaking as she goes. I stuff Simon's details into my pocket, and head back to reception.

Tom, Zach and I sit at the kitchen table, playing a game of Uno. I'm terrible at it – don't understand most of it in all honesty, but my son loves it, so I just crack on.

'That market man came back to school today,' Tom says.

'The market man?' Visions of a man clutching baskets of carrots or lettuces invade my mind, but then it dawns on me who he means, and my shoulders turn to ice.

'Y'know, that man who talked to us about his job. Today, he was visiting Margaret and some other teachers, in the office. I saw him when I took the register down this afternoon.'

Zach shoots me a look, and my mind spins in circles. Why was he there again? To see me? To see Tom? Did he recognise his son in assembly and work the whole thing out? Is he going to the principal to ask for her help in winning custody?

I doubt it, but still, I feel sick thinking about it.

'Do you see that man often?' Zach asks, and Tom shakes his head.

'Just today and yesterday. I remembered him because he was

wearing the same shirt as he was wearing yesterday. I never wear the same clothes twice, do I, Mum?'

I shake my head, and Zach squeezes my hand under the table.

'I won!' Tom throws his arms up in the air and squeals. 'Woohoooo! What do I win?'

'A bath,' I say, and my son groans.

'That's not a very fair prize.'

I laugh and kiss my scruffy little prince on the head. He cuddles into me, okay to show affection when he's away from his teasing friends.

'Come on,' Zach says. 'Let's get these cards put away. If your mum says that it's bath time, then it's bath time.'

Tom pouts.

'I hate baths,' he says. 'When I'm a grown-up I'll never have a bath.'

'Then remind me never to visit you without a nose peg.' I laugh. 'Come on, if you go into the bath without any fuss, you can have a hot chocolate when you get out.'

'With marshmallows and cream?'

'We'll see.'

Tom scoops up the cards and dumps them back into the box. I think about my work clothes, with Simon's number scrawled onto a piece of paper in the pocket. It's just a coincidence that we bumped into each other in Waterstones, and that he's been at the school twice in the past two days. It's all a coincidence.

Isn't it?

'There are no such things as coincidences,' I say out loud. Zach turns to look at me, while Tom peeps out from behind the Uno box.

'What did you say, Mummy?'

'Nothing,' I reply. 'I was just singing a song to myself.'

The next few days pass in a blur, and consist of mornings looking out for Simon at school, and afternoons wondering if he's in school. Every time Tom says he's got something to tell me, I imagine that he's about to relay some kind of 'market man' tale, and even nothing-bothers-me Zach has taken to asking every now and then. It's horrible to feel so paranoid, but what else can I do? After ten years of freedom, his appearance has sent my nerves spinning, and it makes me want to vomit that he's been so close to his son – even if he doesn't know anything about him.

'If you're that worried, why don't you just ask Margaret how she knows him?' Zach stares at me during one of our regular over-the-fence chats. I suspect he's sick of hearing about the principal at this point, but he's my friend, so he puts up with it as best he can.

'I can't come out and just ask her. She'll think I'm a lunatic! Besides, I checked her diary again, and he hasn't been into school since Tuesday, and it's now Friday night, so hopefully that's the end of it.'

I hold my crossed fingers up over the fence, and Trevor the lab barks in appreciation. Zach crosses his own fingers in reply, and then gets back to raking the pile of leaves that have gathered in his garden overnight.

I thank God for good friends, and then head to the kitchen to make Tom's favourite Friday night dinner – lasagne again.

'For fuck's sake, ref! Get a pair of glasses! That should've been a penalty!!'

A middle-aged, bald bloke shouts at the skinny referee, who

is wearing a thick pair of glasses, and running up and down the football field. One of the mothers swings around and eyeballs the bald dad, shoves her fingers to her lips and hisses 'Shush!' at the top of her voice.

'Mind your own business,' the man snarls, and then turns his attention back to the game.

'Can you please refrain from swearing?' she barks. 'There are children all over this field.'

The man tuts and then swears under his breath, just loud enough for the mother to hear. I expect her to turn round again, but she doesn't say anything more.

On the field, twenty-two under elevens swerve around each other, trying to grapple the ball and score the elusive goal. It's a bright autumn day, but the wind is still managing to suck the breath out of me. I pull the zip of my coat up to my neck, and wish I'd brought my gloves. Just as I'm wondering if I should nip back to the car and find my emergency pair in the glovebox, I see her.

Monica Travis stands on the other side of the park, and her eyes are trained on me. I rub my own eyes and think I must be seeing things, but no – as I squint, I can see her even clearer. It's definitely Simon's wife. My legs feel like string, and the coldness in my stomach no longer has anything to do with the autumn wind. I take my phone out of my pocket, but my hand is shaking so much I almost drop it. I grip it with both hands, open the camera and pretend to take a photo of Tom, while really snapping Monica.

The complaining woman from before sees what I'm doing and squawks.

'You shouldn't be taking photographs of the kids. It's against club rules.'

I slip the phone into my pocket.

'Get a fucking life,' I snap, and the bald man applauds me.

'You better not put any photos on social media,' she shouts as I walk away.

I know that the last thing I should do is approach Monica Travis, but now that my feet are moving, it's impossible to get them to stop. I look up and she's still in the same place; still watching; her face contorted and stern.

As I round the end of the field, there is a gigantic cheer. I look up and see that Tom has scored a goal and is leaping around with a group of friends. I stop to give him a clap, and as I do, Monica throws her hood over her head, and walks towards the park exit.

'Charlotte! How are you? I haven't seen you in ages!' Debbie Martin bounds over, waving her hands as though I'm miles away. Debbie is a parent at school, and the biggest pain in the arse you can imagine. If there's something to complain about, she will be first in the queue. If her son doesn't get a part in the school play, or if another child gives him the slightest of dirty looks, you can guarantee that Debbie will be rapping on my glass partition, demanding to have a word with Margaret. Socially, she seems to think we're the best of friends, and whenever she sees me, it'll take at least thirty minutes to brush her off.

But not today.

'I'm so sorry, I can't talk – I have to catch up with someone.' I rush past, and Debbie sighs.

I leave the crowd of parents behind, and ten seconds later, I clock Monica with her back to me, just about to make it through the gate that leads to the car park.

'Hey! Monica! Stop!'

My ex-lover's wife halts, lowers her hood and pulls out her earbuds.

'Oh, hello. Charlotte, isn't it?'

'Yes, it is.'

We stare at each other; strangers and yet not quite. Then when I think of something to say, we both end up talking at the same time.

'I'm sorry,' she says. 'You go first.'

Despite the autumn chill, I can feel sweat tickling my right eyebrow, which threatens to drop into my eye at any moment. I rub at it with my sleeve.

'I was just wondering why you are here. You don't have any kids on the team, do you?'

Monica purses her lips and then smiles.

'No, Charlotte, I don't have a child here. But my husband does though.'

Her words land like a knife in my stomach, and my throat feels as though it's full of pins and needles. I open my mouth to reply, but Monica throws her hand out to stop me.

'Don't bother denying it. I know you gave birth to my husband's child. Tom, isn't it? The little redhead over there.'

She motions towards the pitch, where Tom is leaping around like an excited frog. He hates to be described as a redhead. He's strawberry blond, that's what he always tells me. The skin on my cheeks tingles and I wonder why I'm thinking about my son's hair colour, instead of what Monica has just told me. She knows I have a child! She knows I have her husband's child! I can't believe this.

I turn back to confront her, but the woman has gone. I race to the gate, but I'm too late. Monica is already in her car, and there's no way I'll be able to catch up with her.

'Did you see me, Mum? Did you see that goal I scored? Wasn't it fantastic? Bobby said it was just like the kind of goals David

Beckham used to score. Do you think I might be as good as David Beckham one of these days? Do you, Mum?'

Tom bounces up and down on the back seat as though he's just won the World Cup. He has no idea that today our lives changed forever, and I have no wish to tell him.

'I think you'll be the best football player in the world,' I say. 'Now pop your seat belt on, and we'll get going.'

'Can we have pizza?'

'Yes, we can have pizza. But please put your seat belt on, or we can't go anywhere.'

Tom clicks his belt into place, and I fling the car into reverse. Asda is five miles away, and as my son rattles on about goals and penalties and free kicks, I can't stop thinking about what Monica has told me.

How does she know about Tom, and how long has she known? Has she told Simon? And if so, was I right and that's why he's been at school twice this week? Is he going to force me to give him access? My throat contracts. I can't believe this is happening.

After all these years.

Why now? Why, why, why?

'Mum! I said, did you see when the referee blew his whistle at me?! He thought I'd gone offside, but I hadn't. I know more about the offside rule than he does, don't I, Mum?'

Tears spill over my lower eyelids, and splash onto my cheeks. I wipe at them with the back of my hand and try to hide my despair from Tom, but it's hard. In fact, it's impossible.

'Are you okay, Mum? Why are you crying?'

My son strains against his seat belt and just manages to touch my shoulder. I grab his hand and squeeze it. If I could, I'd hold on to it forever.

'I'm okay,' I say. 'I was just thinking about how proud I am of you, and I think you're a magnificent football player.'

'Thank you, Mummy,' he says. 'But please stop crying. You're making my eyes feel watery.'

I pat his hand and return my own to the steering wheel. He's right. No good can come from my tears. I'm made of stronger stuff than this. My life is spinning, but it's not yet out of control, and I have to make sure it stays that way. I think about the phone number hidden in my bedside cabinet, and know what I have to do.

I have to speak to Simon.

I have to be sure he doesn't know about our son.

After Tom goes to bed, I pick up my phone, but my hands shake so much, I can barely function. After thirteen attempts, I get up enough nerve to press the call button, although I feel so out of breath that I wonder if I'll ever be able to speak. What if Monica picks up? What if one of their grown-up kids pick up? It rings four times and then a man's voice booms down the line.

'Hello?'

Simon.

His voice hits me in a way I didn't expect, and I hang up and then regret calling at all. Although I withheld my number, I still fear that he'll somehow figure out who was calling, and call me back. Stupid I know, since I wanted to speak to him in the first place, but I've never been one to let facts get in the way of a good dose of paranoia. I grab a glass of wine and take a large gulp. Medicinal purposes... I need this for medicinal purposes...

Six minutes after the failed phone call, my phone rings, and it's an unknown number again. I click the accept button, but don't speak, waiting for the caller to either announce themselves or hang up. There is no sound, so I press my ear against the handset and wait. There is a breath.

'Who is this?' I ask.

Another breath. Small and serene. A woman for sure.

'Whoever this is, make yourself known, or I'm calling the police.'

'This is Monica,' says the voice. 'I'd like you to meet me.'

7

'That was a lovely dinner, Mum.' I rub my stomach, to show appreciation, and my mum smiles.

'That's good, love,' she says, and then straightens her blue flowered dress. My mum may be nearing her seventies, but she still likes to wear a fancy outfit for Sunday dinner. May she never change.

'I'm glad you liked it,' says my dad. 'We'll send you the bill in the post.'

Tom bursts out laughing. Dad says the same 'joke' every week, but somehow Tom still thinks it's the funniest thing ever.

'Do you need any help with the washing up, before I shoot off?'

Mum gives me a quizzical look, as she picks up the gravy boat from the table.

'You're leaving so soon?'

'Yes, remember I told you I was meeting one of my friends from work? We're going over some stuff we need to do tomorrow.'

My mum wiggles her head.

'Oh yes. Sorry, dear, I was half asleep when you called last night. You go when you need to. I'll be more than happy to spend the afternoon playing ludo with Tom, and your dad will be fine doing the dishes on his own.'

My dad raises his eyebrows in mock disgust, and Tom laughs again.

'Poor Granddad! But maybe you could bill Mum for that as well!'

'Good idea!' My dad takes an invisible pen out of his pocket, and pretends to scribble against his hand.

'Don't encourage him, Tom!' I say. 'He really will send me a bill, one of these days.'

I get up from the table, throw my handbag over my shoulder, and kiss Tom on the top of his head. His hair smells like tea tree oil – a shampoo we've been using for the past year because they say that it's good at keeping nits at bay...

'See you later,' I say. 'Love you all lots.'

'Love you too!' my family's voices ring out as I make my way down the hall. I bite my lip, as a mixture of guilt and regret ripples through my head. I wish I hadn't had to lie to them just now, but what else could I say? Tell them that I'm going to visit the wife of my ex-lover? A lover by the way, who is the father of my son?

No thank you.

Not today.

Not any day.

The Garden of Olives – the restaurant where Monica has decided we should have our meeting – is not one I would normally go to. As a (fairly) young single mother, I'm used to sitting on a plastic chair in the Northampton branch of McDonalds, or hanging out with other mothers in the local coffee shop or family-friendly pub. This place is located on the outskirts of our village, and while I have driven past it many times on the way to somewhere else, this is the first time I've stood inside.

The first thing I notice is the array of bright chandeliers, hanging from the ceiling. They send rays of light across the entire restaurant, illuminating the child-free couples, enjoying a long Sunday lunch. Every dining party sits in large, round booths, with cloths and fresh flowers on the tables. This restaurant is way out of my league, and I'm embarrassed that I'm supposed to be having coffee here. Is that even allowed? Everyone seems to be engrossed in huge meals, and my stomach lurches with a mixture of nerves and indigestion from my mother's cooking.

A man in a pink uniform bustles over.

'Can I help you?' he asks without making eye contact.

'Yes, I'm supposed to be meeting somebody,' I say.

'Did you book? We're very busy as you can see.'

I don't care for this guy's attitude, but I'm so intimidated by him that I don't dare ask what his problem is.

'She's with me. Monica Travis. I have booked.'

I swing around and there is Monica, dressed to impress in a cream suit with a gold trim around the lapels. My jeans and red shirt are out of place here. I'm dressed for a barn dance, stuck in a world better suited to *The Real Housewives of Beverly Hills*. The waiter checks for Monica's name in a large white book, and then smiles for the first time since I arrived.

'Very good, Mrs Travis,' he says. 'Follow me, please.'

The waiter grabs two menus and saunters over to a booth in the corner of the room, right next to the window. The last time I drove past this window, I was heading to Northampton, and my infamous trip to Waterstones. Who knew that I'd soon be sitting here with the wife of my son's father? Not me.

I sit down, and I'm immediately thrown by the blue neon strobe, lighting up the back of the chair. As if that isn't fancy enough, the wall next to me is covered in lilac-and-white flowers, and I have to resist the urge to reach out and see if they're real. The table is set for two people, and includes tall, thick-bottomed wine glasses, a wealth of shiny cutlery and three tiny candles in glass holders. If I wasn't so nervous, I'd be mesmerised by the decorations, but as it is, the whole place is nothing less than a sensory overdose.

Monica sits about three feet away from me, and plonks her huge black handbag on the seat between us. Then off comes the suit jacket, and that gets shoved on there too. I feel as though she's building a wall between us, which is maybe just as well – at least it will keep her from launching a physical attack.

'Can I get you something to drink?' The waiter seems enthralled by Monica, which isn't altogether surprising. She's a stunning woman, and even though she is in her forties, she has glowing, wrinkle-free skin and immaculate make-up. Her black bob is pinned back on one side, and she wears the kind of jewellery I've only seen in movies – or on members of the royal family.

'We'll have a pot of tea, thank you,' she says. 'English breakfast if you don't mind. And we won't need the menus, as we're not going to be eating anything.'

The waiter's face falls, as he realises his tip won't be as big as he expected it to be. He nods, gathers the menus and then heads to the kitchen. Monica and I sit in awkward silence, until she takes a breath, leans her head against her hand and turns her body to face me.

'So,' she says, 'you had Simon's child.'

Her bluntness hits me in the core, but I guess it breaks the ice.

'Yes. Yes, I did.'

'Tom.'

She says my son's name, and my blood freezes.

'How did you know that?'

'It's not hard to find out these things,' she says, but offers no further explanation.

The waiter arrives with a tray, and decants everything onto the table: Green, white and red teapot; a silver pot which I presume houses hot water; green cups and saucers; sugar; milk; and two tiny biscuits in red wrappers.

'Can I get you anything else?' he asks Monica. She shakes her head, and he trots off to a bigger, better table. Monica pours the tea into both cups, then adds milk and hands it over. Seems I don't get a say in how I take my tea, but I thank her anyway.

'How do you know I had a child?' I stir the tea with a tiny silver spoon, and prepare myself for the answer.

'I've known since the day you were supposed to go for the termination,' she says. 'I overheard Simon making the appointment for you. Stupid sod phoned them while I was in the bath... Must have thought the bathroom was soundproof or something. Anyway, he made the appointment, and repeated the details back to them. That's how I found out.'

As simple as that.

Monica takes a sip of tea, and stares at me from the corner of her eye. She swallows and then her eyebrows knit together.

'Our relationship was complicated at that time, for reasons that I won't go into here, but anyway, on the day of the termination, I made sure I was at the clinic way before your appointment. I sat in the car park and watched as you both pulled up. You looked so young! Just a baby yourself, and while I hated you for being pregnant with Simon's child, it seemed clear in that second that he was taking advantage of you. You didn't look old enough to have any kind of opinion of your own.'

I squirm in my seat. I'd take exception to that, if it wasn't true.

'You're right, I was young, and Simon did take advantage of me. I didn't know that then, but I do now.'

'Age brings wisdom,' she says. 'At least it does for some people. Not all, unfortunately.' She pours more milk into her tea, and takes another drink. 'I must say that I couldn't believe it when he dropped you off and drove away. But maybe I shouldn't have been surprised. That kind of behaviour was Simon all over. Anyway, you went into the clinic and I walked over the road with the intention of following you in.'

'You followed me in?'

Monica picks at a piece of fluff on her coat. One of her bright-red nails is chipped, but otherwise her hands are immaculate. I get a whiff of Daisy perfume. It's the same as the one my mum wears.

'I wanted to ask you for a favour. I wanted to ask you not to go through with the termination.'

My stomach flutters at the casualness of her voice. She didn't want me to go through with the termination? How does that make any sense? It doesn't.

'Why... Why would you do that?'

Monica laughs and stirs her tea with a tiny, silver spoon. I've never seen anyone quite as obsessed with their drink as she is.

'Because I had this crazy notion that I could pass the child off as my own. I had it all worked out. I'd pay you to end it with Simon, and then you and I could go away and in nine months' time, I'd bring the baby home with me. I thought that if I had a child, I could force Simon to be with me exclusively, that it would make him settle down.'

My mouth falls open, and Monica laughs and waves her hands in the air.

'I know, I know! It's like something out of a bad TV movie,

isn't it? But when you're desperate, you think about all kinds of nonsense. You might not go through with it all, but you think about it nonetheless... However! Just as I reached the door to the clinic, it slid open, and out you came. I knew straight away that you had changed your mind about the termination, but I was so shocked to see you, that my idea went straight out of the window. Probably just as well.'

I pick up my cup, but my hand shakes so much that I have to return it to the saucer.

'You think I'm crazy.'

Yes, yes, I do.

'No,' I lie. 'I don't think you're crazy, but you should know that even at the age of nineteen, I'd never have given you my baby. And that still applies by the way!'

Monica grabs my arm, and my bicep contracts under her touch.

'Don't worry,' she says. 'I think I'm a bit too old to pull off a fake pregnancy, don't you?'

I brush her off, by pretending to scratch my arm.

'Does Simon know about Tom?'

'Not that I'm aware of,' she says. 'He's got no reason to think you had the baby, and he's never mentioned you.'

There is a hint of joy as she implies how little I meant to Simon, but I know she's right. I was nothing but a quick fling; his naughty little bit on the side.

I hate men sometimes.

'I want to know why were you at Tom's football match the other day, and also why Simon has been to his school twice in the past week.'

Monica sits bolt upright.

'He's been at his school?'

'Yes, I saw him. I work on the reception desk. He was there to speak in assembly, about his job.'

She nods her head.

'Oh, that's right. He said he was doing some kind of career talk. I didn't realise it would be at your son's school.'

'How could you?'

'Quite.'

We sit in silence for a moment, and I play with the tassels on my handbag. This is awkward, but what can I do? We still haven't got to the point of the meeting yet, or maybe we did and I didn't notice. Either way, I just want to go home.

'I want to ask you for a favour.'

Her statement makes me jump. A favour? What can I give her that she doesn't have already?

'I want to tell Simon about his son.'

I jump forward in my chair, and my teacup rattles and sends liquid into the saucer.

'You want to tell him about Tom? No! Why would you do that?'

My heart rattles in my chest. I can't believe this. Almost ten years I've kept my son to myself, and now here is Simon's wife, saying she's going to reveal all. Why? Why would she do that? She grabs my arm, but I'm too quick and pull away.

'We're not perfect,' she says. 'But my husband deserves to know that he's a father.'

'No! No, he does not.'

Monica finishes her tea in one gulp, and then dabs at her mouth.

'Think about Tom,' she snaps. 'He's had almost ten years without a dad, and look at all the things he's missed!'

'Yeah? And look at what he would have missed if Simon had had his way in the beginning.' I lower my voice and the words come out as a snarl. 'He'd have lost his whole life. His whole life!'

Monica lowers her eyes, and flares her nostrils.

66

'I know that,' she says. 'But he's not going to do that now, is he? You need to give us a chance. Tom deserves to have an extended family.'

My legs bounce under the table. I can't believe that I walked into this situation, but I do know one thing – I'm walking out as quick as I can. I grab my coat and bag, and slide out of the booth. How I'm able to stand upright is a mystery, my whole body is shaking so much. Monica bolts forward, and her arms shoot up into the air.

'You're leaving? Why?'

'I'm going home. I've got a headache.'

Monica slides out of the booth, as the waiter appears back at our table.

'Everything okay here?' he asks.

I'm gone before Monica – or I – can answer.

On the way home, I can't help but think about what Monica said. What did she mean, Simon deserves to know his son? How dare she! He deserves nothing but the slowest, most painful death that can be inflicted on him. He used me, he continues to use her, and she wants to give him access to a child? My child? She must be insane.

My meeting with my ex-lover's wife was nothing like I expected. I am left with more questions than I had at the beginning, and the story of how Monica wanted to pass off my baby as her own was creepy to say the least. Why is she following me around? Why does she want access to my son? What's in this for her? There must be something. All these years I've been worried about Simon finding out about Tom, but Monica's behaviour makes me wonder if I've been looking for danger in the wrong place.

I'm so confused.

By the time I arrive at my mum and dad's, my paranoia has hit fever pitch, so that when I let myself in and discover the house empty, I panic. I send Mum a WhatsApp message, trying to keep it as calm as I can.

I'm back. Where are you? I need to get Tom home for his bath.

I wait to see the double ticks turn blue, but nothing happens. The message has been delivered but not seen. I message my dad:

Are you coming back soon? Where are you?

Once again, the ticks remain grey.

I tap my phone on the counter and try to calm my nerves. There's no reason for me to be concerned or worried. It's Sunday afternoon, my son is with his grandparents, and it's a crisp autumn day. They've gone out for a long walk, that's all. Probably borrowed next door's Pomeranian and took him to the park.

After twenty-two minutes, the back door flies open, and my family pile into the kitchen.

'Where have you been? I was worried sick!'

All three look at each other and then my mum throws her arms in the air.

'Why on earth would you be worried?' Mum fills the kettle and switches it on. 'Pass me the cups, will you? We all need a hot drink after that walk. Tom, don't forget to wash your hands!'

A walk. They've been on a walk. The sensible part of my brain was right. They just went out to blow the cobwebs away. I lean against the cabinet and try to catch my breath.

'Charlotte! Cups please! What's wrong with you this afternoon?'

My mum shakes her head, while Tom and my Dad take their raincoats off. I open the cupboard, take out four mugs and hand them to my mum. She smiles in approval.

'How was your friend?' my dad asks.

'My friend? Oh, she was fine. We just had a quick coffee in the end because she had to get back to her husband.'

'Get all your work done though?'

'What?'

'For tomorrow. You said you were doing work?'

I rattle my head. I need to get better at lying.

'Yes, yes, all good.' I turn to Tom. 'Did you have a nice walk? It wasn't too cold, was it?' I stroke my son's cheek. It is pink and freezing to the touch. I rub it with the back of my hand, but Tom flicks me away.

'I'm fine, Mum,' he says. 'I'm not a baby.'

'Tom met one of his teachers,' Mum says, as she pours hot water into the cups. Tom puts his hands on his hips and tuts.

'Grandma, it wasn't my teacher. It was a man who came to school to talk about his job. His market job, remember?'

'Oh yes. Silly Grandma.'

'What do you mean, you saw the man who came to school?'

My heart beats so fast that I feel like I'm about to faint. My mum shrugs and stirs some hot chocolate into Tom's cup.

'Did you wash your hands? Wash them before I give you this.'

Tom turns on the tap, and a torrent of water cascades into the sink. He squirts far too much liquid soap into his hands, and proceeds to scrub as though he's a surgeon, about to perform an operation.

'Is anyone going to answer my question?'

'He was just out with his dog,' my mum says. 'Having a nice Sunday afternoon walk by the looks of it. He seemed like a friendly man. Told us how nicely Tom sat during the assembly.'

My mum turns her attention back to my son, and I can hear them talk about being careful because the cup is hot, and exchanging questions about cookies or muffins, but I feel as though I can't respond. Tom saw Simon? Close to my parents' house? While I was having coffee with his wife? The same wife who wanted me to give her my baby ten years ago? My neck and shoulders feel as though they're filled with ice, and as my mum tries to hand me a mug of tea, I dart out of the door.

'Where you going?'

I can hear the voices of my three family members rattling down the path as I reach the gate, but I can't stop. I have to run. I have to find Simon. I have to know what's going on with him, with his wife, with everything!

I have to know!

I'm halfway down the lane when I realise, I didn't even ask where they saw him. It could have been anywhere, and I could be running in the opposite direction, but I can't slow down. My feet refuse to stop, and I can't turn back to the house and ask where he was, so instead, I carry on.

Running.

Running.

Running.

I reach the river as it starts to rain, and the drops splash into the water and hit me in the face like wet bullets. I try to wipe them away, but it's no good. The raindrops get heavier and heavier until my glasses are covered and I can't see where I'm going or what I'm doing.

And then I trip and fall.

And my legs and hands are covered in puddle water, mud, grime and yellow, slimy leaves.

But there is no sign of Simon.

'Charlotte! Charlotte!' My dad's voice echoes down the river path, as I am still slumped on my hands and knees. I look up, he waves and then helps me get back onto my feet.

'Come on, silly.' He speaks to me as though I were Tom's age, and that's fine with me. 'What's got into you today, eh? Have you had a bad dream or something?'

I shake my head, and flick the leaves from my jeans. They reveal wet, muddy prints, and I notice that one leg has a rip at the knee, and a trickle of blood seeps through the fabric.

'I'm bleeding,' I say, as though my dad hasn't noticed.

'Let's get you home,' he says. 'We'll get you all cleaned up.'

8

In the safety of my mum and dad's kitchen, I sit on an old dining chair and spill out my heart. Tom has gone next door to play with their dog, after telling me that I'm even clumsier than him, and I should never go out for a run in the rain. God bless him, he's so innocent and I hope he always stays that way.

My mum bathes my knee like she used to do when I'd fallen off my bike aged eight, while I tell them the entire story. Everything.

Every... Little... Thing...

And my world feels lighter by the end of it.

'Do you think I'm being dramatic, by not wanting them to have access to Tom?'

My dad shakes his head.

'No, I think you have good reason to believe they might be here to cause trouble, especially after hearing about the wife's fake pregnancy. Nobody we know would ever do something like that, would they, Anne?'

My mum places the plaster on my knee and pats it.

'Not that I know of,' she says. 'Right, there you go. All done.'

'Thank you.' I rub my leg and it stings under my touch.

'Do you think badly of me for going out with a married man?' I look down at the floor, as though I'm that same teenager who got herself 'into trouble' with the wrong guy. My mum shakes her head, while she washes her hands.

'Charlotte, we've always known that Tom's father was an older man, so to hear that he was married comes as no surprise. Besides, it sounds to me as though he used you. He knew what he was doing, but you were just a kid. It's not your fault, but it's not his wife's fault either, so go easy on her if you ever see her again.'

I roll my eyes. Typical that even on hearing what I've just said about Monica, my mum is still concerned about her well-being. My dad had a brief flirtation with a work colleague before they were married, and my mum has never forgiven him for it. I imagine she still lies in bed, plotting the woman's demise, but then again, I probably would as well if I was in that situation.

My dad gathers up all the medical supplies; throws the used ones in the bin and pops the rest into the box.

'I think the best thing you can do is to ignore what she said about having access, and to try and stay away from that man, *and* his wife.' He emphasises the word as a way of chastising me for meeting up with her today. 'I've seen stories like this on the television, and the parental responsibilities soon get boring in the end and they back off. But if I see Simon lurking around again, he won't be able to see straight, once I've finished with him.'

My mum bursts out laughing, and even I can't help but smile. Once again, my little dad thinks he can beat up anyone who upsets his daughter, and God love him for it.

'Oh, shush, Bernard,' Mum says.

'I'm being serious!'

'Well, I don't have any bail money, I hope you know... So, you'll just have to run fast so the police don't catch up with you.'

My mum winks, and for a moment all is well with the world. But I'm not sure how long that will last.

Three hours later and I'm at home. Tom is in bed and Zach and I are slumped on the sofa, drinking tea. Zach grabs a cookie from the plate on the coffee table, and stuffs it into his mouth.

'You know what I think you should do?' he says through a mouthful of snacks.

'No, what would you do?' I roll my eyes, because whenever Zach has a great idea, it's something outrageous that nobody in their right mind would ever attempt.

'I know, I know, you're gonna think I'm crazy, but I think you should go and speak to Simon. Tell him that his wife has been lurking around, and it's made you wonder about his motives as well. Tell him if he doesn't leave you alone, you'll go to the police.'

'It's not as simple as that.'

'Why?'

Crumbs fall onto Zach's chest, and he brushes them off onto the floor.

'Because I don't want to get in the middle of his marriage problems. If I'd wanted to do that, I'd have done it ten years ago when I was sleeping with him.'

Zach licks his top lip, and sighs.

'Got it.'

I tut, and pat his arm. Is that a hint of jealousy from my friend with benefits? Do I want it to be? I'm not sure.

'Anyway... Perhaps I'm thinking too much into this. Simon hasn't done anything wrong, has he? All he's done is come into school for a career talk and then my parents saw him walking his dog near to their house. I have zero evidence that he knows anything about Tom, and if Monica does go ahead and tell him, then I'll just have to deal with it – one way or the other.'

Zach takes out his phone.

'Do you know where they live?'

'No. As I told you, I thought they were in London, and I've no idea how long they've been back here. In fact, when I saw them in Waterstones, I just presumed – or hoped – that they were visiting Northampton. I had no idea that they'd come to Bromfield, but there you go!'

'What was the number you had for him? Can you remember it?'

I reach into a nearby drawer and take out the crumpled bit of paper that holds Simon's phone number. I hand it over and Zach stares at it.

'Great. Having a phone number could make things easier.'

'Easier for what?' I ask the question but Zach doesn't answer. Instead, he inputs the number into his phone, smiles and then hands it over.

'Voila!'

I take the phone and stare at a listing for a Mr Simon Travis, 16 Donovan Grove, Bromfield-on-the-water.

'How? How did you find this?'

Zach grabs another cookie, and sits back into the sofa.

'Just call it journalistic skills... He must have advertised something in the small ads at some point. We keep the name, address and phone number of every person who advertises in the newspaper – for security reasons. We're not supposed to pass the details along, though, so if anyone ever asks, you didn't get the address from me.'

I stare at the page, and can't believe Zach found the listing so quickly. It's true what they say – there is no such thing as privacy anymore.

'Shall we go and pay him a visit?' Zach asks. 'See what – if anything – he's up to? We don't have to mention Tom. After all, at this moment, he's only seen you as a receptionist at the local school. We could ask a few discreet questions, and see what's going on. What do you think? We could go over there tomorrow afternoon, after you've finished work.'

'Why would I do that? I don't want this man to be in my life. If I go round there, he'll know he's got to me.'

Zach leans forward, pops the cookie back onto the plate, and pushes up his sleeves.

'Or he'll know you're onto him. If his wife has already told him about Tom, it'll give you the upper hand, because he'll know you're not scared. You'll have some kind of power.'

That is the most ridiculous thing I've ever heard, especially as the first thing I want to do is run far, far away. My heart falls into my stomach, and my first reaction is to say no, but then I think of all the upset this week has caused, and I decide to do the right thing. Even if it just gives me a feel for what's going on, it'll be better than nothing.

'Okay,' I say. 'Let's pay him a visit.'

Donovan Grove is one of those streets where every house is magnificent, individual and set back from the road. Built in the 1950s, I walked down here all the time during my teenage years, and once dreamt of owning number 12 – a white-bricked home with green shutters and roses around the door. Cliché perhaps, but that kind of thing excited me when I was fifteen years old. I once went out with a boy just because his cousin lived in that house. I was hoping I'd be asked to a party there or something, but one thing I learned during that time is that if you have a house as magnificent as number 12 Donovan Grove, the last thing you do is have a teenage party in it.

We amble past the once-coveted house, and I notice that the shutters are now brown, and the roses have long since been pulled out. The colourful flower beds have made way for pebbles, and even the beautiful green front door is now black and rather foreboding. It's a shame what time can do to a place – or at least our memories of it.

Zach grabs my hand.

'You okay?'

I'm not okay, but I don't want to show it. If I admit to Zach that I want to go home; that I'm frightened and about to throw up, he'll just stick me back in his car and take me away. As much as I'm scared and want to head home for a nice cup of tea, I also want to see what the deal is with Simon Travis. Seeing his crazy wife at Tom's football match, and then hearing how she once coveted my child was terrifying. I need reassurances that they're not here to cause trouble, and if that means speaking to Simon again, then it's something I need to do.

We stop just as we reach the huge hedges that surround number 16. I can see the front door, and it looks intimidating and terrifying. I can't go up there. What am I going to say? Zach swings around to face me.

'Fuck, Charlotte! You're as white as a sheet. Was this a bad idea? Do you want to go home?'

My breath catches in the back of my throat, and I cough.

'I don't want to go home, but at the same time, I'm not sure why I'm here. I've spent the past ten years hoping I would never see Simon again, and now I'm going to knock on his door? What the hell am I thinking?!'

Zach rubs my shoulders, and his touch soothes and comforts me.

'Look, we've been over all this, but if you've changed your mind, just say the word and we'll get out of here. We can always come back another day, if that's what you decide. It's no problem.'

He gives me that funny, wide-mouthed smile that he has, and I wonder in that moment why we've never made things serious between us. I shake my head. What a stupid thing to think about, when I'm about to walk up my married ex-lover's driveway. I'm such a bloody idiot. All of this is idiotic. Every single bit of it.

'Yes,' I say. 'Let's go home.'

My friend nods, kisses me on the head and we both turn to go back to the car. Before we can get away from number 16, however, the door swings open, and there is Monica. She scowls at us with her arms crossed.

'Charlotte? What are you doing here?' Her voice echoes down the drive and lands with a painful thud in my already freezing ears. Zach and I stand cemented to the ground.

'Is that her?' he asks. 'Is that his missus?'

I nod my head.

'Yes, but let's just go. This was a huge mistake.'

Zach breaks away from me and ambles up the driveway as though he's on some kind of peacemaking mission. I can either run back to the car and look like an utter fool, or follow him and risk upsetting my life even more.

I follow him.

'Hi,' he says. 'I'm Zach, and this is my friend...'

'I know who she is.' Monica looks over Zach's shoulder. 'What can I help you with, Charlotte? Have you changed your mind about what we discussed in the restaurant?'

She smiles, but I shake my head.

'No. No, I haven't changed my mind.'

'So why are you here? I don't understand.'

Monica sucks in her bottom lip, and narrows her eyes as she stares at me. Although she wasn't expecting us, she's still as immaculate as she was in the restaurant. With her hair pulled back off her face, and wearing a simple green dress, she looks younger than her years. She's not wearing any make-up that I can see, but her skin is perfect. It looks like peaches and cream, and she's exactly the kind of person I would expect to live in Donovan Grove.

'I'm really sorry to rush you,' she says, 'but I'm about to go to a yoga class. So, if there's anything I can do for you, you better tell me now, because…'

She taps on her watch, and shrugs. Zach steps forward and I can see Monica staring at my friend's multicoloured, tie-dye T-shirt, underneath his black leather jacket. He's the one who looks like he's on his way to an exercise class, and I'm sure his casual attire is not lost on the ever-perfect Monica.

'Mrs Travis, my friend – who appears to be mute right now – just wants to know what the situation is with you and your husband.'

'What do you mean?'

A stream of strength appears to me from nowhere, and now it's my turn to jump in.

'He means, are you in Bromfield so that you can create problems for me and my son?'

Monica sucks in her cheeks, and snorts.

'Creating problems is the last thing I intend to do,' she says. 'But as far as I'm concerned – and as I told you the other day – Simon deserves to be told about his son, and then if he wants to see him, that's something we'll work towards down the line.'

'But why now? Why after ten years of silence? It makes no sense to me at all.'

Monica shakes her head and prods her long fingernails into her forearm. Her fingers are covered in large rings that sparkle in the sun. They look real to me, but then again, what do I know about jewellery? Not much.

'Because if we wait any longer, Tom will be a teenager and it will be much harder to develop a relationship with him. I'd love to get to know my stepson, and I know that given the chance, Simon would love that too.'

The word stepson rings in my ears. This woman will never be my son's mother – step or otherwise.

'You have no idea if he'd love it,' I say. 'He didn't love it ten years ago, and I'm not sure what's changed. Plus, what's in this for you, anyway? Why do you want to have a connection with Tom? It doesn't make any sense.'

Monica dabs her nose with a whiter-than-white handkerchief, and sighs.

'I have no ulterior motives, other than I think it would be good for Simon to have Tom in his life.'

Suddenly it all makes sense.

'I'm so stupid! Of course you think Tom will be good for Simon! You're worried that your beloved husband is screwing around again, and you think he'll settle down if he has a kid – just like you did when you followed me to the termination clinic. You're using my child's life to try and improve your own! Well, you can forget about that!'

Monica's lips close into a tiny ball, but before she can say anything, Zach steps forward and hands her his business card.

'If you do decide to tell Simon,' he says, 'please consider contacting us first. This is my number, and I think you already have Charlotte's. If we could just organise this together, it will be much better – particularly for Tom, who is still a child after all.'

Zach's calming attitude causes Monica's shoulders to relax. She scratches her chin, nods and stuffs the card into her pocket, without looking at it.

'It was nice to meet you,' Monica says to my friend, 'but I do have to get going now.'

I turn away without saying goodbye. I can't bear to look into her eyes any longer.

The wind stings my face as Zach and I traipse back to his car. I throw my hood up over my head, but the freezing air cuts straight through me.

'How do you think that went?' Zach asks, and I roll my eyes.

'What do you think? She wants Tom in her life, so that Simon will stay in hers! She's evil.'

Zach bites his lip.

'In her defence, she didn't say that – you did.'

'Oh, come on!' I snap. 'You know as well as I do that that's why she's doing this. There can't possibly be anything else in it for her.'

We slide into Zach's battered old Beetle, and he starts the engine. The windscreen is covered in condensation, which he mops up with an old yellow cloth. The rubbing results in tears of wet running down the glass, and he turns the fan on to full blast, in an effort to dry it.

'Do you think she'll leave me alone now?' I ask, although I already know the answer.

'Nope,' Zach says, and then we take off from the kerb. As we pass Simon's house, I peer inside, and see Monica standing next to the window, phone pressed to her ear.

A shiver runs through me, and it has nothing to do with the weather.

9

The next morning, I'm back behind the reception desk. I've got to sort numbers for the breakfast yoga club, but all I can think about is what happened yesterday afternoon. I shouldn't have let Zach talk me into going round there. Monica is never going to leave me alone, and going to her house has just cemented that fact.

But it's too late now.

'Charlotte, please could you make a start on the monthly newsletter? We need to get one out before the kids break up for half-term.'

Margaret's voice makes me jump, and I knock some of the yoga slips onto the floor. I move to retrieve them, but there's so many that it would be rude to disappear under the desk while the principal still stands in front of me. I just leave them where they are.

'Charlotte? I need you to print the newsletter today, if that's okay?'

I shake myself back to reality.

'Yes, that's fine,' I say. 'Is there anything particular you'd like me to include this time?'

Margaret hands me a buff folder, which is so thin that it can't have more than a sheet or two of notes inside. Gosh, if this is all there is to go into the newsletter, I'll have to make some stuff up.

'There's not much this month,' she says, 'but I'm sure you can whip it into something interesting.'

She spins her hands in circles, which just makes it look as though she's miming along to that 'Wind the Bobbin Up' song. I stifle a laugh, but Margaret catches me.

'Something funny?'

Beads of sweat pop up on my forehead, and tickle my hairline. So much for my oil-resistant foundation. The manufacturers obviously haven't heard of Margaret's wrath.

'No, nothing funny,' I say. 'I was just thinking about something Tom said this morning, that's all.'

Margaret sticks her nose in the air, and stares at me as though I'm something she just found on the end of her toilet brush.

'Thinking about family is always enjoyable,' she says. 'I just wish I had the time.'

And with that, Margaret disappears back into her office. I ignore her sarky remark and instead, scoop the yoga slips off the floor, stick them to one side and then open the newsletter folder.

The first photograph makes me want to throw up.

There is Simon, standing with a group of children – one of them being my son. The note underneath describes the picture:

We were thrilled to welcome Simon Travis to school this week. He told the children all about his career in marketing and PR, and the children thought his presentation was entertaining and fun.

Six of the children smile at the camera, while the seventh – Tom – looks up at Simon.

I grab the scissors and try to stop my hands from shaking, as

I trim my son from the photograph. There's no way he's going into this month's newsletter. It's bad enough that Simon will be in there! I shove the photo of Tom into my handbag, and then spend the next hour compiling the newsletter. There is news about the yoga lessons, the trip to Whipsnade, a new craft club and then the visit from the 'market man' as Tom calls him. I print it off, throw it onto the photocopier and make 230 copies; enough for every child plus some spares, just in case.

I leave the copier running, and head back to my desk, in time to see Tom and his friend, Charlie, looking for me.

'Hey, you,' I say. 'What are you doing here?'

'Miss Love sent us down to see if the newsletters are ready yet. She's leaving early this afternoon, so wants to give them to us this morning instead. Can we have them?'

I look towards the copy room.

'No, not quite, but they're being printed as we speak.'

'Great!'

Before I can stop him, Tom rushes into the room, and comes back, waving a handful of yellow newsletters in the air.

'I'm so excited, Mum! Mrs Holmes says my picture is going to be in it this time! I forgot all about my photo with the market man, but now I've told all of my friends and I can't wait to show Grandma!'

My little boy stares at the first page, and then whips it over to the back. The blood runs from my head, as I watch the smile fall from his face.

'Where are you?' asks Charlie. 'I can't see you!'

Tom stares at the picture, and I feel rooted to the spot. No matter how long he stares, he'll never find himself in that photo, and I feel awful. I had no idea he'd even know he was going to be in the newsletter. Shit! I shouldn't have chopped him out. What the hell was I thinking?

'I'm not there,' Tom says, and then he bursts into tears.

~

'Why did you cut him out of it?' My mum gawps at me from across the table. 'You know how sensitive he is... And how excited he gets by things like that.'

I collapse my head into my hands.

'I know, I know. I wasn't thinking. I just wanted to get rid of the evidence that he was standing with his father. It was a spur-of-the-moment thing.'

'And you couldn't stick him back on and run them off again?'

I trace my finger around the flower pattern on my mum's tablecloth, and shake my head.

'I tried, but when I fished the cutting back out of my handbag, it was too crumpled to do anything with. If I'd stuck it back onto the photo, it would have looked ridiculous.'

My dad wanders in from the living room, carrying an empty mug of hot chocolate.

'Tom's watching *SpongeBob*. The hot chocolate seems to have calmed him down a bit.'

'That's good.' My mum looks at me and lowers her voice. 'You'll need to be careful, Charlotte. It's one thing to not want this man to be involved in Tom's life, but it's another to hurt the child's self-esteem.'

My dad nods, as he rinses out the mug.

'It's a fine line,' he says. 'A very fine line.'

No shit! Well, tell me something I don't know. I see the disapproving looks on my parents' faces and just want to cry. I shouldn't have cut Tom out of the photo. At the end of the day, just standing next to Simon was no evidence at all that he was his son. I was stupid, but when instinct takes over, even the craziest of decisions seems normal.

I guess this is just another element of mum guilt to add to my roster.

As if there wasn't enough already.

~

'I heard you tell Grandma that you cut me out of the picture. Why did you do that, Mum? Charlie says his mum would never do that!'

Good for Charlie, and his perfectly perfect mother...

'It's a long story,' I say, as I try and navigate the traffic as well as my son's emotions.

'It's not a story at all,' Tom shouts. 'You cut me out of the newsletter because you didn't want me to be in there, that's it!'

My car hits a puddle, and in my mirror, I can see a soaked, disgruntled pedestrian, shouting at me from the pavement. She thinks she's got problems? She should be in this car!

'It wasn't that at all, Tom! I made a silly mistake. I was trying to trim the photograph to fit onto the page, and I accidentally cut you off. It was all just an accident.'

'You treat me like a baby.' Tom turns his head and stares out of the window. He doesn't believe a word I'm saying, and I can't say I blame him.

~

'So, I had a few spare minutes this afternoon, and did some digging into Monica and Simon.'

'You did? That was very investigative reporter of you.'

I smile at Zach, and he laughs.

'I have my moments,' he says, 'although in this case it didn't come to much.'

He hands me his iPad, and a newspaper report stares up at me, about the launch of Simon's London marketing company. I had already seen this years ago, so it's nothing new. I scroll and there is another pic from just six months ago, this time announcing the expansion of his company, to include a branch in Northampton. There is a photo of Simon and Monica cutting a ribbon outside the office, and it describes her as a housewife. I can't imagine that went down very well. Even though I've only met Monica several times, she comes across more as a socialite than a housewife, but that's just my point of view.

I hand the iPad back to Zach.

'Was that it?'

'That and the small ad I told you about the other day. Simon was selling a bicycle for £200 or nearest offer. Nothing exciting, I'm afraid.'

Before I can reply, the living-room door bursts open, and Tom marches in, holding a green notebook.

'Hello, Champ!' Zach smiles at my son, but Tom averts his eyes from us both.

'You have to sign my homework book,' he says, and drops it onto my knee. I grab a pen from the coffee table, sign it and hand it back. Tom takes the book, and heads for the door.

'Aren't you going to say thank you?' I ask.

'Thank you.'

He leaves the room, and the door slams closed behind him.

'What's wrong with Mr Happy?' Zach points towards the hall, and I shake my head.

'I managed to upset him,' I say, and then I grab the iPad again. 'Okay, at least the expansion of his company explains why they are back in Northamptonshire, but is it the only reason they're here? Could you find anything else at all?'

Zach reaches for the plate of chocolate digestives, and sticks almost an entire biscuit into his mouth. He crunches down, shakes his head, and crumbs fly out of his mouth before he answers.

'That's it, except for some company records for Simon. Oh, there was this too, but how useful it is I don't know.'

Zach brushes the digestive crumbs from his knees, and they scatter over my pristine floor. This is why we could never be partners. The way he eats his food would drive me bonkers. He presses the screen of his iPad, and up pops Facebook. It is a page for the Bromfield and Surrounding Areas Networking Group, and there in the middle of the screen is a photo of the latest meeting. Simon stands in the middle of the picture, and Margaret is three people away.

'Simon and Margaret... So that's how they know each other. Some crummy networking group. I guess she must have seen him as a good candidate for our careers assembly, and asked him to take part.'

'Sounds feasible. Well, at least you've cleared that up.'

'Did you find out anything about Simon's children? They'll be grown-up by now, but they may be able to provide some clues as to what's going on.'

Zach shakes his head.

'Nothing at all. They obviously fly under the radar, which is not surprising, with people like Simon and Monica as parents.'

Zach stares at my wall clock. 'Hey, I better get going. I have to take Trevor out for his walk, and then get some dinner.'

We both stand up, and he shoves his iPad under his arm.

'Thanks for doing that research for me,' I say.

'You're welcome. Even if I didn't find anything interesting. But then again, maybe their lives are none of our business anyway.'

He laughs, we say goodbye and then Zach disappears into my kitchen and out of the back door. His words linger in the air. Maybe Simon and Monica's lives aren't any of our business, but I have every right to know what their intentions are towards my son. Is Monica going to keep the whole thing hanging over my head, ready to explode at any moment? Or is she going to tell Simon straight away, and enjoy seeing him go off at me. After all, as far as he's concerned, I did what he asked me to do, and terminated his child. What will his response be if he knows I walked out of that clinic, and into a life of motherhood?

I have so many questions...

And despite my terror, I need to have some answers.

I write and rewrite my email at least ten times, but as I read through the latest version, I think I have it right:

```
Dear Simon
    It's Charlotte here, (the receptionist
at Bromfield Primary School). I need to
speak to you about something rather
important, and wonder if I could see you
maybe before the weekend. If you're okay
with that, we can meet at the Mistletoe
Inn, on the corner before you reach the
old thatched cottages. I can do any
afternoon, so please could you let me
know? Thanks.
    Charlotte.
```

I close my eyes and press send before I can change my mind. The email makes a swooshing sound, and I imagine it whizzing its way across space, and landing in Simon's iPhone with a massive Hurrah! I place the phone onto the table and watch, begging him not to reply, and yet at the same time, willing him to.

My phone buzzes and I almost jump off the couch. I grab it and stare at the message.

It's from Simon.

```
Hey!
   The receptionist at Bromfield Primary
School? I think I know you as more than
that! LOL! Do you want to see me about
school business or personal? Happy to
meet    you    at    the    Mistletoe    Inn,
regardless, but I'd rather it be for the
latter, than the former.
   Friday at 1.30pm?
   S.
   Xx
```

The kisses and the informality of the email cut into my eyes. I wonder if I did the right thing by asking him to meet, but as with everything I do recently, it's too late now. I press reply, confirm that 1.30pm Friday is fine, and then send the message. A reply comes straight back, informing me that 'S' is looking forward to seeing me again.

Oh God.

What am I about to do?

I don't tell my parents or Zach about my meeting with Simon, because I don't want any worries – aka judgement. This is going to be hard enough as it is, without my dad telling me he wants to come with me; my mum warning me not to upset his wife; and Zach pretending not to be jealous that I had other sexual partners before him... No, maybe that's not fair to my friend.

He's not really the jealous type, but the way he looked at me the other night when I mentioned my 'fling' was like a little puppy dog who's been chucked out in the rain. I can't cope with that. His reaction is the reason why I don't go in for serious relationships anymore.

If they work for you, terrific.

But they've never worked for me.

10

F riday morning, and while I'm supposed to be making plans for some kind of school fund charity event, all I can think about is my meeting with Simon. What am I going to say? What will he say? Will he turn up? Will I turn up? So many questions swirl around my head, and it's hard to concentrate on anything except my anxiety, but I have to get on with this bloody list, before Margaret gets on my case.

Again.

I'm so sick of her sarcastic comments and snappy little remarks recently. The other day she even told me off for padding around the reception in my stockinged feet. Okay, so it might be unorthodox to slip your shoes off under the desk, but I'm sure I'm not the only one who does it. It was just bad luck that I happened to need something from the filing cabinet, when Margaret appeared, and questioned where my shoes were. When I explained that I'd left them temporarily under my desk, I received a lecture on my recent unprofessional attitude to my work. I had no idea what she was talking about – except maybe lopping my son off the newsletter photo – but in any case, she carried on, telling me how terrible it would look if a guest or a parent arrived in reception and saw me barefoot.

Oh, the horror of seeing a shoeless woman in the workplace!

I shake my head at the thought of it, and then get back to my list of events to raise money for the school funds. I have four things so far... Cake sale, pop quiz, parents'-and-kids' bingo, and a sponsored walk around the school field. It's not the most original fundraiser in the world, but it's the best I can come up with just hours before my meeting with Simon.

'Charlotte, how far have you got with the events list?'

Margaret appears from her office; a bundle of files under her arm. I try to hide my inadequate notes, but it's too late. The principal plonks the folders on the desk, and reads the paper over my shoulder.

'Cake sale? Didn't we do one of those last week? Pop quiz? Definitely not. Parents'-and-kids' bingo? How exactly are you planning to run that, without the parents being in the building?'

'I... erm... It was really just an idea. I hadn't got round to the logistics yet.'

Margaret prods her finger onto my note about the sponsored walk around the field, and scowls.

'Have you seen the field recently? It's like a swamp out there, since it is autumn after all. So, unless you're offering to clean all the muddy shoes, trainers and trousers afterwards, I suggest you delete it. The last thing I need in this school is a trail of footprints, and crying children because they've caught a chill, traipsing round the field in minus degrees.'

'Of course. Sorry, I didn't think.'

I try to stop my hand from shaking, as I score the walk off my list, and then I end up deleting the rest of my ideas too.

'I'll look forward to seeing more ideas, later,' Margaret says, and then stomps off down the corridor. If I wasn't so uptight about my meeting with Simon, I might take offence at the way I've just been treated, but right now I can't give it a second thought. Margaret will get her stupid list soon enough, but for now, I'm on a Simon countdown.

God help me.

∼

The Mistletoe Inn is a sixteenth-century building, perched on the corner of Bromfield High Street. It's kind of funny to describe it as a high street, since the only shops on there are a butcher, a gift shop, a too-expensive clothes store, a café and a newsagent. But anyway, for us villagers, it's the centre of everything. Our version of Times Square, if Times Square was fifty feet long and made up of crumbling old buildings.

It's not even Halloween yet, but there is already a Christmas tree standing in the tiny window of the inn. It's covered in bright-red baubles and silver lights, and there is a massive star perched on the top. I'm sure it's there to get us in the mood for seasonal dinners and celebratory events, but it just makes me even more nervous. It's the same with those fish tanks that they have in dental surgeries. The fish are supposed to give off an aura of calm and peace, but seeing them dart around like that, does nothing but bring on my anxieties.

As weird as that may be.

I catch my reflection in one of the windowpanes, and try to study it without anyone realising. It took me ages to get ready today, though goodness knows why I have gone to so much trouble. What do I want Simon to think? That I'm still pretty? That I'm still interested in him? That I still think about him, even now after all these years?

Yes.

No.

I don't know.

It's three minutes before Simon is due to meet me, so I push the heavy door, and go inside. The heat hits me with so much force that my glasses steam up. Thank goodness I'm a mother and always have a tissue in my pocket. I give them a quick wipe, order a lemonade from the bar, and then take it to a table in the corner. It's far enough from the door that I won't get a draft, but it'll be close enough to see Simon as soon as he enters the room. The varnished table is sticky beneath my touch, and I wonder when it was last cleaned, but there is no time to dwell on that, because within seconds of me sitting down, the door swings open, and Simon walks in.

He's wearing a heavy overcoat, gloves and a flat cap, giving him the look of a country gentlemen, even though he is originally from London. He stares at me from across the almost empty lounge, gives me a wave and then orders a cider from the bar. I can feel my heart pounding in my chest, and a minute later, he stands across from me.

'Hi, Charlotte,' he says. I'm surprised that he called me by my real name, instead of Lottie, which he knows pisses me right off.

'Hey.'

There is no question of him greeting me with a hug or a kiss or even a handshake, and I'm happy with that. He takes off his outerwear, settles them onto the wide, low windowsill and then sits opposite me.

'I can't believe they have their Christmas tree up already.' He laughs. 'Is it me, or does that event get earlier and earlier, and more commercial every year?'

I nod in agreement, but all I can think about is how my parents say that kind of thing all the time. God, I used to think he was so cool, but now he's middle-aged. I guess time catches up with all of us eventually, but I always imagined that Simon would stay cool. He takes a gulp of cider, and eyes me over the top of the glass. When he's finished, he wipes his mouth with the back of his hand, but a thin strand of liquid still glints on the top of his lip. I can't take my eyes off it.

'So, how've you been?'

Actually, I've been raising your son for the past ten years. How've you been?

'I've been okay. You?'

He nods and takes another mouthful of cider.

'Good, good. Can't complain as they say. You married? Kids?'

His nonchalant questioning makes the hairs on the back of my neck stand on end, and I pray that my face doesn't give away the answer.

'No, not married. I see you are though.'

He laughs.

'Yeah. In name anyway, if nothing else.'

This again. A decade later and he's still saying the same thing; still desperate for people to think he's a misunderstood husband, rather than a serial philanderer. I pity him. I pity him and his stupid wife.

'So, what can I do for you?' He smiles and reveals those perfect, white teeth of his, and it puts me on edge.

I have no bloody idea what he can do for me. Have I ever known?

'Well, I... I don't know to be honest. I just... I just... I thought... Well... I wanted...'

'Christ, Charlotte, have you developed a stutter since I last saw you? Do you think you can spit it out before closing time?'

'Okay, I want to know what you're doing here.'

There, I said it.

'What I'm doing here in the pub, or what I'm doing in Bromfield?'

'You know what I mean.'

The pub door swings open, and a blast of cold air whooshes down the lounge and straight to our table. So much for the corner protecting me from the elements. I cross my arms around my chest, but I'm still freezing.

'Monica and I decided to move back to Bromfield about six months ago. We'd both had enough of London. It makes me sound like an old geezer, but it's a place for youngsters, not middle-aged cronies like myself. Besides that, I wanted to expand my business, so now I have an office in London and another in Northampton.'

I have to bite my tongue to stop myself admitting that I already knew about the company expansion. Christ, if Simon knew my friend had investigated him, his ego would be out of control.

'Okay, I understand you wanting to get out of London, but why did you come here? Bromfield has a population of what? A couple of thousand? Maybe not even that. It's not the centre of the universe, is it? If you wanted to open an office in Northampton, you could have moved there.'

Simon rubs the corner of his eye. His fingers are immaculate. They've always been immaculate.

'No, Bromfield isn't the centre of the universe, but we wanted to avoid living in a big town again. Besides, Monica's parents are just down the road in one of the villages, so it seemed like a perfect choice. Plus... I kind of hoped I'd bump into you one day. I felt like I needed to apologise to you.'

'To me?'

'For the way I treated you, ten years ago. It was unforgivable.'

I take a sharp breath and the air hits me at the back of my throat. I was hoping that the conversation would go nowhere near the events of a decade ago, but I guess that just makes me naïve. He was bound to mention it. Why wouldn't he?

'Don't worry about it.' I pick at the corner of my beer mat, and try to restrain myself from tearing it into a thousand pieces. Simon grabs my hands and I jerk and pull them back. He notices the inappropriateness of his behaviour, retreats, scratches his head and makes a weird sucking sound with his lips.

'Look, I need you to know that I never meant to leave you at the clinic that day. It was always my intention to come back and collect you.'

'It's okay...'

'No, it isn't. You see, as soon as I got back to the office, my wife messaged me.' He lowers his voice and tilts his head towards me. 'She had taken a fucking overdose.'

'She what?'

His words rattle around my brain. An overdose? An overdose just after she had seen me walk out of the clinic, still pregnant with her husband's baby? More guilt. More ever-increasing guilt.

'She had found out that I was seeing someone.' He waves his hands in the air. 'Don't worry, she didn't know it was you. Anyway, she was devastated that there was somebody else in my life, so took an overdose and then rang me. I had to race home, get her to the hospital and by the time all that had happened, it was too late to pick you up.'

I take a sip of my lemonade, to try and cleanse myself of this information; of this conversation; of this whole fucking episode. I have no idea what I'm supposed to say now, but my mouth just snaps out the first stupid thing that enters my head.

'That's such bullshit.'

The words come out louder than I expect them to, and an old man in a green waxed jacket looks up from his beer and scowls. Simon straightens up, surprised at my defiance. I don't think I ever dared speak to him like that when we were together.

'It's true, Charlotte! When I got home, she had already

vomited all over the couch, but I still took her to hospital, and they pumped what was left of her stomach. It was awful.'

It's horrifying to think that my actions caused another woman so much pain, but in my defence, I was just a teenager, with no ties, and no responsibilities. That can't be said for Simon, however. He told me the marriage was over, that he had had enough and was leaving. If the overdose is anyone's fault, it's his... And hers for staying with the wanker.

I just need to keep telling myself that.

'Look,' I say. 'I can't make any judgements on what your wife did that day. If I was in her position, I'm sure I'd have felt the same way. But why didn't you contact me after that? Couldn't you even send me a text? Let me know what was happening? You owed me an explanation after what you'd put me through. Even a simple goodbye would have been better than silence. Ten years of silence!'

Simon grabs my hands again, and this time I don't take them away. I'm too angry, and upset, and yet I have no idea why I feel this way. Is it because he chose to stay with his wife, or because he saved her from death? Perhaps if she'd died, we'd have been able to make a go of things.

Shit! I can't think this way. It's cruel and it's selfish, and yet I can't help but wonder.

'Don't you think I've regretted that day ever since it happened? I have! I'm not a monster, Lottie. I had feelings for you. Real feelings, and I know that what I did makes me look like an asshole, but you need to know that if I could have called, I would have. The reality is, my phone corrupted and I lost all of my contacts. Then I moved to London and had no way of getting hold of you. That's just the way it was. I'm sorry. For everything. I'm sorry.'

It takes me all my time not to laugh out loud. His phone deleted his contacts? How old is that story? And he had no way of contacting me, and yet he knew where my acting college was, and he knew where I'd be rehearsing every day until the play opened. It's all crap, and while his charm might have worked on that little nineteen-year-old girl who fell in love with him all those years ago, it's not going to work on me now.

And yet I want to believe that it's true.

The voices in my broken heart still wonder if there's a chance of us living happily ever after with our son, while my mind screams back in despair. For fuck's sake! Of course there isn't. But isn't it weird that no matter how old you get, all it takes is a loving look or a few choice words to turn you back into a giddy, loved-up, gullible teenager? I saw it with my aunt. Her husband cheated on her, and then the moment he apologised and told her he'd change, she reverted back to the young girl who had fallen in love with him in sixth form. Until it happened again, just three weeks later.

'So, that day aside, are you really in Bromfield for your own interests, or are you looking for something from me?'

Simon laughs, rubs his neck and leaves red scratches in his wake.

'Lottie, as much as I enjoyed our relationship back in the day, that's all in the past now. I know I'm a bit of a flirt, but in spite of what I say, I love Monica, and would never do anything to hurt her.' I open my mouth to remind him that he did plenty to hurt her ten years ago, but he keeps on speaking. 'I've moved on, and it's time that you did, too.'

A snort-cum-laugh shoots out of my mouth and the old man on the next table looks up again. He's pretending to do the crossword in the local newspaper, but I suspect this is the juiciest conversation he's heard in many years. His pencil hovers over the paper, but I can guarantee that his eyes are not seeing any of the words in front of him.

'Move on? Oh, believe me I moved on many years ago, so don't even go there.'

I hold my hand like a shield in front of me, and Simon sits back in his chair and smiles.

'Okay, I believe you. But in answer to your question, no I'm not in town to get anything from you. I've had enough drama in my life, and don't have any room for more. Let's change the subject.'

'Fine. How are your children?'

Simon's eyebrows knit together and he rubs the stubble on his chin. It used to be all black when I knew him, but now it's speckled with grey.

'My children? What are you talking about? I don't have any children.'

What? My mind goes all the way back to ten years ago, when we sat in his car and he showed me photos of his kids. Was I dreaming that? No, definitely not. I remember him telling me – wrongly – that he couldn't have kids naturally, and his family had been conceived through IVF. What's going on?

'You do have children,' I say. 'You showed me pics of them when we were alone in your car, remember?'

My hands are shaking, and I rip at the corners of the beer mat, in an effort to steady myself.

'I think I'd remember if I had children, Charlotte! You must be getting me mixed up with somebody else. It can happen. It was a long time ago.'

Simon seems confused. In reality, he's told so many lies over the years that he can't keep up with himself. He probably does have children, but has just forgotten about them.

'But when I saw you in Waterstones, Monica said you had to go and pick up Betty. I presumed that was your daughter.'

'No, that's our dog. She'd been at the groomers.' He throws his hands up, as though in a western movie. 'I can assure you I have no kids. Godchildren, yes, though they're hardly children anymore. I'd show you a pic of them, but it's in my other wallet.'

His godchildren. So that's who was in the photo he showed to me all those years ago. It hits me that the only reason he told me he had kids, was an excuse for why he couldn't leave his stupid wife. That's what men do, isn't it? They can't possibly hurt the children's feelings by leaving when they're so young... Maybe when they're older, maybe when they understand what goes on in the world, maybe when they're actually real. Ugh! This man makes me sick and I can't believe I fell for his patter, back in the day. What an asshole.

Before Simon can say anything else, his phone vibrates against the table. He picks it up, studies it for a second and then stuffs it into his pocket.

'I'm so sorry, but I've got to go.'

My ex-lover gets up from the chair, and it makes a grinding noise against the wooden floor. He throws his arms into his coat, and then sticks his cap on his head.

'It was nice talking to you, Lottie,' he says. 'Let's meet up again soon, okay? I'll message you.'

He reaches over and kisses my cheek, and then marches over to the door. As he opens it, the cold air whooshes in and dries the saliva he left on my skin. I rub at it and then gel my hands, while the old man on the next table sniggers.

'Glad to see the back of him, eh, love?'

'Something like that,' I say, as I look at the closed door.

The former love of my life is gone.

Again.

I finish my lemonade, pop to the toilet and then head back onto the street. I pass by the pub car park, just in case Simon is still there, but he isn't. The space is empty, except for a huge skip, an old blue van and the landlord's Range Rover. A ginger cat eyes me from next to a wheelie bin, and I can't help but think he's judging me for meeting my old married lover.

'You and me both,' I say, as I cross the road and head back to pick Tom up from school.

11

The wind is icy cold against my body as I wait for the school gates to open. In the morning, I'm the person who unlocks these gates and beckons all the children into the playground, but in the afternoon, I'm just another freezing parent, hoping that the receptionist hasn't forgotten about us all.

At 3.27pm, Amy, the afternoon receptionist, trudges across the playground, and unlocks the gigantic padlock.

'Bloody hell!' squawks one of the mothers next to me. 'If she was any slower, she'd be going backwards.'

The doors open one by one, and the children file out. There are unbuttoned coats, PE bags being dragged across the tarmac, knitted bobble hats bouncing with each step, and art projects clutched to chests, or waved in the air.

'Hi, Charlotte!' Harry from Year One runs up to me, waving a red toy lorry above his head. 'Look what I won today! It's a truck!'

'Oh, it's lovely,' I say, and Harry looks so proud of himself.

It's hard to describe how you feel when you work with children. They become a part of your life and you feel happy and protective of them all. I always wonder if I'll ever learn their names when they arrive aged four, and then I cry when they wave us goodbye aged eleven. There's not one of these children I don't care about, but there's one child I hold dearer than any other in the world.

My own.

I strain to see the Year Five door, and as I do, Charlie comes bounding out, holding his coat around his shoulders like Superman, or Batman or some other kind of superhero. I expect to see Tom following behind, but instead, there's an empty space. He must have popped to the loo, I guess.

Charlie sees me staring, stops swinging his coat and looks at the floor. He doesn't want to make eye contact. As he reaches me, he tries to rush past, but I'm too quick for him.

'Charlie! Hey! Didn't you see me?'

He looks up. Sheepish.

'Oh, hello Tom's mum,' he says, and then carries on past.

'No Tom with you today?' I shout.

'He went out of the other door. The Year One door at the back.'

I stare at the building. The Year One door? What's he talking about? I turn to ask, but Charlie has already gone, whizzing down the road with his 'cape' still draped over his shoulders.

I look at my watch. It's 3.40pm. The sun will start to fade soon, and the autumnal weather will be even chillier than it is already. I sigh and make my way around to the Year One door. Why Tom has gone out that way is anyone's guess, but if I stick to the main path, at least we'll meet somewhere in the middle.

Only we don't meet.

Three minutes later, I'm at the Year One unit, frustrated and angry that Tom has given me the slip. He must still be cross at me for lopping him out of the newsletter, though how an almost ten-year-old boy can hold a grudge for so long, is beyond me. Maybe he gets that from his father's side.

'Hey, Charlotte, I didn't expect to see you this afternoon. What can we do for you?'

Jennifer, the teaching assistant for the Bluebirds class, helps a little girl on with her coat. Jennifer's shiny blonde hair swings from side to side as she does so.

'I'm looking for Tom. His friend told me that he came out of the Year One entrance tonight – for some strange reason. Is he here?'

Jennifer scowls, and looks back towards the unit.

'Tiffany, have you seen Tom Baker? His mum is waiting for him.'

I can hear a voice coming through the building, but it's too faint for me to make out what she is saying. Jennifer turns back to me.

'He was here, but Tiffany saw him leave about five minutes ago. She asked why he was leaving out of our door instead of his own, but he rushed out so quickly, that she didn't get an answer. Sorry!'

I smile and try to keep the anger off my face. That's the thing with being a single parent – or at least that's the thing with *me* being a single parent. I always assume that people are judging me for not having a man in my life, so feel that I have to be a perfect, patient and never-cross mother to make up for it.

But when I see my rebellious offspring, I'll go bloody mental.

An hour later, the sun is going down, and I'm standing in the hallway of Charlie's house, shuffling from one foot to the other. The smell of pasta sauce wafts in from the kitchen, but it makes me feel nothing but nauseous.

'I won't be angry with you, I promise, but I need you to tell me why Tom went out of the Year One door, instead of his own.'

Charlie stares at the floor, while his mum rubs his shoulders.

'Come on, Charlie,' she says. 'You need to tell Charlotte everything you know. It's getting dark outside, and Tom needs to get home.'

Tom's friend looks up and purses his lips.

'He said he didn't want to see you. That he was still mad at you for cutting him out of the newsletter. Sebastian Green said that you mustn't love him if you did that, and Joshua Brown doesn't even believe that Tom was going to be in the newsletter in the first place. He called Tom a liar.'

I rub my forehead and groan. The bloody newsletter again. I have no idea why Tom is still so upset about it, but I guess when you're nearly ten, a photo in the school paper is maybe more important to you than grown-ups think. Still, that doesn't excuse him from running out on me. What the hell was he thinking? And where is he now? Where is my son?!

'Was there anything else, Charlie? Did he say where he was going? Anything you can remember at all might help me find Tom. Like your mum says, it's getting dark and he needs to come home.'

'Sorry, that's all he said. Can I go now?'

Charlie gazes up at his mum, and she nods her head. He rushes into the living room and the door slams shut behind him. Seconds later I can hear him chatting with his sister as though nothing has happened. I guess in his little world, nothing has.

'I'm so sorry.' Charlie's mum hugs a tea towel to her chest, and shakes her head.

'It was worth a try,' I say. 'Anyway, I guess I should get back home, in case he turns up there.'

'I'm sure he'll be home before you are.' She smiles and reaches over my shoulder to undo the door. I'm disturbing her dinner preparations, but she's too polite to say it out loud.

'Thanks,' I say, and then seconds later I'm out of the house and back into the cold autumn evening.

Where is Tom? Where is my son?

～

Back home, Zach perches on the arm of the chair, staring at his phone. My parents slump on the sofa, both wringing their hands and grimacing.

'That's all of the neighbours messaged,' Zach says. 'The ones we speak to, anyway.'

'Thank you.' I gaze out of the window, but it's so dark outside that all I can see is a reflection of my living room and its occupants.

'I can't believe he would just walk off on his own,' my mother says. 'It's not like him at all.'

My dad nods and breathes in and out through his nose. It makes a long, whistling sound, which is even more unnerving than the silence.

'Are you sure Charlie said he had gone out that way?' he asks.

I nod.

'It wasn't just Charlie who said it. One of the teachers saw Tom leave, and asked what he was doing.'

'And what did he say?'

'He just ignored her and rushed out.'

My mum springs up from the sofa.

'Does anyone want some tea? Shall I close these blinds? We don't want the whole street seeing our business.'

I say no to both questions, and she sighs and sits back down.

'We should phone the police,' Zach says. 'It's been two hours since he disappeared, and I know it looks like he stomped off in a huff, but better to be safe than sorry.'

Zach is right. I was hesitant to get the police involved earlier, because I was sure he'd slink back into the house as soon as he thought his point had been made. Now though, it's dark and cold and creepy out there. My little boy might be in a strop with me, but he needs to come home. He needs to come home, now.

'Yes, let's call the police,' I say, and Zach nods, while my mum grabs her phone from the coffee table.

'Should we call the local police number, or 999?' My mum stares at me over the top of her glasses.

'I don't think that matters, Anne!' my dad growls, and my mum sits bolt upright.

'I was trying to help, Bernard!' she snaps.

'I'll call 999,' Zach says, but before he does, there is a loud bang at the front door. We all jump up, and I dash into the hallway.

It's Tom! It has to be Tom! He's home, thank God he's home!

I unlatch the door, and as it swings open, there he is. There's my son, staring at the concrete path, aware that he's just put me through two hours of hell.

'Tom!'

I rush forward, and grab my son, but as I do so, my eyes fall on a figure standing in the shadows behind him. She steps forward and I am floored.

It's Monica Travis.

'I found this young man walking down beside the river,' she says. 'I didn't want him to fall in, or catch pneumonia, so I thought I'd bring him home.'

By this time my family and Zach are all crowded into the hall, welcoming Tom and eager to see the woman who 'rescued' him. I can't say anything. I'm rooted to the spot, but my mother reaches past me and pulls Tom inside.

'Tom, you silly boy!' She scolds my son, at the same time as hugging him close. Zach pats him on the head and my dad rubs his arm, but Tom remains mute.

'Thank you for bringing him home,' my dad says, unaware of who he is talking to. 'It's a good job you were passing!'

'Could you take Tom inside, please? Get him some clean clothes and a warm drink?'

'Sure,' my mum says. 'Come on, Grandma's little soldier. In we go.'

Tom scowls as he's dragged into the living room. He hates being spoken to like a baby, but he'd never tell his grandmother that. I watch everyone go, and then I step out into the garden, and close the door behind me. The concrete is freezing against my stockinged feet, and the wind cuts straight into my chest, but I need to speak to Monica. I need to know what she was doing with my child.

'What's going on? Why were you following Tom?'

Monica takes a step back as though she's taken a punch. Her bobbed hair swishes back with her; immaculate even on the coldest of evenings.

'I wasn't following your son,' she snaps. 'I was walking my dog and I saw him wandering along the riverbank. I ignored him at first, but then I saw him tumble in some wet, fallen leaves, and I stepped in.'

I roll my eyes.

'Funny, he doesn't seem to have any mud on his trousers. Surely he would have if he had stumbled.'

Monica ignores my remark.

'It's lucky I came along when I did,' she says, 'otherwise he could have fallen into the river or been picked up by a predator or something. I was just trying to keep him safe. I did what any other woman would have done.'

Is she guilting me right now? This is bullshit, and I won't stand for it.

Zach appears at the door, holding Tom's damp school uniform. There are huge muddy patches at the knees. Muddy patches that I had not seen just moments ago.

'Your mum wants to know if we should put Tom's clothes straight into the washing machine? They're covered in mud. Or do you want them to go into the wash basket?'

'It doesn't matter,' I say. 'Just put them wherever you like.'

'Everything okay here?' he asks. I ignore him and lean into Monica.

'You stay away from my son. Don't come near him ever again, you hear me? I want nothing to do with you!'

She laughs.

'That's funny, because you wanted plenty to do with my husband this afternoon.'

My heart sinks into my legs.

'What do you mean?'

'You were seen at the Mistletoe Inn. My friend's daughter is a barmaid there.'

Monica's voice shakes and I wonder if she's about to cry. I don't know what to say. It's no use denying it, and I can't believe that Simon would be so stupid as to meet me in a place he knows he'll be spotted.

Or maybe he doesn't know about the barmaid.

Or maybe he doesn't care.

I shuffle from one foot to the other, and Zach grabs my trainers from the hall and hands them to me. I stuff them onto my feet, even though my legs feel like floppy pieces of string.

'I need to know something,' she says. 'Did you tell him?'

'What?'

'Did you tell him that he has a son? That you gave birth to his child?'

My phone buzzes. It's Charlie's mum, asking if I've found Tom yet. I stick it into my pocket, and take a breath.

'No, I didn't tell him. Simon knowing about Tom is the last thing I want, and to be honest, I wish that you didn't know about him either. But since you seem obsessed with us both, there's not much chance of that, is there?'

Monica's mouth contorts, and her nostrils flare. I've hit a nerve, but what does she expect? Happy families? That's never going to happen.

'Charlotte!' Zach sticks his hands out, as if breaking up a prize fight. 'Maybe we should just say thank you to Mrs Travis for bringing Tom home. It's late and we're not going to solve all of our problems on the doorstep, are we?'

His superiority annoys the hell out of me.

'Shut up, Zach, this has nothing to do with you.'

'Fine.'

He disappears back into the house, and the living-room door slams behind him. Now Monica and I stand glaring at each other, like a scene out of a bad soap opera, and only the occasional car engine breaks the stifled atmosphere. Finally, she shoves her hands deep into her pockets, and sniffs.

'I did you a favour this evening,' she says. 'In spite of everything, I brought your son home.'

Guilt trip again.

'And I'm grateful. But that doesn't mean I want you in his life, so please – this has to be the end of this nonsense. You have to leave us alone now.'

Monica licks her lips, and trots off down the path, her hair whooshing, her high-heeled boots clip-clopping on the concrete.

I slam the door, rest my head against the glass and silently scream.

12

'You want me to stay with you tonight? Y'know, just as friends.'

Zach smiles at me from the other end of the couch.

'No, it's okay, but thank you.'

My parents are long gone, after exhausting Tom and themselves with hundreds of hugs. As soon as their car turned out of the street, my son stormed upstairs and slammed his bedroom door. He's been there ever since. Silent. Moody. Angry. Since then, Zach and I have gone over every moment of what happened earlier.

'I'm sorry I snapped at you,' I say. 'I was reacting to Monica, not you.'

'I know. It's okay.'

Zach grabs his coat from the back of my dining chair and kisses me on the forehead.

'You think I shouldn't have been so mean to her, don't you?'

'What?'

'Monica. You think I should have been more grateful. And I suppose you think I shouldn't have met Simon, either.'

My friend shrugs.

'It's none of my business. Look, get some sleep and we'll speak tomorrow.'

He disappears out of the back door, and I lock it, grab some clean pyjamas from the pile of washing on the kitchen table, and then head upstairs. Tom's bedroom door stares at me; a massive 'Do Not Enter or Else' sign emblazoned in the middle. I knock, and then wait for an answer.

'Mum?'

My son's voice travels through the wood that separates us, and lands with a thump in my heart. I open the door and stare inside. Tom is in bed, and his night light shines a soft glow over his little things: his bookcase full of volumes on horses and trucks; his posters of Eminem (a new addition, thanks to Charlie) and his curtains with blue dinosaurs printed on them. A month ago, he decided that a Year Five boy is far too grown up for such babyish curtains, so I'm buying him new ones as soon as I get paid, but for now they stay.

'Are you okay?'

'Yes.' Tom's head is turned away from the door, and his voice is muffled and nasal. He's been crying into his pillow, and that knowledge tears me apart. I sit on his football-themed duvet and rub his hair. It's damp with sweat, and sticks up at odd little angles.

'I don't think you are okay,' I say. 'Why don't you turn round and talk to me. Tell me what's been going on?'

'I *am* okay.'

I sigh and pick up his tiny stuffed giraffe. I remember the day we bought that silly little thing. We were in Tesco together, and Tom must have been, what? One maybe? No, a little older than that. We were at the toy section, and he picked up the giraffe and insisted on carrying it around with him.

'Mummy has to pay for that before we leave,' I said, but twenty minutes later, as I scanned my groceries, I'd forgotten all about the giraffe. It wasn't until we got out of the store that Tom waved it in my face and I realised. I went straight back to pay for it, because although it was just a pound, I couldn't bear the thought of being dishonest. Tom has slept with Giraffey-Boy ever since, although now he insists that the toy sleeps on his bedside table, even though there are many times when I sneak in and see him cuddling it – just like the old days.

'I know that you're mad about the newsletter,' I say. 'All I was trying to do was fit the photo onto the page. I never knew you'd be so upset.'

Tom lifts his head and turns towards me. His face is covered in tears, and I wipe them with the sleeve of my shirt.

'I'm not upset about the newsletter,' he says.

'You're not?'

'I was, but I'm not anymore.'

I tuck Tom's giraffe under the duvet, and he grabs and holds on to it.

'So why are you upset?'

'Will you be angry?'

'No.'

I hold my breath, and wonder what Tom is about to say. If he'd been in trouble at school, his teacher would have told me. Wouldn't she? My son sits up and wipes his eyes.

'It was the lady.'

My heart leaps.

'What lady?'

'A lady came up to me when I was walking to Grandma's the other day. And she said strange things.'

My mind goes straight to Monica, and I feel the anger boiling in my solar plexus. She is everywhere. Everywhere! What the fuck is her problem? I try to keep the anger out of my voice because I don't want Tom to think that I'm cross with him, but I cannot believe what he has just said. And I know that it can only get worse.

'The lady told me that she knew who my daddy was, and that if I wanted to, I could meet him today.'

My hand shoots up to my mouth. Oh God. No!

'What did you... What did you say?'

'I didn't know what to do, and you always say I shouldn't speak to strangers, so I just kept walking, but then today she was standing on the other side of the fence when we were in the playground. That's why I went out of the Year One door, because I didn't want her to see me! I told Charlie that I was mad at you, but I wasn't really. Not anymore. I was just scared of the lady.'

Tom bursts into tears, and I cuddle him tight to my chest. How dare Monica step in and tell my son about his father? Is it some kind of revenge?

'You did the right thing,' I say, 'but I wish you had come straight over to tell me about it, instead of running away.'

I wipe Tom's forehead. His hair sticks to his skin.

'I didn't want the lady to see me, so I thought I'd wait at the post office until everyone had gone. But then when I came out, you weren't there either, so that's when I walked to the river. I was trying to get home; I promise I was.'

'I know you were. I know. Shush now, it's okay.'

Tom's little body shakes beneath my touch, and I know he is tired and in need of sleep, but there's a few things I need to get straight first.

'So, the lady followed you. And I know she helped you to get up after you fell, but you shouldn't have gotten into her car. You should have asked her to phone Mummy... or something.'

Tom takes his head from my chest and gawps at me.

'I was wrong about the lady. I asked her why she said I could meet my dad and she said she didn't. She said I must have misheard her, and that she would take me home, before I got into trouble.'

I can't believe this. Monica is gaslighting my son? What the hell is she doing?

'Did she hurt you, Tom?'

My son looks confused, wipes his eyes on his sleeve, and shakes his head.

'No, she was nice, and she dried my eyes and let me pet her dog. It's a little white dog. I know I shouldn't have got into her car, but I was freezing. I promise not to do that again.'

A dog barks outside, and we both jump.

'It's just Trevor,' I say. 'Silly, noisy Trevor.'

We both relax.

'Did the lady say anything else about your dad?'

Tom shrugs, lies his head onto his pillow and sticks his thumb in his mouth like he used to do when he was little.

'No, I told you. When I asked her, she said I hadn't heard her properly. Maybe I'm deaf, like my friend, Jacob.'

'No. No, you're not deaf, but maybe you did hear her wrong. If there's lots of traffic around, I sometimes feel as though I've heard something that I haven't as well.'

It's a complete lie, but I don't want to freak out my child. I want him to go to sleep and never think about Monica again. I gaze back at Tom, with the intention of asking him more questions, but my beautiful son is already falling asleep, his breathing deep and loud. I watch him for a moment, feeling his chest rise and fall against my leg. I love this boy. I've always loved this boy, and now I have to protect him more than I ever have before.

I bend down to kiss his head, and then I tiptoe out of the room.

∼

I lie in the bath and as the water warms my bones, I think about Monica. She was a mixture of caring and creepy on the doorstep this evening, but then again, I can't blame her. I'd kill anyone who came near my husband, and I don't even have one. But what kind of woman must she be, to stalk a child, tell him about his father and then ask if he'd like to meet him?

I can't get my head around it, and I'm thankful that after everything, she brought him home safe and sound. That said, did she put Tom in the car with the intention of taking him to her house? Was she planning to kidnap him and then changed her mind?

Or have I been reading too many psychological thrillers?

Nothing Monica has done makes sense, but what can I do about it? Report her to the police? Tell them that she rescued my son from falling into a river and brought him home? They'd never believe she was stalking him, and without any concrete proof, I only have Tom's word that she asked if he'd like to meet Simon. None of that is a crime, and the police would laugh in my face.

I pour the water over my hair and grab the shampoo.

I don't have any answers to what happened this evening, but I do know one thing...

If Monica ever hurts my son, it will be the last thing she does.

The school reception has been busy all morning, and every time I try to do any kind of research into Monica and Simon, the phone goes, or a random parent pops in to complain about cancelled gym classes or enquire about missed trip payments. When the whole school went into assembly, I thought I had a spare five minutes to investigate, but as soon as I took out my phone, Margaret came storming down the corridor with a Year Three boy in tow. She clocked my phone, and scowled.

'If it's not too much bother, please could you telephone Joshua's parents, and ask if one of them could pick him up? He's just thrown up all over the hall.'

She pointed the little boy in my direction, and I nodded my head and threw the phone back into my bag. Sadly, in spite of the sick child in front of me, it was too late to stop another confrontation with Margaret.

'If you could please confine your personal calls to home time, I'd be very grateful,' she said, and marched back up the corridor before I could even reply.

Now, it's 11.30am, there is a lull in my work, and Margaret is showing some prospective parents around the school. With a little bit of luck, she won't be back in reception for at least another twenty minutes. I swing my laptop around so that it's not visible to anyone heading towards me, and then start tapping Monica's name into Google.

Nothing.

What did I expect? Let's face it, if Zach couldn't find anything on her, what chance do I have? I sigh and start typing again, but as I do, my handbag vibrates against my leg. I look around to make sure that Margaret isn't about to return at any moment, and answer the handset. There's a long, drawn-out sigh on the other end.

'I hear you saw Monica last night. What was that about?'

Simon.

There's no hello, no how you doing, just straight to the point. It's weird but after everything he did to me ten years ago, and all the rage I've stored up since then, it is this phone call that makes me want to tear his throat out.

'Yes, I did see her, but I wish I hadn't. Believe it or not, she's not on my list of people I want in my life.'

He breathes heavily.

'Well, according to Monica, she ran into you last night beside the river. You just happened to be passing while she was walking the dog. I'm not being funny, Charlotte, but I hope you weren't following her. I wouldn't want any trouble.'

Ran into me beside the river? What is he talking about?

'Fuck, Simon, you've got an ego on you! Why would I ever want to follow your wife?'

'Well, if you didn't, how come you ran into her then? Seems a bit too convenient to me.'

I cross my legs, and dart my eyes around the room. What is this about? She followed my son, and is now accusing me of following her? This is bullshit.

'I didn't run into her at all. I saw her when she brought Tom home...'

My words trail off, and I hear Simon swallow on the other end of the phone.

'Who's Tom?'

My ribs feel as though they're turning inwards. What did I just say? What did I just say?! A crippling cold sweat travels up my sides, and tingles over my shoulders. This can't be happening. All these years of silence and secrets, and now I've just blurted out my son's name? Just like that?

'Charlotte?'

I hang up.

13

The wind howls around my ears as I walk up the road towards school. I pray that my son has the good sense to come straight out this afternoon. The last thing I need is for him to do a tour of Bromfield like he did last night. I rub my ears and go over the conversation I had with Simon this morning. I can't believe I said Tom's name out loud. And then I hung up! What was he supposed to think after that? I should have told him it was my friend. Or a neighbour. Or even my dog!

A little voice whispers in my head.

You should have just told him it was his son. If you don't, then Monica will, and that will make things even worse than they are already.

I shake the thought from my head, and as I do, Amy wanders out of the school building, and unlocks the gate. Parents and grandparents flow through like sand in an egg timer, and I throw my hood over my head, and ready myself to join them.

My phone buzzes in my hand, and I look at it. It's a message from Simon.

Can we meet tomorrow? I'd like to talk to you.

It wouldn't take a genius to know what that is all about.

~

'Tom, are you ready for school yet? We're going to be late.'

I hear my son stomping around upstairs, and strain to hear if his footsteps appear to be getting closer.

They're not.

'Tom! Get a wriggle on. Turn off your music and come and get your shoes on.'

At last, his door springs open, and my floppy-haired boy bounds out of the room and down the stairs.

'Careful, or you'll fall.'

'Mum! You just said hurry up, so here I am – hurrying!'

'Cheeky!'

I hand him his shoes, and he plonks himself onto the bottom stair.

'Tie them for me please?'

I bend down to thread the laces together, while Tom fiddles with his gloves.

'Will I still be doing this for you when you're twenty?'

'Yep!'

The doorbell goes, and I look at my watch. Whoever this is, I hope I can get rid of them, otherwise we'll both be late. Tom looks up and squints his eyes, trying to see through the fogged glass.

'It looks like a man,' he says, as he jumps up. I slide my feet into my shoes, grab my bag and then open the door. Simon stands on the doorstep, in the same spot as his wife did, just days ago. I stand rooted to the spot, and he smiles and looks behind me.

'Hello, Market Man!' Tom wanders into sight, clutching his PE bag and lunch box. 'What are you here for?'

Good old Tom, straight to the point as always.

'Hello, Tom,' Simon says. 'Nice to see you again.'

He reaches out his hand, and I can't believe that he thinks a nearly ten-year-old boy would want to shake it. My son stares at it, and then holds up his bag and lunch box.

'I can't shake hands I'm afraid,' he says. 'I've got to carry my stuff, and I'm also getting low on hand gel!'

He scuttles past, and reaches the car. I watch as he writes, 'I love Minecraft' in the early-morning condensation on the window.

'Simon, I can't talk now. I've got to get Tom and me to school.'

'Later then,' he says. 'After work?'

Every pore of my body wants to say no, but instead, I nod. Anything to get him to go away, far away from my son.

From our son.

'Great. See you then. Bye, Tom!'

Tom watches as Simon saunters off down the drive. I open the car and we both slide inside.

'I wonder what he wants to see you about,' Tom says. 'Maybe another school talk or something.'

'Yeah maybe.'

I sling the car into reverse and hope I hit Simon Fucking Travis on the way out.

Five hours later and I walk out of work, and straight into my ex-lover. Fantastic.

'Hi!' He's bright and breezy, as though he meets me from work every day.

'Hey.'

I carry on walking down the drive, and he trails behind, before catching up at the school gates.

'Slow down,' he says. 'I'm an old man, remember!'

He's joking. Even if he was eighty years old, Simon would never consider himself to be old. Old is something that happens to someone else, not him. One of the kids from Year Six comes past and gives me a bright smile.

'Sorry I'm late, Miss Baker,' she says. 'I've been to the dentist.' She pulls the side of her mouth open to let me see the dentist's handiwork, and I smile and tell her to just sign in the late book when she goes into reception. She runs off down the road, and I watch to make sure she gets into school safely.

'You take your job very seriously,' Simon says, as I start walking again.

'Don't you ever have to work?'

'I'm the boss. I can take time off whenever I want to.'

The wind whistles down the road, and manages to find its way into the space between the buttons on my coat. I stuff my hands in my pockets and keep walking.

'Must be fantastic,' I sneer, but it goes right over Simon's head.

'Yeah, it's not too bad. But I'll have to work late to catch up with paperwork and stuff. I'm normally in the office until nine anyway.'

I don't care.

We reach the car park. In an extraordinary stroke of bad luck, Simon's BMW is parked right next to my little Corsa.

'Is this why you wanted to see me? To tell me about your workload? Because if it was something more important, I suggest you get to it. My car is right here.'

Simon leans on his door, and stares at me. His green eyes might have a few lines at the corners, but they still look the same. I used to think they were beautiful when we were involved, but now they make me feel uncomfortable. They're too piercing, and I feel them burning right through me.

'So, I've got a son then.'

His words hit me in the stomach, but there's no point in denying it. The secret – if it ever was a secret – is no more. I stare down at my feet, and bite one side of my mouth.

'Yes. Yes, you do.'

'Tom.'

'Tom.'

I squirm against my car door. After all the years of wondering if this conversation would ever come, and praying that it wouldn't, here we are. When I thought about it over the years, I always imagined that if – and it was a big if – it ever happened, it would be a huge bombshell. An end-of-*EastEnders* moment. At no time did I expect it to be in a grotty old car park, next to the post office.

'Nice name,' Simon says. 'I had an Uncle Thomas. He was a...'

'His name isn't Thomas. It's Tom.'

Simon nods.

'I know. Sorry.'

He shifts from one foot to another, and I'm shocked at how uncomfortable this conversation seems to be making him. Simon Travis is normally Mr Confident. The man who gets what he wants, when he wants, and always has something to say about whatever subject is being discussed. But right now, he's kind of jittery. He's trying to hold on to his ego, but the situation is getting the better of him.

'Am I on the birth certificate?'

'You're joking, I presume.'

My ex-lover pinches the bridge of his nose, and then throws his hands up in surrender.

'Okay, that was a bit naïve I suppose. I just thought maybe you had…'

'Well, I didn't.'

We stand in silence, and one of the school mums wanders past and waves.

'See you at the gates later?' she shouts.

'Yeah, probably.'

She gives me the thumbs up, glances at Simon, and then heads into the post office.

'So, how did you find out about Tom?'

'After the name slip yesterday, it didn't take Poirot to figure out that something was going on. I asked Monica what the real story was behind her seeing you, and she told me that she'd brought Tom home after he'd fallen beside the river. She already knew we'd been involved ten years ago, so she kind of worked it all out.'

I almost burst into laughter. So, his precious wife just happened to recognise me and work out that I gave birth to her husband's child? Wow! No mention of the fact that she followed me to the clinic all those years ago, and is now stalking me and my son. I decide not to say anything. It isn't any of my business, as Zach keeps telling me.

'What a complicated life you lead.'

Simon smiles with one side of his mouth, and raises his eyebrows. He's amused by me, but I'm not altogether sure why. The wind rattles around the car park, and an old Coke can rolls over to my feet. I kick it, and it heads straight under my car.

'She's a good woman, you know. Has a big heart.'

I throw my hand out, and almost hit him in the chest.

'Spare me! I don't need – or want – to know about your marriage. But hey, I hope you're very happy together. Say hello to her for me.'

Simon reaches forward to touch me, but I shrug him off before his tentacles can destroy me once again.

'Goodbye, Simon.'

'Wait, we need to talk about Tom.'

My cheeks burn, and a pain pierces my brain, between my eyes. What do we need to talk about? What is there to say?

Plenty, but nothing I want to get into here.

'I'm not being funny, but we've been standing here for at least five minutes, and you've mentioned him once. The rest of the time you've been discussing your wife.'

'I want to see him.'

'No!'

I open the car door and throw myself inside, but Simon steps forward and blocks me from closing it.

'You can't stop me,' he says, 'I'm his father, and I'm entitled to see him.'

'You're entitled to nothing!' I shout, and then I push him away and somehow manage to close the door.

'I'll do all I need to do to see my son,' he snaps.

I open the window an inch, and glare at my ex-lover.

'You come anywhere near my son, and I'll go to the police and report you for stalking and harassment. Leave us alone!'

The words come out with such ferocity that they leave tiny dots of saliva all over the window. Simon's eyes bulge, as though trying to hold themselves into the sockets, and his face flushes red.

'Charlotte, let's talk about this...'

His voice has changed from one of menace, to consolation, and he even attempts a smile.

'No! Leave us alone. I mean it!'

I start the engine and screech out of the car park before he can say anything else. My heart beats so loudly that I feel as though it's about to explode. I can feel the walls closing in on my perfect little life; suffocating me from within and pressing on my skull.

Crushing me.

Crushing my world.

Threatening to grind up everything I have held dear for the past ten years.

And it has to stop.

A couple of hours late, Tom and I wander home from school, and the bitter wind cuts straight through my old coat. I desperately need a new one, but I'll have to wait until Christmas.

'Why didn't you bring the car, Mum? You always bring the car.'

Tom's teeth chatter, and he pulls his hands up into his coat. I'm glad I bought it a size too big. At least the sleeves are long enough to keep his fingers warm.

'I don't always bring the car,' I say. 'I just needed a bit of fresh air.'

'This is more than fresh air! This is frozen air! Like walking through an ice cube. I need my Minecraft hacksaw to get through this!' My dramatic son spits the words out and bangs his hidden hands together.

'Where are your gloves?'

He shrugs.

'I don't know. Charlie borrowed them at lunchtime, and I haven't seen them since.'

'So, Charlie has them then?'

Tom throws his arms in the air, like some kind of demented judge.

'I told you, I don't know. One of the fingers has a hole in it anyway, so I'll have to get new ones.'

I resist the urge to comment further. Falling out over a pair of hand-knitted gloves is not on my agenda tonight. We round the corner, and our house comes into view. I'm shocked to see that there is a figure hanging around on the driveway, and I screw up my eyes to get a better look.

Oh shit.

It's Simon.

Again.

He looks up from his phone and waves as though he's an old friend, popping over for a cuppa. I don't reply to the greeting, but it turns out I don't need to, because Tom waves and shouts a gigantic, 'Hello, Market Man!'

He nudges me.

'Mum, do you think Market Man has been standing on our drive since this morning? He must be freezing!'

I scowl.

'Of course he hasn't!' I snap, but Tom doesn't seem to notice. Instead, he passes Simon as though he stands on our driveway every day.

'Sorry, I can't talk. I've got loads of maths homework to do.'

Simon laughs, and ruffles Tom's hair as he rushes past.

'Best get to it then, Tommy.'

Tom hesitates for a moment, scowls and then positions himself next to the front door. I let him in and then turn back to Simon.

'Don't call my son, Tommy. That's not his name and he doesn't like it.'

Simon's mouth turns down at the corners, and he raises his eyebrows.

'Noted. I just thought it was cute, that's all.'

'Well, it's not.'

'Noted. Again.'

Simon grins, and I want to punch him. Ten years ago, I was

awaiting the birth of my son, wondering how I was going to survive and how I could afford all the paraphernalia that comes with a child. Luckily for me, my parents bought the cot, the pram and a heap of clothes, but the day-to-day expenses would always be down to me. Simon, meanwhile was living it up with his stupid wife, no doubt going out to fancy restaurants and buying all the luxury goods he wanted. I remember when we were together, he told me he'd bought a thirty-thousand-pound car on a whim. Who does that? I can hardly afford to buy a magazine on a whim. Life must be so great when you're well off.

'Simon, I've had a long day. What do you want?'

He stares at his watch for a moment, and then runs his manicured fingers through his hair.

'I wanted to apologise for this afternoon. I got a bit worked up, and I shouldn't have. I'm sorry.'

'Great. Goodbye.'

I pick up a parcel that has been left behind my big plant pot, and hope that when I straighten up, Simon will be gone. Wishful thinking.

'Can I come in for a minute?' he says. 'I need someone to talk to, and you're the only person I can think of.'

'Oh, come on!'

'It's true.'

He picks at a piece of white paint on my door frame, and it peels off and reveals a layer of the old, green colour. Terrific, now I'll have to add that to my list of stuff I have to sort out – when I've got the time and the money.

'Why can't you speak to Monica? She's your wife!'

He brushes the paint onto the floor, and steps on it, as though hiding it will make it less noticeable.

'We've had a bit of a falling out. She's gone to stay with her friend for a while. Hopefully nothing serious, but who can tell nowadays.'

A falling out with Monica? What was that about? I wonder if it was related to me and Tom, but there's no way I'm going to ask him about it on the doorstep.

'Sorry to hear that,' I lie. 'But isn't there anyone else you can turn to? No other young woman to satisfy your every need?'

I want my words to pain him, but there isn't a hint of regret anywhere on Simon's face.

'Hey, it's been many years since I last had another woman – especially a younger one. They're nothing but trouble, and I'm not getting any younger myself. I need someone who remembers the seventies... Or at least maybe the eighties. Every young woman I meet, hasn't got a clue when I talk about the Thatcher years, or Live Aid, or any of it.'

'Fascinating.'

I step into the front door, and Simon moves to follow me.

'What are you doing?'

'Please, Lottie. I'm a lost cause. I just need five minutes of your time.'

I sigh and step aside. He wipes his feet on the mat as though they're covered in mud.

I pop two cups of coffee onto the table, and Simon grabs his and studies the photo on the side.

'The Rolling Stones? Are you older than I thought?'

'Yes, I'm fifty-five. Just a bit younger than you.'

'Funny.'

I try to remember the last time I sat this close to Simon. The other day doesn't count. We had a table between us, and we were in a public place. Now here we are, sitting together on my leather couch, and the only other person in the house is Tom. Thank goodness he's a nerd when it comes to working on his homework. Any other kid would be sat between us, demanding to know why the latest assembly speaker is drinking coffee with Mum, but Tom doesn't work that way. He just thinks that the Market Man is our friend now. He's been in his school several times, and on our driveway twice, so now he's part of our lives.

But not in the way Simon wants to be.

'So, tell me more about Monica. Has she really gone?'

Simon wipes his mouth on the back of his hand, and plonks his cup back onto the table.

'Yep, it appears so. I think she's a bit pissed off with the whole Tom scenario.'

'My son isn't a scenario.'

I run my finger around the rim of my cup, as Simon picks up a digestive biscuit, and sticks half of it into his mouth. I hope it chokes him.

'I know, I know, but you know what I mean. It's not that she doesn't want me to be in a relationship with my son – she does – but she's just feeling a little overwhelmed.'

'Bless her.'

My sarcasm isn't lost on Simon, and he shuffles in his chair, probably hoping it will swallow him up.

'Anyway, she's taken a suitcase of stuff, but since her closet is the size of a double-garage, I suspect she'll be back – either to stay or to pick up the rest of her clothes.'

'Has she ever left you before?'

'Nope.'

Simon picks up a tiny flowery vase from my coffee table, turns it from side to side, and then puts it back where he found it. He takes another gulp of coffee, and then slumps back into the cushions. This is so, so odd.

A little voice pops into my head, and screams at me.

Simon abandoned me at a termination clinic.

And now he is in my house.

Simon abandoned me at a termination clinic...

And now he's in my house!!

'Shall we talk about the elephant in the room?'

'What elephant?'

Simon's eyes narrow, and his lips disappear into his mouth.

'Charlotte, you know what elephant. The fact that my son – our son – is upstairs right now, and I'm not allowed to mention it.'

'You mentioned it a moment ago. And I don't have a problem with it, so long as you don't say it to him.'

I take a gulp of coffee and try to disguise the shaking in my voice. When I put the cup back onto the table, I'm aware of Simon's eyes studying me; willing me to say something positive. But what is there to say?

'If you'll give me a chance, I can make your lives a lot easier.'

'Our lives are fine as they are, thank you.'

Simon looks around at my cramped living room, in my tiny house. My home is probably smaller than his bedroom, but at least it's mine... And the landlord's.

'I could give you some money,' he says. 'You could buy a bigger house, and get Tom into a better school. Why don't you...'

I jump out of the chair, and Simon stops talking. He's gone too far, and my anger cannot control itself any longer.

'Tom goes to a good school,' I shout. 'And our house is fine, thank you. Okay, so it's maybe not as posh as your palace down the road, but at least it's a happy place to be. Unlike yours.'

Simon stands up and tries to touch my arms, but I slap him off.

'Don't touch me. Don't touch me now or ever. You understand?'

My wobbly legs manage to stumble over to the window, and I stare at a lady over the road, sauntering along with her little boy and a huge bag of bread. They're heading to the river to feed the ducks, and I wish I could grab Tom and go with them. Why did I have to let Simon into my house? He's in my home, and now he wants to be in my life, and that of my son. The idea makes me feel sick, and I hold on to the windowsill in an effort to stay upright.

'Lottie, I'm only trying to help. I want to get to know my son. I just want to be a dad…'

'Oh, for fuck's sake! Where was this fatherly instinct ten years ago, when you dumped me at a clinic and ran for your life?'

Simon rubs his temples, and screws up his eyes. When he next speaks, he does it slowly, in short, sharp bursts.

'I explained about that.'

'No! You told me why you didn't come back, but the fact remains that before that happened, you told me it would ruin your life if I had your child. You couldn't book the appointment quick enough, and then you drove me there, because you didn't trust that I'd go through with it.'

He smirks and crosses his arms.

'Rightly, as it turns out! You should never have made the decision to have my child without telling me. We had agreed not to keep it.'

I slump against the windowsill, and pray that I don't collapse at any moment. We agreed? We agreed? What egotistical planet is this man living on? He thinks that because he decided it wasn't right, that I should have just gone along without any questions asked. What a joke.

'Don't you get it? I never agreed. It was you, all you. Right up to the last minute, I was asking if you would change your mind, but you wouldn't, because it's always all about you!'

My hands shake, and I pick at a loose thread on my sweater, in an effort to keep them occupied.

'Well, I don't remember that,' he says. 'And anyway, that's not the point. The point is that you did have the child, and now Tom is here and I want him to know that I'm his dad. I can give him a terrific life. He deserves to know that I'm his dad!'

'No!'

Simon looks past my shoulder, towards the door.

'Hello, Tom.' He smiles.

I swing around, and there is my lovely boy, holding an old copy of *Tom Sawyer* under his arm. His hair flops down over his left eye, and his mouth hangs open.

'You're my dad?'

Before I can answer, Simon pushes past me and heads over to Tom, as though this is going to be some kind of beautiful family reunion. But I know my son, and this is not going to end well.

'Hey, Sport.' Simon bends down to hug Tom, but he's having none of it. He shoots one last look at me, throws *Tom Sawyer* at my ex-lover, and then storms out of the room, and up the stairs. Simon picks the book up and places it onto the table.

'That went well,' he says, and takes a last swig of coffee.

14

'I want to see my dad, and I want to be a vegetarian.'

Tom, my parents and I, sit around their dining table, eating roast beef and Yorkshire pudding, when my son decides to drop his bombshell. The room goes quiet. Until then, my parents had been gossiping about the woman next door, who is having an affair with the man whose garage backs onto theirs, but now the atmosphere is thick and full of pins and needles.

It's been a week since Simon dropped his bombshell, and since then Tom has been adamant that he wants nothing to do with him. For my own selfish reasons, I was glad. I was ecstatic in fact. Why would I want Simon to walk in and steal my son away? I've spent almost ten years raising him. What right does some stranger have to walk in and be his dad?

No right. No right at all.

But now, in just a few words, everything has changed.

'What do you mean you want to see your dad?'

Tom shrugs and shovels another piece of beef into his mouth. So much for wanting to be a vegetarian. I try to speak, but no more words come out. I can't believe my son wants to see Simon. Just three days ago he assured me that he never wanted to see Market Man again, and that was fine with me. What has changed in the meantime? As if reading my mind, Tom takes a swig of water and then carries on talking.

'Charlie says it's great to have a dad. He sees his all the time. They have dinner together and play computer games and football, and go climbing at that treetop place, and everything.'

The idea of Simon doing any of those things with Tom is laughable. My mum catches my eye and smiles.

'Y'know, Tom,' she says, 'Charlie's dad does all of those things because he lives with him. There's nothing to say that your dad would be able to do those things as well. He might not have the time.'

My dad stands up, and the legs of his chair grind against the tiles.

'More tea anyone?' He gathers the cups before we have the chance to say no, and then disappears into the kitchen.

'I don't care if he doesn't have time.' Tom pouts and folds his arms like he used to do aged three. 'I just want to see if he'll have time. I want to know if he likes football, and watching golf on the telly, and playing games, and all of those things.'

'What brought this on?' I shuffle a roast potato around my plate, and know that I won't eat another mouthful of my dinner. Damn you, Simon. Your presence has ruined my life and now you're ruining my Sunday roast.

'I told you! Charlie says it's great to have a dad, and I want to see that for myself! I'm allowed to have a dad, y'know. Almost every kid in my class has a dad!'

A smile dances on my lips in spite of myself. I can just imagine my son, surveying all of the children on their parental status, and then putting the stats together for future use. My dad arrives back from the kitchen, and plonks down three cups of hot, over-brewed tea.

'Everything okay in here?' he asks.

'I'm going to see my dad,' Tom barks. 'And we're going to spend tons of time together, and there's nothing Mum can do about it.'

'Well, won't that be fun? For all of us.' My dad looks at me, as Tom's words hang in the air like bats.

My mum reaches over and pats my hand.

'Y'know, dear,' she says. 'I think Tom's right. It's maybe time for him to see his dad.'

Well, she's changed her tune! I glare at her, and can't imagine why she would ever think it's a good idea for Tom to see Simon. The man is a womanising, cheating scumbag, who robbed me of my acting ambitions, and dumped me at a termination clinic, but she's conveniently forgotten about that.

'Great!' Tom leaps up and fist-pumps the air. 'I'm allowed to see my dad!'

'Hold on, I never said you could do anything of the sort.'

Tom stares at my mum.

'No, but Grandma did, and she's allowed to make decisions too.'

My mum mouths 'sorry' to me, through scrunched-up lips, while Tom does a happy dance around the dining table.

'Sit down and finish your dinner,' I say, but he takes no notice.

'You know, your mum and I were saying the other day that this would happen.'

My dad stares at me, over the top of his mug. This is something that really irritates me about my family. Whenever anything happens in my life, they have a good gossip about it between themselves, and then they often involve the rest of their associates as well. One time I told them that Tom had got into a fight at school, and my dad's cousin phoned me that night to ask me all about it. I bet she's been kept well informed about the latest goings-on, though after the reception she got the last time she phoned, I doubt she'll contact me again.

'I wish you'd stop gossiping about me,' I say, and my mum tuts.

'For goodness' sake, we're not gossiping, we're just having a conversation. But your dad is right, we did think it would happen, and now that it has, you should think about letting the boy see his dad. It was one thing not having contact with Simon while he didn't know about Tom, but now it's different.'

'Yes!' shouts Tom. 'Now he wants to see me, and he wants to do all of the things that other dads do. So, I'm going to see him!'

I guess it's hard for an almost ten-year-old to see what a sleazeball his dad is, but I'm not about to explain. I gaze around the table, and everyone stares at me. Ugh! This is terrifying, and I don't want any part of it. But as much as I hate to admit it, maybe my mum is right. Now that they know about each other, I can only keep Tom away from Simon for so long. It is a painful truth that Tom will probably find out for himself just how much of a scumbag his dad was and is, but I will just have to hug him close and look after him if that happens. Until then, I've been forced into a corner, and I can be bad cop no longer.

'Okay,' I say. 'You win. You can see your dad.'

'Yay!' cries Tom, and stuffs an entire mini-Yorkshire pudding into his mouth.

A week later and Simon arrives at my door to take me and Tom out for lunch. My son wasn't in the least bit happy when I told him that I'd be coming too – apparently Charlie the parenting guru says that Tom should have alone time with his dad – but tough luck. The only time Simon has seen his son is in assembly and on our driveway, and I can't imagine he has any knowledge of how kids work. So, for now – and maybe forever – they're both stuck with me.

Simon hovers in my hallway, shuffling from one foot to the other. Is he nervous? Is that even a thing in his world? Seems it is.

'Tom is just brushing his teeth,' I say. 'He'll be down in a minute.'

'That's fine,' Simon says. 'The table is booked for one, so we have plenty of time.'

My ex-lover has a George Michael stubble thing going on, smells of Kouros aftershave, and wears a shirt and tie. Who dresses that way for a Sunday lunch with a child? He does apparently.

'Where are we going?' I push my hair behind my ears, as if I don't care, but deep down I'm intrigued in spite of myself.

'I thought we could go to La Petite,' he says, and I laugh a little too loud.

'La Petite? That posh place next to The King's Head in Boughley?'

'Yes. Do you think that's too much? I'm not used to eating Sunday lunch with a kid.'

You don't say. The fact that La Petite sells nothing but pretentious seafood and posh pastries, is lost on my ex-lover. Tom would throw up as soon as he saw the starters, and I'd do the same when I saw the bill.

'It's a little too much,' I say, and Simon's shoulders sag. In spite of everything that has happened in the past, he's trying his best to make today perfect. And it would be if Tom was a twenty-five-year-old, easily-impressed bimbo. But he's not.

'Doesn't Tom like fish?'

'Well, yes, if it's dipped in batter and wrapped in newspaper.'

'Got it.'

I can hear Tom clomping around in his bedroom. He'll be

sorting out the Minecraft characters that he wants to show his dad – so he can be just like Charlie. I can imagine the raised eyebrows if he pulls those out of his backpack in La Petite.

'Look, why don't we just go to the Mistletoe Inn. He likes the chicken kiev and the pasta in there, and he'll appreciate that they've got their Christmas tree up so early.'

Simon runs his fingers through his hair, and then admires himself in the mirror.

'Okay, I'll see if I can book us in.' He reaches for his phone, but I wave him away.

'Don't worry. They don't take reservations in there. It's first come, first served.'

Simon stares over my shoulder, and I can hear the thud of Tom's shoes, clumping down the stairs.

'Hey, Scamp.'

I turn to see how my son reacts to Simon's attempts at being familiar, and as predicted, he's scowling. He thrusts his backpack into my arms, and unhooks his coat from the peg.

'Word of advice,' he says in his best big boy voice. 'If you want to be my dad, you'll need to work on your nicknames. I don't like Scamp, and I don't like Sport, and I don't like Tommy.'

Simon laughs, and scratches his shoulder.

'Okay,' he says. 'I'll work on my lines.'

He winks at me. Tom's funny attempt at being bossy has relaxed Simon, and I'm not sure if that makes me feel good or not.

'Come on,' Tom says, and then pushes past us, and out onto the driveway. 'Are we going in your posh car? Charlie's dad doesn't have a big car like this. His is old and a horrible green colour.' He leans on Simon's BMW and pulls out his phone. 'I'll just send Charlie a photo of me next to this car. He can show his dad and make him jealous.' My son sticks his tongue out and takes the pic. He's enjoying today already, and I don't know whether to laugh or cry.

The Mistletoe Inn is busier than it was when I met Simon the other week, but not so busy that we're turned away.

'Just grab a table anywhere,' the waitress says. 'I'll bring the menus over when you're settled.'

We find a table next to the window, and Tom throws his backpack onto the windowsill.

'Do you want to see my Minecraft figures,' he asks. 'I've got loads and I'll be getting more for Christmas.'

'Minecraft? Is that a pop band or something?'

Simon hangs his jacket on the back of his chair, while Tom looks at him as though he were nuts. He's about to tell Simon off for getting it all wrong, when the waitress comes over with the menus. My ex-lover looks relieved. Menus he is an expert with. Almost ten-year-old Minecraft fans? Not so much.

Still, in spite of the awkward start, the afternoon goes well. Simon and Tom bond over a love of watching golf of all things, and Simon promises my son – our son – that one day he'll take him to the golf course out by the country park, and they'll give it a go. Tom loves the idea of this, because Charlie has never been to the golf course with his dad.

Spending time with my son and the man who ran away from us was never going to be the most relaxing day of my life, but the smile on Tom's face makes it somehow bearable. Still, I can't help but worry that it will end in tears, and I'm already planning my revenge if it all goes wrong. Which it will, let's face it. This is Simon we're talking about.

My ex-lover drops us off outside the house, and Tom bounds out of the car with the words, 'Bye, Market-Man Dad. I'll see you again next Sunday.'

Simon opens his mouth – I'm sure to tell my son that there's no way he can see him two weekends in a row – but Tom is already heading for the house, his head full of dad dreams and possibilities.

'Don't worry about next Sunday,' I say, as I slide out of the car. 'We'll see you whenever.'

'I'll be here if I can, I promise. It's just... difficult.'

'Yeah, I can imagine.'

I slam the door, and head into the house before he can say anything else.

I pull the duvet up past Tom's shoulder, and tuck it in around him.

'Did you have a good day?' I ask. He hasn't said much about it since he got in, but I did hear snippets of his conversation with Charlie, and it sounded positive. I'm not sure how I feel about that.

Mixed feelings.

Mixed feelings indeed.

Tom stares up at me with those huge green eyes of his, and his thick eyelashes whisk up and down.

He's got such beautiful eyes.

He has his dad's eyes.

'It was okay,' he says.

'Just okay?'

'Well, the spaghetti was nice, but the sticky toffee pudding was a bit dry. I needed more custard.'

He smiles and my heart melts.

'We'll make sure you get more custard next time.' I kiss his forehead and then turn off the light.

'I love you, Mum,' he says.

'And I love you right back.'

As I close the door, my mobile vibrates in my pocket. I stare at it as I go downstairs, and I'm more than surprised to see that the name staring back at me is Simon's.

'Hello?'

I reach the living room and close the door. If he's about to say something awful, I don't want his son to hear it.

'Hey, Charlotte, it's me.'

I refrain from telling him that I know already and instead, plonk myself onto the sofa and take a swig of wine.

I need it.

'What can I do for you?'

'I had a good time today. Did you? Did Tom? Did he like meeting me? Did he say anything about me?'

So many questions, and I suspect that Simon isn't interested in any of the answers.

'He said he enjoyed the pasta, but there wasn't enough custard.'

'What?'

I rub my forehead. I've got the start of a headache, but I'm not sure we have any Ibuprofen left in the cupboard.

'Yes, he had a great time. Thanks for paying by the way.'

'You're welcome.'

Silence. What now? What does he want?

'Charlotte, there's something you should know.'

Here we go. This is where he tells me that he's got to move to Yemen, or fly to the moon, or leave for a year of deep-sea fishing. Anything to get away from his responsibilities. The responsibilities that he wanted just days ago.

'I know that Tom would like to see me every week, but... but...'

'Don't tell me, you can't see him again. Is that it?'

'It's not that. It's... It's Monica.'

Monica? I'm confused. What has his absent wife got to do with anything?

'She's back, you see. She was back when I came home this afternoon.'

A freezing chill whips its way up my spine, and lands on top of my shoulders. Why would I ever doubt that she'd slither back into our lives. If Simon notices my silent discomfort, he doesn't mention it.

'We had a good talk this evening,' he says. 'Our argument was stupid anyway – she totally overreacted by walking out and accepts that. So yeah... That's what I was ringing to tell you.'

'So where does that leave your son? The one you insisted on having access to. Remember?'

Simon sighs, and when he speaks again, his voice is lowered to almost a whisper. She's there. She's in his house and he doesn't want her to hear him.

'It doesn't change anything between us, I promise. I won't abandon Tom, and I'll do all I can to see him and help you to raise him. I want to be part of his life, and so does Monica.'

The words stick in my ears. Once again, he says he wants to help me raise my son. The thought of Simon sticking his nose into anything I do with Tom fills me with horror, but to have Monica involved as well, is off the chart. There are many things I could say to him right now, but I'm too emotionally exhausted to get involved. All I want to do is dive into a bubble bath, and then slip into a pair of clean, fluffy pyjamas.

I ignore Simon's comments about being involved in Tom's life; wish him a good night, and pray I never hear from him again.

15

Monday morning is always the worst time for working in a school reception. You can guarantee that even before the gate is opened, there will be parents queued outside my office, telling me how little Harry has got nits, or Maisy hasn't received her letter for the trip to Twycross or whatever. Then there are the phone calls, reporting absences or lateness. The calls wouldn't be so bad if I could just concentrate on them instead of talking to parents in person as well, but no, Margaret thinks I should be able to do both things at once, and who am I to argue?

'I don't think it's fair that Giuseppe should miss out on his yoga class, just because the teacher lost his slip, do you?' A stern-faced mother with pink spiky hair stares at me from behind the glass, and I want to tell her that I couldn't care less about his slip, or his classes. All I can think about is yesterday, and how I let Simon into my son's life, and now him and his awful wife are going to try and take over. But instead of boring the yoga-mum with my problems, I just smile, write down her name and promise I'll sort it out before home time. She nods and pushes her way past the hordes of parents, all waiting to speak to me.

'Can I help you?'

A small brunette woman steps forward and smiles. She looks far too young to be a mother, but who am I to judge?

'I'm here for the assembly,' she says. 'I'm Loretta, the children's author?'

'Oh right. Yes, okay. Just fill in the visitors' book and I'll get you a badge.'

I reach behind me to find a lanyard, but before I can hand it to her, I see Margaret heading out of her office, and straight towards me.

'Charlotte, can I have a word?'

I sigh. Can she have a word? Can she bloody wait until this queue has gone down? Probably not.

'Yes. I'll just finish dealing with these parents, and I'll be with you.'

'I need to speak with you now!' Her mouth turns downwards, showing off the jowls on either side of her face. 'Ask one of the teaching assistants to fill in for you.' And with that, she stomps back to her office.

Shit.

I pick up the phone and call Janet from Year One. Straight away she is pissed off that I would suggest she help on reception, as though the very idea is beneath her.

'I've got work to do as well, you know,' she says, and then hangs up the phone. The attitude on her, just because she is a TA and I'm 'only' a part-time receptionist. If the whole reception could be manned by robots, I'm sure that would please most of the staff in this place. Then they'd never have to speak to me again.

And talking of speaking, why on earth does Margaret want to have a word with me? I pray it's not some kind of parents' questionnaire that will involve hours of my time for little to no response. We haven't had one of those since we came back from the summer holidays, so we're probably overdue. Oh God, I hope it isn't a questionnaire. I don't think I could cope with that on a Monday morning.

'Can I have my visitor's badge please?' The visiting author motions towards the lanyard in my hand.

'I'm sorry,' I say. 'Here you go.'

I hand it over, and the next parent steps forward, just in time for Janet to appear in reception. Her long red hair flops into her eyes, and she pushes it back.

'I'm here,' she says. 'Please don't be too long. I've got a parents' reading session to organise, and a play to rehearse.'

'Believe me, I don't intend to be,' I say, as I open the door and head towards Margaret's office.

'There's been a complaint. A serious one actually.'

Margaret sits behind her desk, examining a piece of paper in her hand.

'A complaint? I don't understand. What kind of complaint? And by whom?'

Margaret places the paper face down onto the desk, and stares me straight in the eye. It's disconcerting, but I refuse to look away. I can feel sweat behind my knees, and my heels jump up and down, but I can't let the principal see how nervous I am. I've done nothing wrong, after all.

'I'm afraid I'm not at liberty to tell you who has complained about you, but the insinuation is that you have been stealing from the school trip fund.'

My heart falls into my stomach, and I gasp. I'm aware that

my mouth is hanging open, but the muscles in my face refuse to keep it closed. I'm in shock.

'Stealing? I've never stolen from anyone in my life.'

Margaret reaches into her desk drawer and brings out a bundle of envelopes, full of money for the students' cinema and burger trip. It's the same bundle that I was counting up on Friday morning, ready for banking this morning.

'There should be six hundred pounds in these envelopes. Broken down, that is fifty children at twelve pounds per head.'

'Yes,' I say. 'That's how much there was on Friday. I remember because I thought it was funny that it should come out at exactly six hundred. For the most part, these things tend to add up to odd numbers. Y'know, with all the twenty-pence pieces and stuff. I was quite surprised...'

I'm rambling, I know I'm rambling, but I can't help it. I can't believe Margaret is questioning my counting skills. Is that what she's doing? It seems that way.

'The money in these envelopes adds up to five hundred and fifty pounds, which means that somebody has filtered off fifty – probably from the loose coins that were in the envelopes.'

'When you say somebody – do you mean me?'

Am I being accused of stealing money from children? Yes, yes, I think I am. Bile rises in my throat, and I can hardly breathe.

'You were the one who first opened the envelopes.'

'I know I was, but that doesn't mean I stole anything. No, that's not right. I would never do that. Perhaps... perhaps some of the parents didn't put the correct money in. Maybe they put ten pounds instead of twelve.'

Margaret shakes her head.

'And yet you've just said that there was six hundred when you counted it on Friday.'

'There was. But maybe I counted up wrong. Maybe I just

thought there was six hundred, and there was only five hundred and fifty.'

I'm so confused. I did count up the money correctly. I know I did. But if that's the case, where has the fifty quid gone? It's not a huge amount of money in the grand scheme of things, but that's not the point. I can't believe this is happening to me. How can this be happening to me? Margaret leans forward and places her hands on her knees. One of her rings catches on her blue tights, and leaves a hole. She rubs at it, as though it will cure itself.

'Charlotte, I know how hard it is to be a single parent – my goodness, I've met enough to know – but if things were so bad, you should have come to me. Under no circumstances should you have taken money out of the school trip fund.'

Rage bubbles up my throat, and I can hardly breathe. How dare she? How dare she accuse me of such a thing, when I didn't do it, and there is zero evidence to say that I did. I stand up, my elbow hits off the bookcase, and pain sears up through my funny bone.

'Margaret, I didn't steal anything from the fund. I've never even stolen a paper clip before.'

The principal rubs her forehead and writes a random comment in her notebook, which I cannot read. She lowers her voice, and her face softens.

'I didn't want to say this until the full investigation had taken place, but you were seen taking the money. Somebody saw you putting it into your handbag.' I open my mouth to speak, but Margaret holds her hands in the air. 'I'm so sorry, Charlotte, but I can't say anything more. Now, as I said, I'll have to investigate the matter, but don't worry, I'm not going to suspend you. That's the last thing I want to do, but I'll have to ask Amy to take over all money issues until we've sorted it out.'

Margaret smiles as though she's done me a favour, and with no more words to say, I nod and head back to my desk, tears threatening to tumble down my cheeks. Janet sees me approach and throws a pen onto the desk. The queue has gone, and the phone is silent. Thank God.

'Right, can I get back to my own job now?'

I nod, and she plods off down the corridor; unaware of my pain, and unconcerned about anything that just happened in the office.

I sit down, turn the school phone to silent mode, and scour my brain for a hint of something – anything – that will prove I'm innocent.

But before that can happen, murky memories hit me like a brick.

It was Friday night... Tom was complaining that his school shoes were letting in water, and I told my parents that I'd have to repair them with superglue until payday. My mum was incensed and offered to pay for a new pair, but I couldn't. I couldn't take money from my pensioner parents, especially when payday wasn't that far away...

But then later, after we had got home, I found some money in my bag and presumed that my dad had slipped some in when my back was turned. That's what he does. It's his thing. I was angry that he had gone against my wishes and put money into my bag, but at the same time, overwhelmed that I have such loving parents, who are always happy to help – even if it leaves themselves out of pocket. How could I not think it was Dad who put it in my bag? It made perfect sense.

And how much money was there?

Fifty quid.

My knees bounce up and down under my desk, as I second-guess myself. I did count up the money correctly on Friday, and I even wrote the number in my notebook. I reach to retrieve the pink book, and sure enough, six hundred pounds is written in bright-blue ink. I hate blue ink, but as I was counting up the cash, it was all I could find. I'm overthinking, and in any case, me writing it down proves nothing. Nothing that Margaret will take as evidence of my innocence anyway.

I rub my face and then my heart leaps as I remember the text conversation between me and my dad, on Friday night, just after I found the money. Of course! This will prove that he put the money into my bag. My mind whirrs, and thoughts twirl like spinning tops. I grab my phone, to convince myself that the conversation really happened, and I can just about make out the words, in spite of the water rising in my eyes.

Message sent at 8.26pm: Thanks Dad. You're one in a million.

Message received at 8.29pm: You're welcome. We're always here for you.

Shit.

The conversation proves nothing.

Despite me thinking that we were both talking about the fifty quid in my bag, there is no mention of money in his message or my own. At the time, I'd just assumed that he knew we were talking about the money, but now I'm not so sure. I think back to when we left their house on Friday, when my dad leaned over, kissed my cheek and told me that if I ever needed anything from them at all, they'd always give it to me. My message was in relation to the money, but Dad's could have been in response to his supportive words.

Oh God.

I switch my phone off, and slide it into my bag. As I do so, Tom runs down the corridor with Charlie, bounding as though it were Christmas morning.

'Look, Mum,' he squeals. 'Look at how bouncy my new shoes are! They help me run mega fast – faster than Charlie and faster than anyone. Even the teachers!'

Margaret appears at her office door, and smiles at my son.

'Good morning, Tom,' she says. 'Ooh, new shoes?'

Tom slides one shoe off his foot and holds it up to the principal.

'Yes, I got them on Saturday. They're not trainers, but they make me run faster than anyone. Even Mo Farrah.'

He turns the shoes over, to show off the sole, and the price sticker shines as though it's made of neon lights.

Forty-eight pounds.

Margaret looks at the price, then my son, and then me.

'You're a lucky boy, Tom,' she says, and then disappears back into her office.

'You think I took the money?'

I glare at Zach, as he throws his leftover tea into the sink. We're hanging out in the kitchen so that Tom doesn't overhear the conversation. It would be the worst thing ever if he knew what was going on.

'Don't be ridiculous. Why would I think you'd taken the money?' Zach sighs, takes my cup from my hands, and rinses it. Water splatters up and leaves great puddles on the counter. Despite my worries, it still bothers me that Zach seems in no hurry to mop it up.

'But you just asked if it was possible that the money had been put in my bag.'

'Yes, by someone else, not by you.'

I shrug.

'Well, someone must have put it in there, but I'm pretty sure it wasn't me.'

'Pretty sure?'

'Yes. But you know what it's like – I keep second-guessing myself. Could it have fallen in when I leaned over to pick up my pen? Could I have picked it up with a piece of random paper, and put in there by mistake? I just don't know.'

Zach puts the cups onto the drainer, and ignores the splatters all over the sink. I reach over and retrieve some kitchen roll. The idea of leaning in a puddle drives me insane.

'And it wasn't your parents?'

'No. My dad messaged earlier to ask if I was sure I didn't want to borrow some money before payday. I asked if he'd slipped some money into my bag on Friday, and he had no idea what I was talking about.'

Tom plods into the kitchen; a Spiderman character in one hand, and a box in the other.

'Hey, Tom. Want a drink?' Zach holds up a glass, but Tom shakes his head.

'No thanks. But, Mum, look at this! I was just checking my bird feeder in the front garden, and I found this package on the step.'

A package? There was nothing there when we got in earlier. I look at the wall clock and it is 6.30pm. Too late for the postman, but not for a courier, I guess. Still, I didn't hear anyone knock.

'Let me have a look.'

I dry my hands, and reach over to take the parcel from Tom, but he clutches it to his chest.

'Nope!' he says. 'Look at the name on the front. Tom Baker. That's me if you don't know! What do you think it is?'

I lean over to look at the label. Sure enough, it's addressed to my son, though how on earth he's getting post, I'll never know.

'You haven't been splurging on Amazon, have you, Tom?' Zach winks at me, and Tom scowls.

'Duh! I don't have an Amazon account. Mum, where are the scissors? I want to open it and see what's inside!'

I reach for the scissors, and then motion to Tom to hand the parcel over. He does, and I look to see if there are any clues as to where it came from, before I skim the scissors over the top. The box pops open, and inside there are hundreds of bits of polystyrene.

'Ooh! Squiggly bits!' Tom grabs a handful and throws it in the air like confetti. 'Mum, let me see what it is!'

I hand the box over, and my son runs into the living room. Zach and I follow, just in time to see Tom jump onto the sofa, and turn the box upside down. Thousands of 'squiggly bits' come flying out, and then a shiny white box thuds onto the cushions. I'm standing four feet away, but even from this distance I can see that there is an apple on the front.

Tom whoops and punches the air.

'It's an iPad, Mum!! A new iPad!!'

'Oh my God.'

Zach stares at me, and rubs his chin.

'You bought him a new iPad?'

'No, I didn't. But I bet I know who did.'

While we were out with Simon yesterday, Tom mentioned that his current iPad was – in his words – 'Embarrassing by its oldness'. He complained that some of his games no longer worked because the device was too old to run the updates, and his music kept cutting out because there wasn't enough memory. I told my son that no matter how much he complained, I couldn't afford to buy him one right now, and he'd just have to put it on his Christmas list, or save up for a couple of years. Either of those options was no guarantee of actually getting a new iPad, but at least he had a chance, and maybe I could sell something to help him on his way.

While we were talking, Simon didn't say a word, and in fact, I even cursed him in my head for spending most of those five minutes on his phone. Now I know what he was doing – buying my son a new device, without any thought about how it would affect our everyday life.

'It's from my dad, isn't it? He bought me an iPad!'

I grab the delivery note, and sure enough, Simon's name and address are emboldened at the top.

'Yes, it would seem that way,' I say, and Tom leaps up from the sofa, and runs for the door.

'Where are you going?'

'I'm going to set this up,' he says. 'And then I'm going to Skype Charlie from my old iPad, so that I can show him my new one. He's going to be well jealous!'

Zach moves forward and picks up a handful of polystyrene bits.

'Aren't you going to help us clean these up?'

Tom shakes his head.

'I'll do it later,' he says, and then disappears into the hall.

'Did you know Simon was doing this?' he whispers.

I kneel down, retrieve the delivery box and scoop the packaging into it.

'No, I didn't. If I did, I'd have killed him!'

'You need to speak with him,' Zach says. 'This is bullshit.'

I look down at the mess on the sofa and the floor, and nod my head. My friend is right, this is utter bullshit, and in so many different ways.

After Zach has left, and Tom goes to bed, I phone Simon. On the third ring, it's picked up.

'Hello?'

Monica's voice trills through my handset, and I squirm. What's she doing picking up Simon's phone? I guess she has so many trust issues, that she doesn't think twice about looking through his calls.

'Hey, it's Charlotte...'

'Charlotte! It's lovely to hear from you! Did Tom like his iPad? We've been thinking about it all day.'

So even Monica knew that Simon had ordered the device. Well, thanks both for warning me.

'Yes, he received it. He's been playing on it all night. Look, is Simon there? I'd like to speak with him about it?'

'No, he's in the shower. There was some kind of work crisis this afternoon, so he was late getting home. I will tell him you called though. Thanks so much for letting us know it arrived.'

I rub my eyes. The moral compass on this woman is totally off. She thinks it's perfectly okay for Simon to pay over three hundred pounds for a gift that isn't even for a birthday or Christmas? My gran would have said that's an example of how the other half live, and she would be right.

'Listen,' she says, 'I'm so sorry to do this to you, but I'm cooking pasta, and it's about to boil all over the hob. But I will tell Simon you phoned. He'll be thrilled to know the gift arrived and that Tom is happy with it. Thanks for phoning! Bye!'

She hangs up before I can even reply.

16

Tuesday, and I'm back at my desk, gazing into space and wondering what I'm going to do about Simon buying the iPad. It was all Tom could talk about this morning, and he's given me strict instructions to charge it up when I go home this afternoon. In truth, I'd rather throw the damn thing out of the window, but I imagine that would be classed as inappropriate. I pick up my mobile to send Simon a text, but before I can do anything, Margaret appears.

'Charlotte, do you have the register for Mrs Wallace's class? I need to check something.'

Shit. I've been working hard all morning, and the first time I pick up my mobile, the bloody principal has to appear. Why does this always happen to me?

'Erm, I'm not sure. I'll check.'

'Are you busy?'

She gawps at my phone, and I throw it back into my bag.

'Yes,' I say. 'I've just finished going through the numbers for the teachers' first aid course.' Not that Margaret is in the least bit bothered about that, but I feel obliged to add it into our conversation. I'm still aware that she thinks I'm a common thief, but I don't want her to think I'm a lazy bitch as well.

I don't make eye contact with her – just rummage through the pile of folders, and hand over the one she's looking for.

'Thank you, that's great.' She goes to walk away and then stops. 'Oh, and Charlotte?'

'Yes?'

She leans in and lowers her voice.

'I won't be taking any further action on the money situation. You're a good employee, and I'm prepared to give you the benefit of the doubt. We'll make up the difference with the money we made from the cake sale the other week, and then draw a line under the whole silly business.'

My heart leaps, and tears spring to my eyes, though I try to hide them from Margaret.

'Thank you. And I didn't take that money, just so you know.'

The words almost stick in my throat, since I know that the missing money was in my bag, but I'm determined I didn't put it there. Margaret nods, and disappears into the office. She doesn't believe me, but what can I do?

'I'm really sorry. I had no idea that sending a gift would piss you off. If I'd known, I wouldn't have done it.'

Simon and I walk along the riverbank, where we have met in an effort to clear up the iPad nonsense. It's cold and wet, and a thin layer of fog hovers over the river, threatening to swallow us up. Still, I can't complain. At least Simon agreed to meet me here, otherwise I might have been stuck in my house with him, and I wouldn't want that again. The wind swirls down the path, and a ripped page from an old newspaper whips around our legs. I go to pick it up, but Simon kicks at it with his foot, and it ends up in the river. So much for looking after the environment.

'It's not that it pissed me off for no reason,' I say. 'It pissed me off because it was inappropriate to give a three hundred pound gift to a child, when it's not a special occasion.'

'I get it. I'm sorry.'

Simon looks forlorn, and I feel a pang of guilt that I brought the subject up. But then again, it had to be said, otherwise where will it end? A Ferrari on Tom's seventeenth birthday? I shudder at the thought.

'I know you're new to this, and you want to make up for lost time, but to give you some perspective, I spent about one hundred and fifty pounds on Tom last Christmas, and it will be the same amount this year. If you carry on spending hundreds more on random treats, it will destroy all the joy he feels at Christmas. You see?'

'One hundred and fifty pounds?' Simon clenches his mouth. 'That's not a lot, is it?'

My chest contracts, and I regret telling him how much money I have to spend on Christmas gifts. I don't trust him to stay in the same budget, and it fills me with horror that I could give Tom a computer game and some books, while Simon and Monica waltz in with a new laptop and designer trainers.

'No, it isn't a lot, but it is reality.'

'What if I give you some? I can transfer whatever you need, and you don't have to tell Tom that it came from me.'

We sit down on an ancient bench, and the slats creak underneath us. I wonder how many conversations have taken place on this bench? A thousand? No, much more...

'Charlotte? Did you hear what I said? I can give you some money for Tom.'

'Yes, I heard you. It's just – and I don't mean this in a horrible way – but I've raised my son for the past ten years on my own, and I'm happy to continue that way. Thank you though.'

I attempt a smile, but it comes off as more of a grimace. A young mother ambles past with a baby in a buggy, and a toddler skips beside her. The tot is dressed as though visiting the North Pole, and she waves at us as she trundles past. The mother looks exhausted, and I empathise with her. I remember those days with Tom. He would have me out of bed at 5am, and would be glued to a CBeebies DVD ten minutes later. I'd try to catch a nap on the sofa, while he watched television, but having a toddler jumping on me every five minutes made it impossible. Thank goodness my son now likes a long lie-in at the weekend. We're both catching up on all the sleep we missed out on all those years ago.

'Monica and I have been talking…'

Simon's voice comes straight into my brain and shakes me out of my daydream.

'About what?'

'We would like to have more input in Tom's life.'

I'm suddenly freezing, and it has nothing to do with the cold weather. Simon and Monica want more input in my son's life? What the hell does that mean?

'What do you mean, more input?'

Simon shifts in the bench, and it creaks again. A jogger runs towards us, and my ex-lover puts his finger to his lips, in an effort to stop me asking questions while we're in earshot of someone else. The runner ignores us and jogs on, but Simon remains quiet.

'Are you going to tell me what you mean, or do I have to guess?'

'It's nothing sinister,' he says. 'It's really connected to what I said to you before. We want to share Tom's life, and give you the support you need to raise him.'

'The support I need?!' I leap out of the bench and point my finger a little too close to Simon's face. 'I don't need any support at all, thank you! The time for support would have been ten years ago, when I found out I was pregnant, but you were incapable of that. Remember?'

Simon cracks his knuckles, and I struggle not to throw my hands over my ears.

'I've done many things I'm not proud of,' he says, 'but I want to make up for the lack of help you've had in raising our son.'

'Our son? Please don't call him that. Tom is my son, okay? If you stick around long enough for him to recognise you as his dad, then you can think about calling him your son. But no matter what, I'll never need your help to raise him, and that goes twice for Monica.'

'Charlotte!'

I storm off down the river path, with Simon's words ringing in my ears. What a joke that man is. What an absolute joke.

My talk with Simon must have sunk in somewhat, because so far there are no more gifts from him, and no mention of him sharing the responsibilities of raising Tom. Thank God for that. Still, it hasn't stopped my son from wondering if he can tell his dad that he wants a new Man United football strip, and a pair of designer trainers. I've told him that under no circumstances must he mention them to Simon, but I have no confidence in him keeping quiet.

It's 5pm, and Tom and I are at my mum and dad's for dinner. The thick aroma of beef biryani wafts up from my plate, and I reach for a piece of naan bread before my dad steals the last piece.

'So, you had a good time on Sunday, Tom?'

Tom stares at my mum, and a thick line of confusion appears between his eyebrows.

'Sunday?' He spears a piece of beef with his fork, shovels it into his mouth, and then a light bulb goes off. 'Oh, you mean the pub with Market-Man Dad? Yeah, it was good, but they should have given me more custard.'

My mum stares at me from across the table, and I shake my head and roll my eyes.

'He means that he didn't get enough custard for his pudding.'

'Oh.'

'Custard is always important,' my dad says. He has a piece of rice stuck to his chin, and my mum tuts and flicks it off. 'But, Tom, don't you think it's time to stop calling him Market-Man Dad? Don't you think maybe Simon would be better?'

Tom wrinkles his nose.

'Simon? I'm not calling him Simon! Charlie calls his dad, Dad. He doesn't say, "Hey, Alfonso!" does he?'

'Charlie's dad is called Alfonso?'

Tom shrugs.

'I don't know. I always call him Charlie's dad.'

Everyone laughs, but the comment hangs in the air. My son wants to call Simon, 'Dad', and after the conversation I had with Simon yesterday, I find this disclosure terrifying. Once this happens, it will be a matter of moments before the subject of helping to raise Tom comes flying back again. I thought I had more time. I thought my son would have no interest in calling anyone Dad, just moments after meeting them, but I was wrong.

I can feel the biryani rising in my throat, and I swallow hard to get it back down. Now is not the time to puke all over my mother's pink, flowered tablecloth.

I've got enough problems.

~

Friday afternoon. I've finished work for the day, and I swing past my parents' house to return a cake tin I forgot to give them the other day. My mum has promised a cake for the village bake sale, and according to her, her reputation hangs by a string if I don't return the tin. I wade through the fallen leaves and muddy puddles on their street, and by the time I reach their gate, my feet are covered in autumnal grime. I stoop down to retrieve an oak leaf that is stuck to the top of my boot, and it is when I stand back up that I notice it.

Simon's BMW is parked right outside my parents' house.

My first reaction is to think I'm wrong, that it must surely be someone else's car that just happens to be parked on the same street. However, when I look through the window, there is a folder on the back seat with 'Simon Travis Market-Me' written on the front. What the hell is he doing so close to my parents' house? I gawp up and down the street, but there is no sign of him. It's only when I hear my dad's voice, and I look into their garden, that I realise – Simon is not only with my parents, but he is also carrying a large, concrete garden ornament.

My dad looks up, waves and then Simon does the same. I clutch the cake tin to my chest and somehow manage to get up the path without collapsing on the way. My dad smiles broadly, while my ex-lover looks sheepish – as he should.

'Hi, sweetie,' my dad says. 'I was just trying to move this new ornament to the front of the pond, when along came Simon, and offered to help.'

'He did? That's not weird at all.'

'Be with you in a minute,' my dad says. 'Simon, come this way, and I'll show you exactly where it needs to go.'

Simon heaves the ornament further onto his chest, smiles at me and then disappears down the side path, and into the back garden. What on earth have I just witnessed? My dad and the older, married father of my son, not only conversing in the garden, but working together? How is this happening? How do they even know each other?

I march down the path and burst into the kitchen, where my mum is busy making tea in the fancy pot that only comes out for visiting royalty... or married ex-lovers.

'Oh hi! We never expected to see you this afternoon.'

I throw the tin onto the side, and it makes a clanging noise, not dissimilar to the chimes of doom.

'Mum! Do you mind telling me why Simon is helping Dad in the garden? And furthermore, why he is here in the first place?'

My mum takes out the posh china from the back of the cupboard, and places it all onto the counter.

'Don't be angry with us,' she says, 'but we decided to get in touch with Simon after we heard that he was seeing Tom. We wanted to make sure he was the right kind of person to hang around our grandson.'

'What?! Why would you do that?'

My mum waves me away, as though it's the most natural thing in the world to contact your daughter's ex-boyfriend, when they've never officially met before. As she faffs around with the cups, I look out at the garden, and see my dad showing Simon around his tiny shed. To his credit, Simon seems to be asking questions and taking some kind of interest, which is surely not a requirement in this situation.

'Mum! Are you going to tell me what's going on?'

She stops playing with the cups, and turns to face me.

'I was hoping your dad would be the one to tell this story, but he seems far too concerned with his shed. Anyway, as I said, we thought it would be best to contact Simon, since he was going to have contact with Tom. We met him yesterday morning at his office, and we didn't expect to like him, but he was very nice to us.' She throws her arms in the air. 'Before you ask, no we didn't mention anything about the past. We all thought it best to concentrate on the present and the future, and not be bogged down with any hard feelings we may have had before.'

I can't believe what I'm hearing. It's as if they've been brainwashed by Simon's patter. And what does she mean, they decided not to talk about the past? That's the very thing they've been furious about for the past ten years. Typical they should draw a line and move on. That little development has Simon written all over it. I lean on the counter and hang my head in my hands.

'Mum, I wish you wouldn't get involved in my business. How many times do I need to ask?'

'Oh, honey,' she says, 'it's not about getting involved in *your* business, it's Tom's business. We've only got his best interests at heart, and thankfully, it seems that Simon does, too.'

I screw up my face, just in time for my dad and Simon to come into the kitchen. My dad removes his gloves and claps his hands together.

'Phew! It's a cold one out there. Did you see the ornament? Doesn't it look nice?'

My mum and dad gawp out of the window, while Simon smiles at me.

'Sorry,' he mouths, but he gets no reaction out of me.

We sit in the living room – my parents, the father of my child and myself – and sip tea out of my mum's dainty little cups. Polite conversation is the topic of the afternoon, and the room is full of stories of garden centres, local cafés and how lovely the river looks at this time of year.

And then it happens.

'I was thinking that Tom might want to come to my house for dinner on Sunday,' Simon says. 'Monica is keen to spend time with him.'

'Oh, how lovely,' my mum gushes. 'Tom will love that, I'm sure.'

I shoot her a dirty look, but it goes straight over her head.

Simon ignores my mum's gushing tone, reaches for a Penguin biscuit, and then stares at me. He's desperate to hear my reaction, but I'm not sure he'll like it when he hears it.

'It's too soon,' I say. 'Tom has only been out with you once, and the last time he met Monica, it was when she drove him home, after following him down the river path, demanding that he go with her to meet you.'

Simon gives me a quizzical look. I'm aware that I'm being rather dramatic, but I don't care. The bones of what I said is true – she did follow him, regardless of what her excuse was. My mum and dad look at each other and then my mum offers Simon another biscuit.

'No thank you,' he says. 'Gotta watch the figure at my age. I'm not getting any younger.'

My mum giggles like a demented schoolgirl. Simon has won her over, and it pisses me off. If it was up to me, I'd tell him to get lost and be done with it, but I won't, because at the same time, I'm aware that the more I protest, the more insistent he'll be.

At least that's what I presume.

'I know Monica didn't have the best start with Tom,' Simon says. 'But she thought she was helping at the time. Besides, all that stuff is in the past now, and we really would love to show Tom the house and spend more time with him.'

The dog from next door starts barking through the wall, and my dad takes the opportunity to tell Simon all about the problems they've had with the yappy pooch.

'You see,' my dad says, 'there is a Pomeranian on one side

and he's fine. We take him out for walks sometimes, don't we, Anne?'

My mum nods, and sips her tea.

'But this dog – this one is another thing altogether. Barks all day and all night if he gets the chance, and the owner doesn't seem to care about it at all. Do you have any noise problems where you live, Simon?'

Simon shakes his head.

'Thankfully, we live in a detached house,' he says. 'But we did used to have plenty of problems in London. Noisy neighbours were nothing compared to the constant sirens and shouts from the street.'

My parents nod in sync, and I can't believe we are having this meaningless conversation in the middle of Simon's request to take Tom to his home. Do they think it is all wrapped up now? Is it all okay, because Simon has had a heart to heart with my parents, and then helped them to move a new garden ornament? This is such crap. Just one pub-bought pasta dinner and Simon thinks he's Dad of the Year. Here I am, struggling to pay the bills, while he lives in a sodding mansion and buys my son an iPad on a whim, and the only one to see the problem is me.

'So,' Simon says. 'Do you think Tom could come and visit us on Sunday? I promise he'll be perfectly safe, and I'll make sure he has a terrific time.'

Everyone's eyes are on me. I want to say no, but it's impossible. My parents would judge me, Tom would be devastated, and Simon would only keep nagging until I finally say yes. I'm backed into a corner, and I can see no way out.

'Okay,' I say. 'Tom can come to your house on Sunday.'

Simon breathes out hard, and makes a raspy noise with his lips.

'That's great,' he says. 'I'll pick him up at one.'

'Hold on,' I snap. 'I haven't finished.'

'Oh?'

'If Tom is coming to visit you and Monica, then I will be there as well. No need to pick us up. We'll make our own way there, and see you at 1.30pm.'

Simon shrugs, as though it's the most natural thing in the world to entertain his wife, his ex-lover and his long-lost son, but deep down I hope he's dreading it.

17

'Do you think I'm overreacting?'

Zach takes a banana from my fruit bowl and turns it every which way before unpeeling it.

'What are you doing?'

'I saw an article online, about spiders living in bananas,' he says. 'So now I have to examine each one before I eat it.'

I roll my eyes and silently wish he'd eat his own fruit instead of mine. Single young men don't seem to know the meaning of the word 'budget'. But then again, neither does Simon, and he's not young at all...

'I wouldn't worry about it. I'm pretty sure that banana spider thing was fake news. Anyway, do you think I'm overreacting?'

'To Simon wanting to have a part in Tom's life? Maybe a little.'

He pinches his fingers together to make a point, but it just makes me angry.

'It's not about him having a part in Tom's life,' I say, as I throw Zach's abandoned banana peel in the bin. 'It's about Simon wanting to help raise him. That's a different thing entirely. Don't you think?'

'Yes, I suppose it is. But then again, it depends on what he means by helping to raise him. If he means giving you a bit of money every now and then, and taking Tom off your hands for a weekend here and there, then I suppose that could be fine. But if he means going for shared custody, and living with him just as much as you do, well that's another issue.'

I slam the bin lid, and take a step back.

'You think he might be going for shared custody? That's ridiculous! Why would you say that?'

Zach swallows the last bit of banana, and puts his arms around me.

'That was the wrong thing to say, and likely a complete exaggeration. I'm sure it's the former. He just wants to give a little help, and we could all do with that occasionally, don't you think?'

I think back to all the help I've had over the past ten years. Gifts, emotional support and occasional money from my parents, friendships from the likes of Zach and the mothers I met during the first years of Tom's life, and little support packages at Christmas and birthdays from my gran. I've had help from almost everyone – even the government – but none whatsoever from Simon. Maybe now it's his time to step up and give some.

Maybe.

'I agree that we all need help,' I say, 'but it seems to me that since he came to Bromfield, my life hasn't been my own. First, Monica follows us around, then Simon reconnects, and buys my son an expensive gift, and now he's even at my parents' house, helping in the bloody garden! The guy who has never got his hands dirty in his whole life, probably! I just feel that it's all getting out of control. I'm not used to this, and I can't help feeling suspicious.'

Zach nods, and rubs my shoulders.

'I understand that,' he says. 'It's all new to you and to Tom. I think the best thing to do is just take it one day at a time. See where it goes. Take all the help you want from Simon, because he's likely to get bored before long anyway, and then you'll have worried needlessly. Just let it run its course, okay? It might be over before you know it.'

I nod and smile and say all the right things, but inside I can't believe that this will ever run its course, and that bloody terrifies me.

I drive towards Donovan Grove, and Tom sits in the passenger seat, singing along to the radio at the top of his voice.

'I thought you hated eighties music,' I say, and he laughs.

'This one is good. Grandma was playing it the other day.'

'Grandma was playing Dexys Midnight Runners?'

He shrugs.

'I don't know, but she was playing this song. I recognise the tune. It's a good tune, isn't it? It has lots of violins in it. At least I think it's violins. It could be fiddles.'

I laugh, and reach over to ruffle his hair.

'It could be both,' I say, and then Tom gets back to his singing. He looks as though he has no worries in the world, and maybe he hasn't, but it's strange that he's so laid-back about his father being in his life after ten years. Is that normal? Is that what kids do? I have no idea.

'Does he have a swimming pool?'

'Who?'

'The Market Man... I mean, my dad. Charlie's mum says that all of the houses on Donovan Grove have pools. They're mansions! Mansions like rich people live in on *MTV Cribs*!'

I turn into Simon's street, and the hedges and fancy gates rise up before me. It's strange to think that this place was what my teenage dreams were made of, and now my son is visiting his father here.

Sometimes life is odd.

Tom sits upright and stares out of the window, taking in every detail of the fancy road.

'Wow, Charlie's mum was right. These houses are huge!! Look! This one looks like the *Home Alone* house! Do you think they do have pools, Mum?'

'I'm not sure. I imagine that Si... your dad... will show you if they do.'

His house beckons on the right, and I pull over. They have an enormous driveway, and the gate is open – just as it was the day Zach and I visited – but it wouldn't feel right to drive in there. It would feel as though we were friends or family or something, and we are not.

Are we?

I park on the street with the rest of the minions, cut the engine, and then turn to tell Tom to remember his rucksack, but it's too late. He's already grabbed it, is out of the car and rushing towards Simon and Monica's drive. I wish I had half of his confidence. Where does he get it from?

His father.

'Tom! Wait for me. You can't go in there alone...'

'Tom! How are you doing, my friend?'

I look towards the house and there is Simon, striding out to meet him. Monica hovers behind, covered from head to toe in designer wear, and smiling as though greeting a long-lost relative.

Which is the truth, isn't it?

Kind of.

'Simon tells me you work in the local school. How do you like it?'

Monica puts a tiny fork of salad into her mouth and smiles. What the hell is she talking about? She knows where I work. We talked about it on that afternoon in the restaurant. I scratch my nose and as I look at her, Monica stares back and opens her eyes wide. Either she has a terrible memory, or she doesn't want Simon to know that we already discussed it.

I don't quite know, but I'll play along.

For now.

'Yes,' I say. 'I work part-time on the reception desk.'

'That's lovely,' she replies. 'I do think it's important to still work when you have a child. It allows you to have a bit of independence. A little school job is perfect, isn't it?'

I swallow a piece of lettuce, and fight the urge to swing for her.

'It's more about necessity than independence, but yes, it's pretty perfect.'

'Good hours?'

'Yes. Part-time, like I said.'

Simon picks up a china bowl, full of roast potatoes, and offers it to Tom.

'Tom, my man, do you want some more roasties? Looks like you've just about finished the ones you had.'

My son's smile spreads the breadth of his face. He can't believe his luck that there are more than a handful of potatoes on offer. It's four biggies or five little ones at my parents' house, and rarely any seconds.

Tom spears six more roasties, and stuffs one into his mouth before it's even hit his plate. Just as he's about to have another one, Betty the bichon jumps up onto his lap, and he offers her one as well.

'Betty! Get down!'

Simon waves his hands towards the dog, and it jumps down and drops the chewed potato onto the carpet. Monica smiles through tight, thin lips. I'm surprised she allows dogs into this posh, uptight house. Even though I've been past it a thousand times, nothing could have prepared me for what the house looks like inside. It's unbelievable. Tom was right, it is like the *Home Alone* house, and every other John Hughes film come to that. My mum introduced me to *Pretty in Pink* years ago, and this house would put the posh kid's house to shame.

The entrance is large and bright, with shiny white tiles running from one end to the other. The moment we entered, I had to stop myself from skidding straight onto my face, and even Tom in his rubber-soled trainers, seemed apprehensive about stepping on them. How does anyone walk on such things? Thank goodness I won't ever need to worry about that in my little semi.

Rising up from the hall is a massive staircase that wouldn't be out of place in *Gone with the Wind*. As I looked upwards at it, I half expected to see Scarlett O'Hara racing down after Rhett Butler. Maybe that's what attracted Monica to this house. I bet she pretends she's a movie star every time she comes down those stairs, and her resting bitch face could outshine Scarlett O'Hara's any day of the week.

The dining room resembles one of those set-ups they have in kitchen and bathroom showrooms. One wall is covered in grey wallpaper, with green swirls all over it. It's too artsy for my taste, but I can hardly take my eyes off it. There are fancy paintings of cats, with multicoloured paint splashes over the top, and a television mounted to the wall, in case they get bored of each other over dinner.

The furniture in this room is grey and modern with sharp edges, which gives off a cold and unwelcoming vibe. There aren't even any photos of Monica and Simon – or anyone else for that matter – it's all very clinical. Almost like a hotel room... if hotel rooms had large dining tables in them.

I gaze up at the ceiling, and notice that there is a chandelier sparkling above my head. I used to have a small one in my bedroom when I was a teenager, but I never dusted it, and before long it was covered in spider's webs and fluff. This one looks as though it's made of diamonds, and I imagine that if a spider dared look at it, Monica would have a freaking breakdown.

'Do you have a pool? My friend, Charlie, says that all of these houses have a pool.'

Tom's voice shakes me out of my daydream, and he looks wide-eyed at his father, begging him to answer in the affirmative.

'No, I'm afraid not,' Simon says, and Tom's face falls.

'Oh.'

'We do have a gym though. I'll show you it later if you like.' Monica takes a sip of her white wine, and stares at Tom over the top of her glass.

'No, you're okay,' Tom says. 'I don't like gym. We do it at school.'

Monica laughs.

'Gym class and a gym room are very different, Tom. I'll show you it later, and you'll see what I mean.'

My son shrugs, while Monica plonks down her fancy wine glass, and traces her finger around the rim. She is humouring him, pretending that they're friends, but I wonder what she thinks. Her husband had an affair – probably one of many – and the result was Tom; a child that she's known about and kept quiet about for almost ten years. And now here she is, pretending to be his best friend.

I don't buy it.

'You know, Tom,' says Simon, 'this isn't our only house. We

also have a house next to a lake, which we can maybe go to one day.'

Tom's eyes light up.

'Does the lake have boats?'

Monica laughs.

'Not at the moment,' she says. 'But perhaps we can buy one just for you.'

'Coooool!'

Simon reaches behind him, pulls open a drawer on the wall unit, and grabs a brochure.

'Here it is,' he says, as he passes the glossy booklet to my son. 'You'd be very welcome to go there one day.'

Tom thumbs through the brochure, no doubt looking for a perspective bedroom.

'You've got a book dedicated to your house? Fancy!'

My sarcasm is not lost on Monica, but she's not going to admit it.

'The house belonged to Simon's aunt,' she says. 'When she passed, it went to him, but we use it so rarely that we've decided to sell. We're hoping it doesn't go until the new year though, as we'd like to spend Christmas there if possible.'

'Can I spend Christmas there too,' asks Tom, and Simon laughs and ruffles his hair.

'Tom!' I snap. 'Don't be cheeky.'

Monica waves off my comment.

'Oh, he's fine! If we still have the house by then, you're more than welcome, Tom. But maybe not on Christmas Day itself. We wouldn't want Santa to forget where you are, would we?'

Tom pulls a face, while I stare at my glass of juice, and wonder if Monica really believes in her role as stepmother to my son. She's doing pretty well so far, but honestly? I can't see it lasting.

What is she up to?

She doesn't seem inclined to tell, and Simon is too busy basking in the ego of fatherhood to notice. What a weird set-up.

And yet here I am, eating their fancy chicken and pretending not to notice Simon staring at me from the corner of his eye. What is he thinking about? What is anyone thinking about? The only person who doesn't seem to be bothered is Tom. He's too busy tucking into his dinner, and no doubt rehearsing his conversation with Charlie about how rich his dad is, and how he got to eat a hundred roast potatoes and no vegetables, except his beloved green beans. I look over and Tom smiles and runs his fingers through his strawberry-blond hair. It sticks up in all directions, but it just makes him all the more loveable in my opinion.

'Can I please go to the toilet?'

Tom stares at Simon, and Monica grimaces. No doubt the thought of a youngster using her polished toilet is too much to bear. She tries to hide her disdain, but it's everywhere. All over her face.

Such a fake, fake, fake.

Simon gets up and points in the general direction of the shiny hallway.

'It's through there – beside the front door where you came in.'

'Your toilet is downstairs? Ours is upstairs next to the bedrooms.'

Monica purses her lips.

'It's called a visitor's toilet,' she says. 'Our main bathrooms are upstairs.'

Tom's eyes almost pop out of his head.

'Amazing! Just wait until Charlie hears about this! He's got one toilet, like a normal person.'

Monica flings her arms in the air, and laughs.

'You're so funny, Tom!' she says, and my son shrugs. He has

no idea what she's talking about, but if there was an Oscar for the best attempt at fake humour, she'd be a clear winner.

'I'll show you where it is.' Simon gets up and shuffles Tom towards the dining room door.

'And after I've been to the loo, can you show me the garden? I bet it's the size of Wembley Stadium!'

Simon chuckles and pats his son on the back.

'It's not that big, but yes, I'll take you out to see. Bring your coat. It's nippy out there.' He turns back to us and smiles. 'Back in a minute!'

Monica watches them go; a broad grin stuck on her made-up face.

'They look so happy together,' she says. 'It's wonderful that they've found each other, don't you think? By the way, that's a gorgeous necklace. I've never seen anything like that.'

She reaches over to get a better look, and she's so close that I can smell wine and cigarettes on her breath. It takes all my strength not to recoil, and no matter how hard I try, I can't stop my eyebrows from knitting together.

My hand shoots up to my necklace.

'It's just a cheap thing,' I say. 'I bought it in Skegness for a tenner.'

Why am I telling her this? I bet her own jewellery is worth thousands.

'It's cheap but cheerful,' she says, and when she smiles again, her wide mouth reveals a tiny piece of lettuce stuck between her two front teeth. I opt not to tell her.

'Monica, what do you want from us?'

The words bolt from my mouth before I can stop them, and she slumps back in her chair.

'I don't know what you mean. I don't want anything from you.'

'Oh, come on!'

'I swear I don't... Except maybe your friendship.'

She bites the skin around her thumbnail, which makes me feel even more uncomfortable than I did before. Is that a tear in her left eye? She's a better actress than I am.

'Call me suspicious, but I just don't buy this being nice business. After everything that has happened in the past, I find it hard to understand.'

Monica pulls out a pink handkerchief from the waistband of her pencil skirt, and dabs at her eyes. She reminds me of one of those socialite women from the fifties. She should be gazing into the window of Tiffany's, not living in a tiny village, talking to the local school receptionist.

'I'm trying to welcome you both into my life, because you – or your son at least – is a big part of my husband's life. I'm a contrary human sometimes, I'll admit. I know I did want to get Simon and Tom together in the beginning, but when my husband finally found out that he was a dad, it made me feel awkward and aware of all my failings. I don't know why, and it's humiliating to even admit it, since I was the one who wanted it to happen, but anyway, I panicked. I'm human, what can I say?'

Her words sound more like a rehearsed sermon than a conversation. Learning lines was my speciality when I went to acting class, and my teacher thought I was so good at it that I would easily walk into an acting job after college. That all changed when I got pregnant with Tom, but now Monica seems to have acquired my talent for putting together words and phrases that masqueraded as her own. She runs her fingers over the embroidered table mat. Was she really aware of her failings when Simon reconnected with Tom? Did she really feel humiliated and awkward? Her words gather in the back of my brain and converge with my thoughts. I must not feel sympathy for this woman... I must not feel sympathy for this woman!

'So, is that why you went to stay with a friend for a while? Because you felt awkward?'

Monica nods, and tucks her sleek bob behind her ear.

'Yes. It was ridiculous really, and I soon missed being at home. Strangely, once I came back and spoke to Simon, I realised how silly I was being. This was a chance for a new life for Simon and myself. It could all work out the way I wanted it to, if I was brave enough to give it a go.'

Another profound speech. This woman should be a writer. She'd make millions.

'Besides,' she says, 'since Tom has been in Simon's life, he seems to be settling down a little, and that can only be a good thing, right?'

There are those words again – settling down.

'You mentioned wanting Simon to settle down when we met in the restaurant. Monica, are you still afraid that he is going to stray? Because if you are, Tom or any other child will never prevent that from happening. You know that, right? If you don't trust your husband, then maybe you need to look at yourself. Get out of here and move on with your life.'

Monica sniffs, dabs her nose and gazes towards the hallway to make sure her precious husband isn't eavesdropping on our conversation. He's already left for the garden, though, so the only thing he'll hear for the next ten minutes, is a low-down of football and the latest YouTube sensation.

'You don't understand,' she says. 'I can't just walk away from my marriage, no matter how much I distrust my husband. I'll lose everything I have, if I do.'

Monica runs her ring-encrusted fingers over her fancy, gold bracelets. I'm not sure if this woman is in love with Simon, but she certainly adores the status of being Mrs Travis. Being the head of a multimillion company brings money, and what does money bring? Everything Monica has ever wanted. Except monogamy.

'I think it's time for Tom and I to be going home. We've taken up enough of your afternoon.'

Monica rubs her neck. Her long, peach-coloured nails make a scratching noise that goes straight into my brain.

'Please don't rush off, you're welcome to stay as long as you like.'

As her words hang in the air, Simon and Tom return from the garden. My son bounds in like a baby deer; he's so excited.

'Mum! You'll never guess what they have in the garden!'

I break eye contact with Monica, and smile at my son.

'No, I don't think I will. You better tell me.'

'A beehive!!'

I'm confused. Simon doesn't look the sort to don a beekeeper's outfit and waft one of those smoke gadgets around, and there's no way I can see Monica doing it.

'You have a beehive?'

I look at Simon, and he waves off my question and laughs.

'It's not ours, but we enjoy eating the rewards.'

Monica stands up.

'Do you like honey, Tom? We've got loads in the cupboard.'

Tom rubs his stomach and licks his lips in a dramatic fashion.

'Yum! Yes please. I can have it on my toast in the morning, can't I, Mum?'

I nod, and watch as he skips out of the room, behind his... what is she? His stepmother? It chokes me to think it, but I suppose she is.

Simon shuffles from one foot to another, and a broad grin runs almost the length of his face.

'He's a great kid!' He taps his temples. 'Bloody intelligent, too. Smart as hell.'

'Yes, he's wonderful.'

My ex-lover steps forward and touches my arm. I tense up and step back.

'You've done a bloody good job,' he says. 'Thank you.'

Thank you? Thank you for raising his child after he wanted nothing to do with him? There's so much I can say in response to that, but I'm anxious to get out of here without a scene, so instead, I nod.

It's all I can do.

Simon and Monica wave us off from their million-pound house, and we plod down the driveway, towards the road. Tom clutches his honey as though it's a pot of gold dust, while I try to hang on to my sanity until we reach the car.

We get to the gate, and Tom turns and waves to his new-found family.

'Bye, Dad,' he shouts.

'Bye, son!' Simon replies, and then Monica's candyfloss voice comes wafting down the drive.

'See you soon, I hope!'

Tom waves again, but I keep walking, resisting the urge to march back in there and puke all over their polished doorstep.

18

Monday morning, and I'm back on reception. Margaret is out of school and as usual, Linda Turner is on the warpath.

'Have you any idea when Margaret will be back?' She presents it as a question, but it's more of a demand. Get the principal back here or else!

'No, I'm sorry. She's gone to the dentist, so she could be out for the whole morning.'

Linda tuts and touches her flower slide, which today is a blue pansy with tiny silver bells hanging off the petals. I'm sure that isn't at all annoying to the other teachers in her unit.

'The dentist? So, Margaret is allowed a dentist appointment during school hours, but we're not? That sounds about right.'

I don't know if she needs an answer to that statement or not, so I choose to stay quiet and let her ramble on. The last thing I need is for me to agree with Linda Turner, and then have her relay that opinion to Margaret. The principal would love that, especially after the whole money scandal.

'I suppose I'll have to leave this on her desk. It's the document she asked me to prepare about school health and safety procedures.' She waves a brown, A4 envelope above her head. 'Please make sure she knows it's there.'

'Don't you want to just leave it in her basket on the shelf? She'll see it as soon as she comes in.'

I point towards the shelf where Margaret's post tray sits, but Linda frowns.

'No, I don't want to risk it getting lost amongst the other post. I'll leave it on the desk, as planned.'

Linda turns towards Margaret's office, and as she does so, a boy from Year One comes bounding into reception.

'Mrs Turner! Chelsea has just thrown up in the hall. Mrs Smith says you're to bring some sand and paper towels right now!'

Linda grunts, rolls her eyes and then throws the envelope in my direction.

'Please put this on Margaret's desk,' she says, and then disappears down the corridor.

I don't mind doing chores for the teachers, but Linda Turner speaks to me as though I'm her own personal servant. I look at the basket on the shelf, go to put the envelope in there and then think against it. If Linda comes back in five minutes and sees that I've just popped her precious cargo on the shelf, she'll kick off, and I don't think I could handle that on a Monday morning.

I head into the office and throw the envelope onto the desk. As I do so, I hear the swoosh of the front door, followed by the click, click, click of Margaret's heels against the tiles. Before I can leave, the principal appears at the office door.

'Charlotte. Can I help you with something?'

I smile brightly – too brightly – and Margaret looks behind my shoulder and towards her desk. She doesn't trust me. Ever since the money incident, she has looked at me funny, and being caught in her office is not going to help my cause. It's well known that Margaret doesn't appreciate anyone going into her office when she's out – hence the tray at reception, for notes and other memorabilia – but try telling Linda Turner that.

'I was just leaving a message,' I say. 'Linda Turner wanted me to give you this.' I hold up the envelope, as though it's some kind of treasure find, but Margaret isn't impressed. She takes the letter out of my hand; looks from it to me, and then drops it onto her desk. I don't know why, but I feel guilty, for no reason whatsoever. Ever since the money incident, Margaret just has to look at me and I feel as though I've done something wrong. I don't know what it is, but I'm sure I'll find out.

I turn to leave, but Margaret's voice stops me.

'Charlotte?'

'Yes?'

'From now on, please leave all messages in my tray on reception. It will work better for both of us that way.'

Margaret still doesn't trust me. While it's true that I've never had a particularly friendly relationship with the principal, we've always been cordial to one another. After all, we have to work close in proximity and relationship, so it's always made sense to do what she asks, and respect her decisions, even if I do question them every now and then. But since the stolen (or planted) money situation, any kind of relationship I had with her has been ruined. I don't think she'll ever trust me again, or at least she won't until I'm able to prove that I didn't take anything that wasn't mine. Should I just lie down and accept the fact that I've been branded a thief? I don't think I should, but then again, what else can I do? It all seems pretty hopeless at this point.

'I normally do leave your post in the tray, but Linda Turner was insistent that I hand deliver it. She was going to do it herself, but then one of the kids came and...'

'Charlotte?'

'Yes?'

'Just do as I ask, okay?'

'Yes, Margaret,' I say, and then slope back off to reception.

~

It's Wednesday morning, of the longest week in history. Ever since Monday, Margaret has been on my case, and it doesn't seem to matter what I'm doing, it's wrong, or late, or unneeded. I've been told off for allowing Tom and Charlie to sit in reception during wet play; I've been too friendly while talking to parents on the phone; I've been too slow at getting the registers back from the classrooms... And on it goes.

I thought I was being paranoid, but then when Amy and I were doing the changeover yesterday, Margaret bounded out of her office to demand to know why I was being so noisy. I wouldn't care, but it was Amy who was talking loudly, not me. Afterwards, Amy asked what the hell I'd done to upset Margaret, and I had to say that I had no idea. For someone who was supposed to be drawing a line under the money situation, the principal seemed reluctant to forgive and forget, but I didn't want to get into that with any of my colleagues.

'She's been super-nice to me lately,' Amy said. 'She even offered to cover the reception for me the other day, while I popped to the staffroom for some coffee. She never does that. As I'm sure you know.'

I did know that. Normally I have to make coffee when Margaret has her back turned, or else seek out a kind teaching assistant to cover me while I'm gone. No way would I ever ask the principal to cover for me, or even expect her to ever ask if I needed a break. It just isn't the done thing – at least with me.

But now it's Wednesday and halfway to the weekend. The thought of a nice cup of coffee fills my mind, and I look at my watch. It's nearly 11am, and the likelihood of a parent arriving in reception is pretty low. I stretch my legs and just as I'm about to sneak out of my office, I hear Margaret's voice.

'Charlotte, can I see you please?' The principal stands at her office door with her arms crossed, her breasts resting on them like a shelf. Shit. What have I done now? I turn on the answerphone, check the CCTV to make sure nobody is on their way down the drive, and then head towards the office. Margaret steps back to let me inside, and then closes the door behind me.

'Is everything okay?' Dear God, please don't tell me there has been more money missing. I can't cope with that. Not again.

'I'm afraid it isn't.' She beckons for me to sit down on the orange chair reserved for naughty kids and annoying parents. I perch on the very edge of the seat, as if sitting back will prevent me from ever leaving again. My palms sweat, and I wipe them on my trousers, but that only seems to make them worse.

'What's wrong?' My voice is far sterner than I want it to be, but I can't take any more guilt, when I haven't done anything wrong.

Margaret sits down, leans forward and stares at me.

'Charlotte, something has been preying on my mind since I found you in my office the other day.'

Here we go.

'What do you mean?'

'You said you were in here to deliver an envelope, but when I returned to my desk, my paperwork was disturbed, and my diary was not on the page I left it on. Furthermore, an envelope containing the Year Five end-of-term exam papers was missing. I've spent all week trying to find it, but it's completely disappeared.'

I'm confused. Why would messed up paperwork and a missing exam paper have anything to do with me?

'I don't understand.'

'Tom is in Year Five.'

'Yes. So?'

'So, he'll be taking the exams himself, won't he?'

Margaret leans forward and takes a stack of envelopes from the shelf above her desk. She plonks them down and starts going through them.

'Year One... Year Two... Year Three... Year Four... Year Six...'

She counts as she places each envelope onto the desk, but as she predicted, Year Five is missing.

And it's clear that she thinks I took it.

'Margaret, are you accusing me of taking the Year Five exam papers for Tom? Because he's a bright kid and he would never need – or want – to see them before exam day.'

'I'm not accusing you of anything at all,' she says. 'I'm just stating that it has gone missing, and the only person who was in here on Monday morning, was you.'

Before I can stop myself, I'm on my feet, wringing my hands and rubbing my face. This must be a joke. I've never stolen anything, and yet here I am for the second time in as many weeks, being accused of something terrible.

'I didn't steal anything,' I say; the words bubbling in my throat like gigantic tears. 'And anyone could have come into the office that morning, not just me.'

'Did you see anyone come in?'

'I don't think so. I don't know... But Linda Turner was about to, before that kid came and...'

Margaret stands up and places her hands on her hips.

'Charlotte! You must understand that I'm not accusing you of stealing the exam papers. I just need to get all of the facts straight before I investigate further.' Her voice softens. 'Now, let's get ourselves together and think about it. Apart from Linda, did you see anyone come into the office when I was out on Monday?'

I shake my head.

'No. No, I'm sure I didn't see anybody.'

'Okay. Well, maybe it's all a huge mistake.' Margaret's phone rings, but she continues as though nothing is happening. The incessant buzzing goes straight into my head, and I have to hold on to my hands to prevent myself from pouncing on it myself. As the principal stares at me, tears bubble out of my eyes and pour down my cheeks. I've never been in trouble at work before, and now here we are.

'Oh, Charlotte, please don't cry. I'm so sorry if I've upset you. I just need to cover every avenue. You understand?'

I nod, and the tears keep coming. Margaret rubs my arms and smiles through her thin, orange-painted lips.

'Let's go and take a look in reception, shall we? Maybe the envelope made its way out there with the registers or something. We'll take a look through them all, and it's bound to turn up. Come on...'

Margaret motions for me to exit her office, and I somehow manage to leave, despite my legs having turned into spaghetti.

As we reach my desk, Frankie Williams from Year Two comes running along the corridor.

'Frankie!' snaps Margaret. 'Let's not run in the corridor, shall we? We don't want any accidents.'

The little boy stands as still as a soldier.

'Sorry, Mrs Holmes,' he says. 'My mummy is picking me up for the doctor. I don't want to be late, or I won't get my sticker!'

Sure enough, there's Frankie's mum, waving at us from the front door. I press the button to let her in, and she takes one look at my puffy eyes, and whips her son out as quickly as she can. I can't say I blame her. Once they've gone, Margaret heads straight for my desk.

'Okay, where are the registers? Ahh, here they are.' She whips them down from the shelf and rummages through, but I know she won't find the exam paper among them. The folders have been in and out of reception more times than I can count.

Why would the exam envelope turn up there? It would make no sense whatsoever, and sure enough, Margaret gets to the end of the pile, sighs and lifts them all back onto the shelf. Her eyes are all over reception, and I feel guilty, even though I've done nothing wrong. Why is this happening? Anyone could have taken that folder, or it could have just fallen down the back of her desk or something.

Margaret is about to give up looking, when I notice her eyes fall on something under my desk. She crouches down and pulls out the tote bag I keep for lunchtime shopping purposes. The words 'Save the Arts' stare up at me from the side, and my emergency umbrella pokes out of the top.

'What's this?'

'It's my shopping bag. I leave it here in case I need it after I finish work.'

She nods and holds it open. I don't need her to make any further comment, because I can see what she's looking at. A brown, A4 envelope stares up at me from the depths of the bag, and Margaret pulls it out and holds it up.

'It's the exam papers,' she says. 'And the envelope has been opened.'

'I don't know how it got there,' I say. 'I have never seen it before in my life.'

The principal throws my bag back under the desk, and sticks the envelope under her arm.

'I think we have a problem,' she says, and although I have no idea what's going on, I have no option but to believe her.

I've been asked to keep off school property until further notice. 'Pending investigation,' Margaret said, though I'm not sure what that means. I didn't take that envelope, but how do I prove my innocence? I walked myself straight into this disaster. I was the one person to go into that room, and all because bloody Linda Turner can't bear her important messages to be left in the tray.

I tell Zach about the suspension, while he's playing with Trevor, the dog, in his back garden. He says he's shocked, but I can tell in his voice that he's wondering if I did do it. Or maybe he isn't, but my paranoid heart tells me he is.

'Are you going to tell your parents?'

'Hell, no! They'd go mental. I can't stand their lectures at the best of times, never mind now.'

'And Tom?'

'What about him?'

'Isn't he going to wonder where you are, when he doesn't see you in reception tomorrow morning?'

Shit! In all the upheaval, I hadn't even thought about what Tom would say.

'I'll have to think of something before tomorrow.'

'And then hope he doesn't tell your parents.'

I rub my head.

'It just gets better and better, doesn't it?'

19

The next morning, my tears of pain have been replaced with an unbearable, bubbling rage. Way back when my mum was going through the menopause, she used to tell me about this hormonal feeling where her temper would seem to take over her entire body. She could feel it in her arms, her legs, and even her fingers, and would scratch her limbs just to try and relieve the overwhelming urge to punch a hole in the wall. I used to think she was being dramatic, or attention-seeking or both, but now? Now I understand that feeling more than I ever thought I would. Fury spirals through my entire body, and I'm nowhere near menopausal.

No, I'm just bloody furious that I've been suspended for no reason whatsoever. I did not steal those exam papers, and I am determined to prove it, one way or the other.

Tom and I march up to school; him talking about a YouTuber who does unboxing videos of wigs – and me wondering if any minute now, Simon is going to pull up in his swanky car, and haul my son inside to start a better life. I grip onto Tom's hand, and he pulls himself away.

'Mum!! Don't hold my hand on the way to school! I'm almost ten now. What if someone sees?'

'Sorry, I didn't think. Come on, let's cross the road here.'

We both look left and right, and then trot across the street, where the school looms in front of us. I've already told Tom that I won't be in for a week or two, and had a whole story planned about annual leave, and having to help Zach decorate his living room. In the end though, I didn't need to go any further than, 'I'm taking two weeks off,' because then *Doctor Who* came on the telly, and Tom told me to shush so that he could watch it. Thankfully.

'I'll be okay here, Mum,' he says. 'I'll see you later.'

Tom runs over to Charlie and they both rush inside. Charlie's mum turns and waves, but I have no time for a moment of idle chit-chat today. I disappear into the crowd of school mums, dads, grandparents and kids, and then find myself at the gates. Do I dare go up to reception when I've been suspended?

Yes, I do. I bloody well do.

'You're not supposed to be in here! If Margaret finds out, you'll be fired for sure.'

Amy's voice is barely audible through the reception glass, and she ducks down in her chair, as if she's terrified of even talking to me.

'Relax,' I say. 'I'm here in my capacity as a parent, not a receptionist. I'm quite within my rights to be here for that.'

'Okay, so what can I do for you?'

'I need to check the visitors' book and the CCTV.'

Amy's head darts towards Margaret's office, and her mouth falls open.

'For God's sake! How the hell does that have anything to do with being a parent?'

'It doesn't. But if anyone asks, I'm here to ask about Tom's after-school club. He wants to do kick-boxing after Christmas, and I want to check if there are still spaces.'

Amy shakes her head.

'It's bad enough that I have to come in here full-time, but now I have to lie as well? When are you coming back? I hate working in the mornings.'

A mother comes up behind me, and I stand aside so that she can hand in her son's trip money.

'It's for Joel Daniels,' she says. 'I forgot to write his name on the envelope. Shall I do it now?'

'Did you put his name on the slip?' Amy asks.

'Yes, but not the envelope. Maybe I should write it on there as well.'

The woman hovers next to me, and I can smell her cheap perfume. It goes straight up my nostrils and into my brain.

'That's okay,' Amy says. 'I'll sort it.'

The woman hesitates, opens her mouth, and then decides to let Amy do her job. As if to hurry her departure, the exterior door swings open, and out she goes.

'Where's the visitors' book?' I look past Amy and into reception. It's still on the shelf, where we put it in the evenings. Heaven knows why we do that, but we do.

'You can't look in there, it's confidential. Please, Charlotte, you're going to get both of us in trouble.'

My job-sharer looks over her shoulder and grimaces. She's always been a bit of a wimp, but this is ridiculous. Is she the one who is setting me up? It wouldn't be so far-fetched to imagine that she could steal the money and plant that and the exam papers in my bag. As much as she denies it, I bet she's really enjoying being the main receptionist on duty. It gets her closer to Margaret as well, which has always been important to her.

It's an interesting thought...

'Look, all you need to do is put the visitors' book out here on this shelf. It should be out here anyway, because if you don't, and someone gets into the building without signing in, you're going to get yourself into trouble.'

Trouble will be the last thing Amy wants, and so she grabs the book, swooshes open the glass partition and throws it onto the shelf.

'Here! Now I'm going to go over to the filing cabinets, and by the time I get back, you need to be gone.'

'What about the CCTV?'

'No! I'll be fired if I let you watch that. What is this all about anyway?'

I flick though the pages of the visitors' book, while Amy glares at me.

'For God's sake, Amy, I'm not asking you to hack the school's mainframe or bring down the website. All I'm asking is for you to look and see if the camera has picked up any strangers, coming into reception during the past two weeks. If I can show that an uninvited guest has been in here, I could be halfway to proving my innocence... It's surely not that hard for you to help!'

'For someone who needs my assistance, you sure know how to put me off doing it.'

Amy stands with her hands on her slim hips. What size is she? A zero? A two at the most. I feel a twang of jealousy, as I don't think I've been that size since I was twelve. But that's not important right now.

'It doesn't matter,' I snap. 'Just get to your filing cabinets, and leave me to it.'

Amy sighs and wanders over to the other side of the room.

No, I don't think she could have set me up. She's too prim and proper for that.

I take the book and crouch down underneath the counter, just in case Margaret comes out of the office, and I flick through each page, starting with the day the fifty quid decided to jump itself into my bag. There is a visiting author, the yoga teacher, the football coach, a man who brings exotic pets to show off in assembly, and various parents, coming in for meetings and reading sessions.

Not one of these people would ever find themselves in my office, and even if they did, they'd have no reason to set me up.

It's a dead end. A stupid, infuriating dead end.

'It's someone in the building then. That teacher who hates you? The one who always tells you off for leaving your desk... Hairslide Woman!'

I laugh. I've never heard her called that before, but it's fitting.

'That's Linda Turner. I don't think she hates me. She just thinks I'm incompetent.'

Zach shrugs and pours Sauvignon Blanc into two gigantic glasses.

'Same difference. If you worked in journalism, you'd suspect her straight away. There's always some bastard out to stab you in the back in my office. Cheers.'

'Cheers.'

We clink glasses, but I'm not feeling very cheerful. It's a school night, and yet here I am, drinking wine to dull my pain. That can't be healthy, can it? I take a gulp, and the smooth, sweet liquid rolls down my throat. I don't care if it's not healthy. I need it.

'What about that other receptionist then? Out to get your job, maybe?'

'I wondered about her this morning, but no. As annoying as she is, she's not that kind of person. Besides, she would never have the guts to do something like that, just in case she got caught.'

I push a stray strand of hair out of Zach's eye, and he stares at me. I've seen this look many times over the past few years, and I know where it will lead. I don't care. I need this. I need to feel a body on top of mine.

'Are you sure Tom's out all night?' Zach's lips brush mine, and I feel it deep in my stomach.

'He's not out, out. He's at his grandparents. Yes, all night. Won't be back until tomorrow, after school.'

Those are the last words I utter, and moments later, I grab at Zach's shirt, trying to unbutton it while his lips reach my ears, my neck, my shoulder. He unclips my bra with one move, and his hands are under my T-shirt, cupping my breasts... I want this... I want this more than anything in this moment...

Bang! Bang!

Zach and I spring apart, like teenagers hearing parents coming upstairs.

'What was that?' Zach stares at me, my lipstick all over his lips.

Bang! Bang!

The noise vibrates through the wall and it's then that I realise – it's the front door.

'Someone's outside.'

'Just ignore it. They'll go away.'

I dive off the couch, and adjust my clothes.

'I can't. It might be Tom.'

I dart to the door, open it without looking through the peephole, and there in all his glory is Simon.

'Hey, I haven't come at a bad time, have I?'

'No,' I say, but I am aware that my bra is still undone, and my breath smells of wine.

'So, can I come in?'

I stand back from the door, and he steps into the hall, brushing his feet on the mat with a dramatic flair that only he could get away with.

'I saw this book about golf when I was out this morning, and thought that Tom might like it. Don't worry, it wasn't expensive. It was actually in a charity shop in town...' He strides into the living room – uninvited – and his voice tails off, as he sees Zach lounging on my sofa.

'Oh, hello. Sorry, I didn't know you had company. I'm Simon. Tom's dad.'

My throat contracts to hear him introduce himself like that. He reaches over, and Zach takes his hand.

'Zach. I live next door.'

'Nice to meet you.' Simon smiles in my friend's direction, but his eyes are on the coffee table. The same coffee table that has two half-full glasses, and two bottles of wine – one almost finished.

'Friday already? I was sure it was only Thursday.' He grins, but I know he isn't joking. My heart sinks into my stomach. Although I shouldn't care, I want Simon to know that I'm a good mother, but this doesn't bode well for me. A man in rumpled clothes on the sofa; alcohol on a school night; smeared lipstick and my bra unfastened... What is he supposed to think?

'It's my birthday,' Zach lies. 'I popped round for a quick one... I mean a quick drink.'

'Happy Birthday! Hey, is Tom around? I'd love to see his face when I give him this book.'

I point towards the clock.

'It's nearly 9pm. He'd be off to bed even if he was here, but no. He's… he's on a sleepover.' I'm hesitant to tell Simon that my son is at his grandparents' house, for fear that he'll march over there and take him away.

Stupid thought, I know, but a thought nonetheless.

'Ahh right. Yes, of course. It's a bit late. I'm just on my way home from the office. Got a lot of work on at the moment.'

'What do you do?'

Zach sits upright, as though talking to the headmaster. Why is he asking Simon about his job, when he knows already? Why is he prolonging this agony?

'I run a marketing firm,' Simon says. 'We've got an office in Northampton, and another in London. You?'

Zach looks from Simon to me, and back again.

'I'm a journalist at the local paper, nothing fancy. Just school fetes, golden weddings, that kind of thing.'

Simon licks his lips. That revelation will have pleased him. God forbid if my possible love interest has a better job than he does.

'Great. And hey, you're still young. There's plenty of time to make it on a national newspaper. I have a few contacts in London, if you want me to put a word in for you?'

What is Simon doing? He met Zach about ninety seconds ago, and already he's offering – or pretending to offer – to help him get a better job. Thank goodness my friend isn't that shallow.

'It's okay, I'm happy where I am.'

'Well, if you change your mind, you can get in touch.' Simon hands Zach a business card, which he stares at and drops onto the table. 'Nice to meet you.'

Simon goes back into the hall, and I follow him to make sure he leaves.

'So, where's Tom's sleepover?'

'What do you mean?'

He stands with his hand hovering over the catch on the front door. My head begs him to unlatch it and just disappear. Just disappear from our lives forever.

'Is it a friend? Someone he knows well? Have you met the parents?'

No! No, I'm not doing this.

'Are you seriously asking this question?'

He throws his hands in the air.

'Just wondered, that's all.'

'Good night, Simon,' I say, as I hurry him out. He turns and opens his mouth, but I close the door before the words have a chance to fill my house with any more paranoia and worry. As I go back into the living room, Zach is peeping through the blinds at the front window.

'Well, he's a bit of a jerk, isn't he? Pretending he wanted to help me get a better job, as if the one I have isn't good enough. Tosser.'

'He'll be able to see you at the window, you know.'

Zach steps away and grabs his wine glass.

'Yeah, I know. I just wanted to make sure he leaves.'

'What did you think of him?'

'Shifty.' Zach picks up the business card, and runs his fingers across the embossed lettering. 'Simon Travis Market-Me. What kind of a name is that?'

I shrug, and he tucks the card into his back pocket, drains what's left of his drink, and then grabs his coat.

'I better be going,' he says. 'Up early for work and all that.'

He kisses me on the top of the head, promises that he'll call me tomorrow, and then disappears out of the back door before I can say anything else.

20

Friday morning, Tom is at school and I'm watching *This Morning* and wondering what happened to my life. There's still no word about whether or not I can go back to my job, and the thought that I'll be left with no income because of somebody's vicious lies leaves me cold. As Holly Willoughby interviews the star of a new sitcom, the phone rings. It's Simon.

'Charlotte! I didn't expect you to be home at this hour. I was going to leave a message.'

'I was owed a couple of days off,' I lie. 'I worked overtime a few months back, and didn't get paid for it.'

There's a pause on the other end of the line. I know that Simon will suspect that's not the truth, but he's willing to go along with it anyway.

'Okay for some,' he says. 'I'm working like a dog.'

'Sorry, the line crackled – did you say working like a dog, or behaving like a dog?'

He laughs, though I doubt he finds it very funny.

'Could be one or the other, I suppose, but in this case, it was the former.'

'So, what can I do for you?'

There's a crinkling of paper, and a pause. As I wait for Simon to respond, I stare out of the window and watch two pigeons chatting to each other on the fence. Their little grey heads bop up and down as they converse, interrupted only by the occasional peck. Gosh, even pigeons have a better social life than I do.

'Yeah, here's the thing...' Simon's voice goes up an octave, and I wonder what's coming next. 'Monica and I have been talking about Tom's birthday.'

His words hit me straight in the middle of my brain. What does Tom's birthday have to do with him?

'He's going to be ten, right?'

'You need to ask?'

There's a pause, and then Simon chuckles.

'Yeah, stupid question. More a comment, really. Anyway, his tenth is a huge milestone and we'd like to do something special for him. We were thinking of taking him to see a show in London, the week before his big day.'

London? My son has never been to London before. Knowing that his dad lived there, I always made a point of declining any invitations to the city, just in case we were to somehow bump into him. That seems like a ridiculous worry in a city of millions, but the world is much smaller than we think. One time my parents flew to Los Angeles, and ended up being in the same hotel as a man my father once worked with. Not only that, but they decided to gossip about their philandering neighbour, only to discover that she was the man's cousin. So, you see everything is connected in one way of another, and even in the most remote of places, you can still bump into somebody you know.

'Charlotte? Are you still there?'

'Yes. Sorry. To be honest, while I appreciate the invitation, I'm not sure how Tom will get on in London. He's not very street-smart yet.'

'Don't worry,' Simon says. 'We'll take good care of him. We'll do a bit of sightseeing, have lunch, then a nice trip to the theatre. If you're up for Tom going, we can stay overnight and come back the next day. There's this hotel down the road from where we used to live. It's been renovated... new floors, replacement windows, all new furnishings...'

The postman waves at me from the street, and I smile back, desperate for him to come down the path and put me out of this misery. He doesn't, though, and turns into Zach's garden instead.

'Simon, is there a point to this story, or are you auditioning for a role in *Homes Under the Hammer*?'

He laughs.

'Watching daytime TV while you're off, are you?'

'Simon!'

'I'm just joking.'

The idea of Simon and Monica taking my son to London fills me with horror. He's been in touch with them for such a small amount of time, and I don't think he knows them well enough yet. And vice versa. What if Tom misses me? What if he forgets to take his giraffe, cries and gets told off for being silly?

What if...

What if...

What if...

Besides, it should be me who is organising my son's birthday celebrations. It's been my job for the past ten years after all. But then again, how am I going to pay for it, with the threat of being fired looming over my head. My brain throbs at the very thought of it.

'Y'know what, Simon? As I told you when you said you wanted more of an input into Tom's life, I don't think we're at that place yet. It's fine for you to see him on occasional weekends, but I'm not ready for you to organise an overnight trip to London. After ten years of silence, it's too much.'

Simon sighs on the other end of the phone.

'I knew you'd say that,' he says. 'But yes, I get what you mean. Okay, we'll forget London, but would you mind if we at least buy him a nice gift?'

'I don't mind you buying a gift. So long as it isn't a pony, or a race car.'

'I think we can manage that,' Simon says, and I can hear the disappointment in his voice, that he isn't getting his own way regards London. For a moment I feel sorry for him, but that soon passes. I say goodbye, and then pick up a photograph of Tom aged eleven months. His hair was strawberry-blond from the very beginning, and his eyes were huge and enquiring. He loved nothing more than watching *Peppa Pig* (though he would deny that now), and playing with his trucks. How can my baby be heading towards ten already? Soon he'll be off to secondary school, and who knows what will happen after that. Time marches on too quickly for my liking. Why can't it stand still for a while? Why can't I hold him close forever? Why did I let Simon Travis into our lives?

I have no answer to any of those questions, and doubt I ever will.

'Aww, it would have been nice for Tom to have a little get-together with his dad.' My mum stares at me from behind her copy of *The People's Friend* magazine. 'Why did you say no? He'd have enjoyed that.'

I can't believe what I'm hearing.

'You're joking?! Up until a couple of weeks ago, you didn't think Tom should have any kind of contact with Simon at all! Dad even threatened to punch him if he were to ever lay eyes on him. Now you both act as though he's your new best friend.'

My mum lowers her magazine, rolls her eyes, and tuts.

'Don't be ridiculous. We've only seen him a few times, and as we already told you, we made contact with him for Tom's sake. Besides, I've always thought Tom and Simon should have some kind of connection. I just didn't mention it to you, that's all.'

My dad strides into the room with the teapot.

'Any more tea?'

I shake my head, and he pops it onto the coffee table.

'Dad, can you believe that Mum thinks Simon should be able to organise a birthday celebration for Tom?'

He hesitates, grabs a biscuit from the tray, and plonks himself onto the sofa.

'Yes, I heard from the kitchen. Do you think you'll say no?'

'I've already said no! And can we please keep our voices down. Tom's in the garden, and could be in any minute. I don't want him to know about any of this.'

Mum goes to the window and waves at Tom, who is busy battering a football off the wall. That will please the neighbours.

'It's a shame though,' she says, as she sits back down. 'He'd have loved to go to London, and it's not as if it's on his actual birthday anyway. It would be the week before, as I understand it.'

'Wait! Who said anything about location? Or the date, come to that! I said that Simon wanted to celebrate Tom's birthday, but I'm pretty sure I mentioned nothing about what he wanted to do. Who told you about London?'

My mum and dad exchange glances, but remain mute.

'I'm waiting.'

Dad swallows his biscuit, and grabs Mum's hand.

'We heard it from Simon,' he says. 'He had just bought a new office chair, and wondered if we'd like his old one for the study. We did, so he popped it round.'

It takes me a moment to work out exactly what she means by 'the study'.

'You mean the spare room with the desk in one corner and the exercise bike in the other? And two seconds ago, you said that you'd only seen Simon twice. Why are you still seeing him? And more to the point, why are you lying about it?'

'He's very nice,' my mum says. 'And I said we'd seen him a few times, which I think means three.' She picks up her magazine again, flicks through the pages in an attempt to look unconcerned, and then drops it onto the coffee table. 'To be honest, we don't see anything wrong in keeping in touch with our grandchild's father. It would be stranger if we didn't want anything to do with him, really.'

Is this a joke? My parents have continued to see Simon behind my back, and now they approve of his plans for Tom's tenth birthday? This is bullshit! I spring up out of my chair, but my legs are shaking so much that I'm not sure how I can keep upright.

'Why would you do this? What gives you the right to stick your noses into my business?'

My dad glares at my mum, his chest rising and falling in tune with his deep breaths.

'I told you we should have told Charlotte we were keeping in touch with him,' he says, and my mum tuts again.

'You wanted to keep it quiet just as much as I did, so don't give me that!'

My dad gets up and tries to hug me, but I shrug him off.

'We just want to make sure that you and Tom are safe,' he says. 'You've got to understand that it's difficult for us. After having you both all to ourselves for so many years, it's not easy to let somebody else in, without knowing him for ourselves.'

I have so many words to say, but they're all stuck in my

throat. I can't do this. I have to get out of here. I grab my handbag, and my parents look dumbstruck.

'Where are you going?' my mum asks, as if that isn't obvious.

'Home. I'm going home, where my private life can remain just that.'

She goes to hug me, but her knee catches on the coffee table, and sends her tea flying all over the carpet.

'Ugh! Bernard! Get a cloth!'

My dad is rooted to the spot, unclear what to do. Family drama is not his thing. Normally, he'd be headed to the allotment at the slightest hint of an argument. I throw my handbag over my shoulder.

'Don't mention anything to Tom about Simon taking him to London,' I snap. 'Whatever you think, he's not going.'

'I'm going to London?!'

I spin around, and there is my son in the living-room door, muddy football under his arm and mouth agape.

Brilliant.

It's a rainy day in Bromfield, and I have no plans to go out before the school run. Instead, I cradle a cup of tea and wonder if the carpet really does need vacuuming or if it can last another day... Or two. Is my suspension making me lazy? Probably, but in my defence, this whole period has been one long journey into depression, and if I didn't have Tom, I don't think I'd even bother getting up and showered in the morning.

My hair needs a wash, but I can't be bothered to do it. I have tied it back in a ponytail, but I'll have to wear a hat to school later, to hide the fact that I'm inept at taking care of myself right now. I can't bear any more daytime TV, so instead, I am watching a video of Tom that was taken when he was at nursery, aged three. It was shot by a visiting production company, who popped the kids on a pretend tractor in front of a green screen, and had them wave at all kinds of imaginary animals and people. Tom needed no encouragement to act out his role of Farmer Giles, and the result has entertained me ever since.

As my little boy waves at a cartoon cow, the doorbell goes. I'm expecting a parcel for Tom's birthday, so I'm not too concerned about what I look like, but as I open the door, my heart plummets. It isn't my package at all. It's Monica.

My ex-lover's wife wears a bottle-green raincoat with the hood pulled tight around her face. Clumps of black hair poke out over her forehead, and water dribbles down into her eyes. She's shaking and holds her arms around her chest, as though trying to comfort herself. Her short, black skirt sticks to her legs like an old dishcloth, and her tights glisten with moisture. I'm sure her outfit cost hundreds – maybe thousands – of pounds, but right now she looks like a mess. But still more glamorous than me.

'Hey,' she says. 'Please can I come in? It's really coming down out here.'

I shake myself out of my daydream, and move aside.

'Sorry, I was miles away for a moment.'

Monica comes into my tiny hallway, takes off her coat and shakes it outside before hanging it onto my wall hook. The remaining raindrops run down the fabric, and drip onto the floor, while Monica kicks off her shoes and rubs her skirt.

'You want a towel?' I ask, although I hope she says no, since the chance of me having any clean ones is remote.

'No, it's okay, thanks,' she says. 'Listen, I can't stay long, but I wanted to have a word with you about London.'

My throat contracts. Why did I know this would happen? Ever since Tom found out about Simon's plans, he has been begging me to let him go. One minute he'll be doing chores in an effort to win me over, and the next he's stamping his feet and telling me how much he hates me. He even texted Simon to tell him how much he wanted to go, and the two of them went back and forth as to the fun they could have if only I'd let them. I know this not because I stalked my son's phone (although I frequently do), but because Tom showed me the conversation in another attempt to get me to comply. All it actually did was earn Simon a phone call from me, telling him to stop winding my son up.

Things wouldn't be so bad if it was just Tom that wanted the trip to happen, but my parents are so taken in by Simon that they think no harm can come from it at all. I'm surprised they haven't booked themselves on the trip just to spite me, and I can't believe how hypocritical they are. They wanted to kill Simon for what he did to me, but the moment he went sniffing around them, he won them over. How do they think that makes me feel? They don't seem to care.

But now here comes Monica, with another attempt to change my mind.

'Monica, I've already said no, and I meant it.'

'I know,' she says, 'but I'm hoping I can change your mind.'

I assure her she won't, and then close the living-room door for fear that she'll see the state of my carpet. There is a small wicker chair in the hall, which my parents gave me when they upgraded their conservatory, and Monica takes no time in plonking herself on there.

'I never had children, as you know,' she says. 'So, after my initial reservations, I was all for Tom coming into our lives, because I knew it would make Simon happy.'

This again. Didn't we go through all this when I was in her house for dinner? The only difference with this conversation, is that she's saying she wanted Tom in her life because she knew it would make Simon happy? Didn't she previously tell me it was to provoke him into settling down?

Whatever. I can't keep up with her.

I can't keep up with anything.

I look at my watch and grimace. I really need to change Tom's bed, and if I don't get it done before the school run, it'll never happen. Monica sees my face crinkle, and stands up.

'I'm sorry if I'm keeping you from something.'

'It's okay. I just have a few bits to get done before Tom comes in from school.'

'Of course.'

She sits back down and plays with a tiny piece of wicker that sticks out from the arm of the chair. It breaks off in her hand, and she drops it onto the floor.

'Look, I know this could be a difficult situation, but it doesn't need to be. We would love to take Tom to London for his birthday, not only as a celebration for him, but as a well-earned break for you.'

I bristle at the idea that I would need a break from my own son, and my sharp intake of breath causes Monica's eyebrows to shoot upwards. She knows she's pissed me off, and before I have chance to reply, she carries on talking.

'Simon has missed out on so much during the past decade – yes, his fault I know – but he is desperate to make up for it now. I promise we'll take good care of Tom, if you're willing to give us the chance.'

I brush some imaginary fluff from my trousers in an effort to seem unconcerned, but I'm sure Monica can tell that I'm not happy with this request. You'd have to be brain-dead not to know it.

'Monica...'

'Please! Just think about it, okay? I know I might not come across as the most maternal of people sometimes, but that's only because I'm not used to being around children. But having said that, I do enjoy Tom's company, and he does make Simon happy. That's so important to me, because it's a rare occurrence for my husband to feel like that about anything.'

She emphasises the words *my husband*, and then gives me a tiny, thin-lipped smile. I rub my temples. I feel a migraine coming on, and I need to get this woman out of my house.

'Listen,' I say, 'if I tell you I'll give it some thought, will that make you happy?' Monica's face lights up.

'Definitely! And if you do decide to let him come, you won't regret it, I promise.'

'I better not,' I say. 'Because if my son is ever hurt or upset while in your care, your world won't be worth living in anymore.'

She rolls her lips into her mouth, and wafts her long, damp eyelashes up and down.

'I believe you,' she says, and then goes out of the door.

21

A week later, and I have admitted defeat on the subject of Tom's birthday celebration. It seemed that out of everyone I know, I was the only one who thought it could be a bad idea. The only one who understood my hesitation was Zach, but then as Tom reminded me, our neighbour has no say on what he can and can't do.

But anyway, the conclusion of over a week's worth of agony, guilt and begging from my son, is that Simon is getting his way. A week before Tom's real tenth birthday, there will be a London weekend. Or a birthday extravaganza, as he calls it. Not only that, but my son will have a sleepover at Simon and Monica's home, the night before they go. That way they can head to London early on Saturday morning, and then they'll have all day to see the sights before the show. Big Ben, the Tower of London, Buckingham Palace... All the places I would love to take Tom for his birthday, if only I could afford it.

But now as Monica and Simon remind me, I don't need to worry about paying for such a trip, because they've got it all sorted out.

Lucky them.

~

It's the day of Tom's sleepover, and there's a freezing wind racing around the school playground, as I wait for him to come out. Beside me, a group of mothers discuss a true crime show that has just launched on Netflix. I try to tune into their conversation, but before I'm able to decipher which programme they're talking about, I see Geraldine Butler, racing towards me, waving her arm off.

Geraldine has two girls at school called Fifi and Levi. We call them Kylie and Danni, because of their celeb status in Years Four and Five. If there's a club to join, they're there; if there's a band to play in, Geraldine's buying them a trumpet; and if there's a play to perform in, Fifi and Levi are first in the queue for auditions. If they don't get the main parts in each end-of-term production, well God help the teacher who made that decision. Tom became fond of Fifi a year ago, but when he asked if she'd like to play Roblox with him, Geraldine almost fainted.

'We don't do computer games,' she squawked. 'The girls are too busy planning their creative careers.'

If those girls leave school and work in an office, I swear Geraldine will have a nervous breakdown, and I just hope I'm around to see it. The woman bounds towards me; her long red hair swinging from side to side, and the tassels on her coat vibrating all around her. She looks like a demented, wintery flapper girl.

'Charlotte! Is it true that you've been fired? I can't believe it!'

The mothers next to me stop their conversation and stare, and I feel as though the entire playground is watching me.

'No, I haven't been fired,' I say. 'I'm just taking some days off, for personal reasons.'

Geraldine throws her hand to her chest, and gasps. She's going for an Oscar with this performance.

'Oh, thank goodness! When Fifi told me you'd gone, I panicked. Nobody takes care of reception like you do, and don't get me started on how incompetent Margaret Holmes is, when she tries to fill in for you.'

'What do you mean? Margaret never fills in for me on reception. If I need anything, I have to put the phone on silent and run. I'd never think of asking her to cover.'

Geraldine stuffs her hands in her pockets, and shakes her head.

'Well, she was definitely on reception a few weeks ago. I went in to see if there had been any more thought about my idea of a macramé club, but you were nowhere to be seen. Margaret was there, though, and she had a pile of envelopes in her hands. When I pressed the buzzer, she dropped the whole lot, and a tonne of money rolled out of the envelopes and went all over the floor. It looked like a scene from a Vegas casino, where some high-roller is lounging on the bed with their winnings. I hope she managed to find it all again. I hate to think of how much money must have rolled under the counter...'

Geraldine continues her rant, but my ears tune her out. I'm too busy wondering why Margaret would be handling envelopes full of money on reception. It's never been her job to do so, and why was she jumpy enough to drop it all over the floor when the door buzzed? Thoughts spin around in my head, and pool in the centre of my brain.

Could Margaret be the one who put the money into my bag?

No, that's crazy. She wouldn't do that.

Would she?

Tom bursts out of the Year Five door, and before he knows what's happening, I've grabbed his hand, and the two of us are queuing up outside the main reception doors, waiting to be buzzed in by Amy.

'What are we doing, Mum?' Tom asks. 'I need a wee, and I need to get ready for my trip!'

'You can go to the loo when we get into reception. I just need to talk to Amy.'

Tom tuts and grabs his phone from his rucksack.

'What have I told you about bringing your phone to school? If your teacher finds it, she'll confiscate it.'

He ignores me, and bursts into laughter at some meme or gif that has popped onto his screen.

Ten minutes, and seven parents later, it's our turn to go inside.

'Amy, please. I need you to give me access to the CCTV files. It's important.'

'I've already told you. I can't do that. Margaret could come out at any moment, and I'll get fired.'

I roll my eyes. Tom has disappeared into the toilet, and there's a matter of minutes before he'll be back again.

'I know that Margaret has already left. I saw her driving off before school had even finished.'

'Oh.'

The door flies open behind me, and one of the dads comes in, with a toddler wrapped around his shins.

'I'm just here to drop off Joshua Brown's karate slip. Shall I pop it here?' He points to the shelf, and without a word, Amy sticks her hand out of the glass partition, and takes if from him. He nods and disappears out of the door, trying to get the toddler to give up her clutch on his leg.

'Amy, I swear... I wouldn't ask you to do this if it wasn't important. Somebody has set me up, and I need to know who.

It's going to cost me my job, and if that happens, I won't be able to afford to live. Please! Please, help me.'

Amy purses her lips, and pushes her hair behind her ears.

'Look,' she says. 'I can't let you into reception, but I suppose I can give you the disk of files.'

I clap my hands together, but Amy responds by wagging her finger in front of my nose.

'You must promise me that you'll put the discs through my letter box by Sunday morning at the latest. That way I can get them back here and nobody will ever know.'

I cross my heart and smile.

'You're a lifesaver. Thanks so much!'

Amy hands me an envelope, full of disks.

'Stick them in your bag, and for God's sake, don't tell anyone that I gave them to you. And don't ever mention this to me again!!'

'No problem,' I say. 'No problem at all.'

'Right, Mum, I'm off! I'll see you on Sunday night! I don't know what time though. Simon says we'll be busy all day, so it'll probably be late. About midnight I'd say!'

Tom bounds down the stairs with his rucksack over his back. God knows what he's got in there, except for a *Doctor Who* colouring book and his toothbrush. He rushes past me, and straight out of the front door, where Simon is waiting.

'Hey! Don't go without giving me a kiss.'

My son groans, but lets me plant my lips on his cheek.

'You be a good boy, okay? Do whatever Simon and Monica say, and do not wander off.'

I hand his little suitcase to Simon, and he nods and smiles.

'He'll be fine,' he says. 'Don't worry, I lived in London for years, and I know every inch of it. Tom will be perfectly safe.'

Tears spring to my eyes, but I blink them away. This is the first time my son has been out of town for the night without me, and it's hard. Even more so since he is spending time with the man who didn't even want him in the first place.

As if reading my mind, Simon brushes my arm with his hand.

'It's okay,' he says. 'I promise he'll have the time of his life. I'm not the enemy, you know.'

'I didn't say you were.'

Tom climbs into the car without giving me a second look, and Simon throws the suitcase onto the back seat.

'Seriously, please don't worry,' he says. 'My only concern is to give my son a trip that he'll remember forever... For all the right reasons. Plus, I'll text you when we get there and you have my number, in case you want to speak to Tom or me, or Monica.'

My forehead clenches into a scowl, and my hands shake. What on earth would I want to speak to her for?

'It's okay, Tom has his own phone, and I'll be calling him on a very regular basis.'

Simon laughs.

'Whatever makes you happy,' he says, and then slides into the car.

'When I was a teenager, I always thought that weekends in my twenties would be all about clubbing and chasing women. But this? I could never have imagined anything as exciting as this!'

Zach holds his head in his hands, while he stares at the black-and-white picture on the screen.

'Will you stop! I need to know if it's Margaret that's setting me up, and the only way I'll know is if it's on these tapes.'

I look at the screen, and watch as I talk to a parent through the reception window. Thank goodness the camera points that way. It isn't there to record anything in my actual office, but because of the angle, I can see part of my desk, including the area where I keep my bags. If anything has been planted by Margaret or anyone else, it should show up here.

'This is the Friday morning when I think the money made its way into my handbag. If Margaret did it, it will have been when I ran to the staffroom to get a cup of coffee. That was at about 10.15.'

I fast-forward through the picture, and sure enough, at 10.17am, I check the clock, press a few buttons on the phone, and then disappear from view.

'Gosh, you were two minutes late for your break,' Zach says. 'Hope you put that onto your overtime.'

'Shush! This is where it's going to happen… If it did.'

We both watch the screen, our fingers pressed to our lips, and eyes almost crossed from the concentration. Sure enough, at 10.20am Margaret appears, holding some keys in her hand, and then she disappears.

'Look! It's the keys to the safe! Now, watch. If she comes back into view with envelopes in her hands, we'll know that what that parent told me is true.'

One minute later, Geraldine appears at the front door, and buzzes. As predicted, a mound of envelopes falls onto the floor, and what looks like pieces of cash, appear on the carpet. Margaret comes into view, buzzes Geraldine into the building, speaks for a moment, hustles her out, and then looks towards the corridor. The principal then bends down to pick up the envelopes and money.

'Here we go.' Zach and I are so close to the screen that our heads are almost touching, but it's worth the eye strain. As Margaret scrambles on the floor, her hand moves to under my desk, and for a split second, disappears into my bag.

'Bingo! Oh My God!! Did you see that? Did you see it? Look!'

'Show me again.'

I rewind and play the whole thing again. This time we watch in slow motion, and the camera shows Margaret dumping something – the money – into my bag. My heart beats so fast that I think it's going to jump out of my chest. I can't believe this. My own principal wants to sabotage my career. But why? What is the purpose of it?

'Where's the tape with the exam paper?' Zach has gone into investigative reporter mode, and we both sort through the bundle of discs until we come across one close to the day in question. We watch two separate days and nothing, and then on the third there it is – Margaret enters reception, sorts through the exam papers and drops one of the envelopes into my shopping bag.

'This is unbelievable!' My head spins, and my back is in actual physical pain. Why did she do this? Why does this woman – who I have worked quietly with for years – suddenly want me to lose my job? It doesn't make any sense.

'Seems we've found the culprit.' Zach rewinds the film and watches it again. 'Wow, I know we have some back-stabbers in my office, but I'm not sure even they would go this far. What did you do to her, to make her hate you so much?'

'What did I do to her?! I have done nothing, except pander to her every wish, for the last five years, that's what I've done! This makes no sense!'

I get up so quickly that my chair knocks off the back of my knees, and Zach reaches over to catch it before it tips into the fireplace. He stares at the screen again, and then puts on his reading glasses, as if that's going to help anything.

'What are you going to do?' he asks, and I shrug, as I pace up and down the living room.

'What can I do? I'd say go to the police, but I'm not sure this sort of thing is even their department, is it? Sabotage of a career is not the crime of the century in a criminal sense. So, what else is there to do? I'm just so confused.'

Zach grabs a huge salt-and-vinegar crisp from the bowl I put out for refreshments, and crunches down so hard that a million crumbs fly out of his mouth and onto the table. I try to ignore his bad table manners, but it's hard.

He presses a few buttons on the laptop, and the evidence is downloaded onto a memory stick. He hands it to me.

'Put this somewhere safe, and we can figure out what to do about it over the weekend.'

I run my fingers over the plastic stick, and then throw it into a drawer, as if it's on fire. The thought of what's on there is nauseating and I can't bear to hold it in my hand.

'What do you think I should do?'

'I'm not an expert at this kind of thing, but I'd say maybe go into school and tell her you know what's happened, show her the evidence and then demand your job back. If she says no, we go to the governors or the union, or the police. Maybe even the Citizens Advice people could help. Believe me, someone will have an answer as to what to do, and then Margaret will be screwed.'

I nod, though I have no idea how I'm going to emotionally prepare for any of that. But whatever we do won't happen until Monday anyway. For now, I've got to get through the weekend, knowing that my son is going to be in London with his father and stepmother. I have to survive that before I can even think about getting my job back. I take a glug of wine, and hope for the best.

~

Zach has gone home. I'm watching a *Friends* marathon on Comedy Central, and trying to forget about Margaret, and the fact that Tom has embarked on a weekend away with Simon and Monica. Why did I ever agree to it? I must be raving mad.

When I was a teenager, my mum used to say that I was the kid who was easily led. If my friends needed anyone to buy cider from the off-licence, using a bag of ten pence pieces, it would be me who was sent. If they got drunk and didn't want their parents to know about it, I'd be the one who volunteered to hide them in my house until they sobered up. It was a constant cause of complaint from my mother, who wondered what high building I'd throw myself from, if my friends suggested it.

Thinking back, I wasn't as bad as she made me out to be, but I must say that I didn't have many questions when asked to do something for somebody. That's what got me into trouble with Simon if I'm honest – not that I would ever admit that to my parents. But anyway, in this case I had stuck firm and said that Tom could not go away for the weekend with Simon and Monica, but somehow, I had been railroaded into it. Not only that, but my parents – who always believed I was easily led – were now completely under Simon's spell. I wish that I had remained firm about this trip, but what can I do about it now?

Nothing.

Tom phoned me just after seven, to tell me all about the huge bedroom he's sleeping in. Apparently, it has Tiffany-blue walls (Monica told him that), and white carpets. They had lasagne for dinner, but it wasn't as good as mine, because it had peppers in it. My son hates peppers, and left them in a pile on the side of his plate. I'd love to know what Monica thought about that! When Tom called, he had just finished playing Wii golf with Simon, and Monica had made him a hot chocolate before he got into bed for an early night.

'I have to be up at 6am tomorrow,' he said. 'That's even earlier than I get up for Christmas!'

He was so excited, and couldn't wait to get to sleep, so that his big day would come quicker. I said goodnight, told him I love him, and that was that. I haven't heard from my son since, and my last two messages have gone unread.

Should I text him again? No, best not. It might wake him up and then he'll be frightened and will want to come home. Would that be a bad thing? Not in my eyes, but in everyone else's for sure.

Still, the urge to talk to someone in the house is unbearable, so I dial Simon's number, and listen as his phone goes straight to voicemail. I look at my watch. It's 10.42pm. He must be in bed now, too, all of them giddy for their perfect birthday trip. I hang up and phone Zach. He picks up with a yawn.

'Were you in bed?'

'No, I fell asleep on the sofa. I was watching *Catfish* and must have nodded off. What can I do for you?'

That's a good question. What can he do for me? Why am I ringing him at this hour? I have no idea.

'I'm not sure,' I say. 'I've been wondering if Tom is okay, and he didn't see my last two messages, so I think he must be in bed, but then I phoned Simon and...'

'Charlotte!'

'Yes?'

'I know this is the first time you've ever let Tom out of your sight, apart from sleepovers at your parents' house, but I'm sure there's no need to worry. They'll all be in bed – which is where you should be by the way – and I'm sure if you ring them in the morning, you'll get to speak to Tom.'

Zach's right, I know he's right, but even so, I can't help but worry. He has no idea what it's like, since he's never had children, but one day he'll learn just how hard all of this is. As I bid him goodnight, I spot my boots, sitting next to the stairs.

Donovan Grove isn't too far away from me. If I drive over and have a quick peek down the drive, nobody will ever know. I'll be happy that I'm just feet away from my son, and then I'll head back here and get to bed.

I slip on my boots, grab my keys, and head out of the door.

22

I pull up outside Simon and Monica's neighbour's house, for fear that if I stop at the end of their drive, my son's new family will see me and declare me nuts. It would be a hard thing to deny, to be honest... Sitting alone in a car at 11pm on an autumnal Friday night is not the behaviour of a sensible human being.

I turn off the engine and pull my coat around me, trying to savour the last of the waves of heat, coming from my fan. I stare towards Simon's house, but I have trouble seeing through the hedge. Damn it, I should have parked a few feet closer, and then I'd have had a perfect view, but it's too late now. If I start and stop my engine again, it might wake up the Neighbourhood Watch and I don't want that.

I grab my bobble hat from the passenger seat, pull it down low, and get out of the car. I only need to walk six feet, and I'll get a proper look at Simon and Monica's house. Then I'll be able to put my mind at rest, jump back in the car and head home.

I lock the door and stroll towards the mansion, but as I turn into the opening of the driveway, something strikes me as not being right. The garage door is open, and Simon and Monica's cars are both gone. For a moment, I think my eyes are playing tricks on me. The garage can't be open. It must be a trick of the light, making me think that the space is empty. I walk closer and closer, but there is no mistake. Apart from a garden hose, an artificial Christmas tree and a white plastic bench, the garage is empty.

Where is the car that drove Tom from our home just hours ago?

Where is the car that is supposed to drive them all to the station tomorrow morning?

My heart races, and I beg it to stop. There must be an explanation. Perhaps Monica went out for the evening and her car broke down, and Simon had to go and rescue her. He must have taken Tom with him, and didn't bother to tell me because, why would he? They'll all be back in a minute and I'll have to run for cover, so that they don't see me.

That scenario buzzes around in my mind as I make my way to the patio doors, at the back of the property. It's damp, and I can feel my hair getting frizzier by the minute, but if I can just see some sign of life through the door, then I'll be on my way. What kind of sign I don't know, but there must be something that proves I'm being a paranoid, anxiety-ridden idiot.

As I reach the door, I'm stunned to see that the curtains are open. Who leaves their curtains open in the middle of the night? Surely that's an invitation for any old pervert or criminal to take a gander into your private life. But still, it's better for me, because now I can see straight into the room, and convince myself that everything is okay...

Only it isn't okay.

As I stare through the large window, my breath catches in the back of my throat and I struggle to breathe. Whereas just weeks before there had been a dining table, chairs and posh units, now the room is empty. To a stranger it would seem as though the house hadn't been lived in for months, but I know better.

Where is the furniture?

Where are Simon and Monica?

Where is my son?!

'Have you checked the front of the house? Maybe it's a trick of the light. Darkness can do some strange things to our vision.'

Zach's voice is relaxed – disappointed even – no doubt wondering why the hell I've gone round to Simon's house so late at night. I hold the phone closer to my face, so that I don't have to shout, but even before I speak, I can feel my voice going up an octave.

'I looked through the letter box. Everything is gone. The table next to the door, the armchair in the corner, and even the rug.'

'What about the living room? Can you see through that window?'

'Hang on, I'll check.'

My breath is short as I move to the front window. Leaves crunch underneath my feet, and I can feel the damp soil moulding itself to my shoes, but I don't care.

'Are you there yet?'

'Yes.'

There are no curtains to hide the view, and I hold my hand up to the glass to hide the reflection from the lamp post. Once again, the room is empty. The only thing left is a lampshade hanging from the ceiling, and the thick carpet.

'There's nothing here at all.' The words stick in my throat and I can hardly get them out. 'It's gone. Everything is gone.'

~

'Have you tried to contact Mr... er... Travis on the telephone?' Constable McGarvey flicks through her notebook and then stares at me. She thinks I'm an idiot.

'Yes, I phoned him and I've phoned my son. Neither one is answering.'

'That may just be because it is the middle of the night, and they've got their phones turned off. I'm sure that if you try again in the morning, there will be an answer.'

I run my fingers through my damp hair. I want to reach inside my head and pull my brain out. I'm in so much emotional pain, and nobody will listen to me. Why won't they listen?

'The point is that the house is empty! They've gone and they've taken my son with them.'

'And you knocked on the door?'

'Yes! It was the first thing I did when I realised the furniture had gone. There was no answer – as your colleague saw for himself when he knocked just a moment ago!'

Across the road, a curtain twitches in one house, while the front door opens in another. Nobody is even pretending to be discreet with their nosiness, and I just want to tell them all to get lost – or words to that effect.

'Charlotte, let's go and sit in here, and we can talk in private.'

The policewoman points to her car, and I follow her. She shows me into the back seat, while she sits in the front. It's still cold in here, but at least it isn't raining.

'I'm going to take down a few details, okay?'

I nod, and even though I've already told her everything, I go through it all again... And again.

'Did Mr Travis say that he was bringing Tom back to this house?'

'Yes! He said that Tom could stay at his house overnight, so that they could get up early tomorrow.'

Constable McGarvey swats at her fringe as though it's a fly, flicks through her notebook again and then turns to me.

'I know Mr Travis told you that he'd take Tom to his home, but did he say it was this actual house? Did he give you an address?'

Her words rattle in my brain. What is she talking about?

'No, he never mentioned this particular house, but this is where he lives. I've visited him and his wife here several times. We had lunch here a couple of weeks ago.'

Constable McGarvey shakes her head.

'It may be that they moved out in the meantime, and didn't tell you. I'm sure there's a logical explanation, and Mr Travis has taken Tom to his new house, wherever that may be.'

A car pulls up behind us, and the headlights shine straight into the back window. Constable McGarvey shields her eyes and we both stare to see who is in there, but it's too dark to see. The policewoman's partner speaks to the driver, and then comes over to Constable McGarvey's car. He taps on the window and she opens the door.

'The owner of the house is here.'

The owner of the house? Oh, thank God, it must be Simon. I dive out of the car, just as a woman exits the vehicle behind us. My first thought is that it's Monica, but she's too broad to be her...

'Charlotte. What on earth are you doing at my house in the middle of the night?'

Lights dance in front of my eyes, and I feel as though I'm about to pass out. This can't be right. How is this possible?

'Margaret. What are you doing here?'

~

The principal stares at me, and I stare straight back.

'Do you two know each other?' Constable McGarvey looks from me to Margaret, and we both nod.

'Charlotte is a receptionist at my school.'

'Your school?'

The policewoman takes out her notebook, as though this is exclusive information that needs preserved.

'Margaret is the principal of the school where I work,' I say.

'And you own this house?'

Margaret nods.

'Yes, that's right.'

'But there is no furniture inside.'

The principal laughs and shakes her head.

'I'm decorating the entire bottom floor,' she snaps. 'All of the furniture has been moved into the gym, so that the decorators have full access to the rooms. Why? What's the problem here, constable? Has something happened?'

Margaret looks over my shoulder at the house. How can it belong to her? Nothing makes sense. Constable McGarvey snaps her notebook closed.

'I think this is a case of mistaken identity,' she says. 'Miss Baker thought that her friends lived here, but that doesn't appear to be the case. Do you have anything that would confirm that you own this house?'

'Of course I do!' Margaret reaches into her handbag and brings out several envelopes. 'Here are some letters with my address on them. I also have the front door key and all of my belongings inside.'

She pulls out her key and jangles it in front of the policewoman's face, while McGarvey stares at the letters.

'This isn't possible!' I shout. 'Margaret does not live in this house. This must be some kind of set-up! This woman has been setting me up at work, and now this!'

Both women stare at me, while the policewoman hands the letters back to Margaret.

'These seem to suggest that this house does belong to Margaret,' she says. 'What do you mean she is setting you up?'

The principal throws her hands into the air and shrugs.

'I'm afraid that we've had a few problems with Charlotte at school, and we've had to suspend her, pending investigation.'

'Investigation into what?'

'Theft of school money, and an exam paper.'

My chin hits the floor, and I stuff my hands into my pockets for fear that I'll thrash out at any moment.

'Both of which you set up!' The words burst out with such force that the nearby policeman steps in and tells me to calm down. 'I can't calm down! I'm tired and confused and worried about my son. Where is he? What have you done with my son?'

Constable McGarvey steps between us.

'I know you're worried, but shouting isn't going to get us anywhere.' She turns to the principal. 'Miss Baker thinks that she may have brought her son here several weeks ago, to visit with his father. Do you know anything about that? Has anyone else lived in your house recently?'

'Yes, my sister has been staying here with her husband.'

'And what are their names?'

Margaret stares at me before continuing.

'My sister is Monica Travis and her husband is Simon.'

My heart falls into my stomach. Monica is her sister? How is this possible? PC McGarvey takes out her notebook again, and writes the names onto a clean sheet of paper.

'Please could you let us into the house so that we can speak with them?'

Margaret shakes her head.

'I'm afraid that's not possible,' she says. 'They moved out last week.'

The rest of the conversation is just a blur, as Constable McGarvey asks me question after question. Yes, I gave permission for my son to go to London; once again, no, Simon didn't tell me that they would be leaving from this particular house; no, I never asked if they owned this house or were borrowing it for a while; yes, I have been suspended from work; no, I don't have a clue what the hell is going on; yes, I feel like an utter prat. Meanwhile, Margaret claims that she does not have the couple's new address, as they're still settling in; she did not know the couple were back in town for the day, but that wasn't a surprise, since they don't have to tell her everything that goes on in their lives.

After much toing and froing, the policewoman has had enough.

'To be honest, this all sounds like a mix-up, which I'm sure will be resolved in the morning. Once you have called Mr Travis – or your son – then I'm sure they'll be able to explain what's going on. It's clear that you gave Mr Travis permission to take your son to London, and we should still believe that is what he is doing. Whether he left from this house or any other, is not important, and I would say no cause for concern. Mrs Holmes, thank you for your help. Miss Baker, please let us know in the morning if you still can't speak to your son, and we'll take things further. But for now, are we okay here?'

Margaret and I both nod, and Constable McGarvey says goodbye. Before I can add anything more to the discussion, she's started the engine, and the car whooshes off from the pavement, and into the night. Margaret and I watch it go, and one by one the neighbours disappear from their front doors and windows.

'Goodnight. I hope you can sort all of this out in the

morning.' The school principal brushes past me, but I'm in no rush to let her go.

'You set me up.'

She stops and turns towards me.

'What?'

'With the money and the exam papers. That's what I was trying to explain to the policewoman, but she went straight on to a different subject.'

Margaret throws her handbag over her shoulder, and sighs.

'Don't be stupid,' she says. 'Now, I can see that you're upset, but I'm not about to stand here and let you accuse me of something that you're already under investigation for. The school governors will decide what is in the interest of the school, and then we'll explain everything to you at a proper place and time.'

'I better send them the tape, then.'

'What tape?'

A tabby cat appears from under the bush and brushes itself against my ankle. The tiny hairs on my legs stand up, and it takes me all of my time not to freak out. I've always been scared of cats, and the fact that there is one here now, when I'm in the middle of this shit show, terrifies me even more. I try to ignore the fact that its tail is now wrapped around my shin, and stare at Margaret.

'I have a CCTV tape, which shows you putting the money and the exam paper into my bag.'

Her mouth falls open, and she throws her hand to her chest in the most dramatic of fashions.

'Good try, Charlotte, but I know that's not true. We do not have any cameras in reception, as you well know.'

'You're right, we don't have any in the office, but we do have one at the front door, looking towards the window where we greet visitors. Beyond that you can see a small triangle of my area and the floor beneath my desk, which is where I always keep my bag. But you know that already.'

The principal tuts and blows something resembling a raspberry, before striding away from me.

'Don't go around saying things like that,' she shouts. 'Lies can get you into trouble!'

Before I can answer, the principal disappears down her driveway, and then my phone rings. It's Zach.

'Hey! Thank God! Are you okay? I've been trying to get through for ages.'

'I'm on my way home,' I say. 'I'll tell you about it then.'

The drive home is a couple of miles, but with so many thoughts whizzing around my head, it seems like hours. So, Simon and Monica have been living in Margaret's house, and I just assumed that it was their own. But where was she when we went over for dinner? In her bedroom? Out for a walk? In another house entirely? Maybe that's why she's now decorating – to make a new start now that Simon and Monica have gone.

Is any of this any of my business? I have no idea. But Margaret being Monica's sister makes sense regards the sabotage of my job. Monica must have spoken about Simon's affair many times over the years, and then when Margaret found out that the other woman was right there in her office, it sealed my fate. I can't blame her. I'm sure I'd do the same for my sister – if I had one – but it doesn't make it any easier to accept.

I'm so tired that my head feels jet-lagged and full of wool, or fog or something. I know the work stuff is bad, but it's nothing compared to how I feel about Tom. I should never have allowed him to go with his dad, no matter how excited he was, and how much everyone around me thought it was a great idea. Granted, the fact that I never questioned whether they owned the house on Donovan Grove, or whether it was there that they were taking Tom, is my fault, and that makes things worse. But all I can do now is pray that when I call Tom's number in the morning, I hear his excited little voice, telling me what a wonderful time he's having.

But first I have to get through the next four or five hours.

23

6.30am and Zach has already been in my house for twenty minutes.

'You want another cup of tea?' he asks.

I shake my head. I've just finished the last one he made, and what I need now is an espresso.

'If you change your mind, let me know. Have you tried ringing Tom again?'

'Not since you went into the kitchen five minutes ago.'

My friend smiles through thin lips, and I know I'm being snappy for no reason, but I'm so exhausted. I was awake all night, except for five minutes of stressful dozing, every now and then. I lost count how many times I checked my phone, but every time I did, it informed me that Tom had not yet read my messages. When my clock told me that it was 6am, I pounced on my phone again, expecting to see some positive news, but no. Nothing from him or from Simon, who I had messaged through the night. Thinking they must both be up, I tried to call, but I got sent to voicemail again, and since I know that Tom doesn't have any clue how to access that, I didn't leave a message.

'I'll try again,' I say, and dial both numbers. They're still off.

'Do you have Monica's number?' Zach asks, and I shake my head.

'I did, but then she changed it, and I didn't think to ask for a new one. Something else to beat myself up about, I guess, but since I had Simon's and Tom's numbers, it never occurred to me. Why would it?'

Zach shrugs.

'That's screwed up about your boss being Monica's sister though,' he says, 'but it explains a lot about the sabotage.'

'I was thinking about this on the way home, and it does make sense – or at least it would if Monica wasn't so happy about me and Tom being in her life. If that's the case, then why would Margaret still want to screw up my job?'

My friend picks at a loose thread on his jumper but remains quiet.

'What?'

He shrugs, and brushes the thread away.

'I was thinking earlier that if Margaret is still gunning for you, then perhaps Monica isn't as happy as she's pretending to be. Maybe her sister knows Monica's real feelings and is working on her behalf.'

I stare at my friend through narrowed eyes. Why the hell is he saying this to me? As if I'm not paranoid enough about Tom being with his wicked stepmother!

I open my mouth to answer, but my phone rings. My hands shake, and I can't pick it up quick enough. It's Tom.

'Baby! How are you? I've been thinking about you all night!'

There's a silence on the line, and then my son's small voice comes rattling through.

'It's okay,' he says. 'I miss you though.'

'Aww, I miss you too, but you'll be home tomorrow. Are you on your way to London now? Are you on the train?'

I press my ear up to the phone, but I can't hear any train

noises. Instead, I think I can hear bird sounds, but perhaps I'm mistaken.

'No,' Tom says. 'Monica told me we're not going to London now. We have to stay here because my dad isn't well.'

'Your dad isn't well? What's wrong with him?'

My heart beats in my throat, as Tom's voice dips to a whisper.

'I haven't seen him since last night,' he says. 'Monica reckons he's in his room, but she won't tell me which room that is, and now I'm just hanging out on my own.'

He doesn't know what bedroom Simon is in? How big is this house? Is it a hotel? An apartment block? What?

'Tom, where are you? I'll come and pick you up right now.'

My son starts to cry, and I can feel his pain coming through the phone. I knew I shouldn't have let him go. I bloody knew it!

'I don't know where we are. We're not in the house we visited the other week. This one is next to a lake. It's big with red bricks. I loved it when we came last night, but now I don't. Monica says she doesn't like kids to use phones, so I had to hide mine in my shoe so she didn't find it. Now I just want to come home. I don't want to be here anymore.'

What's going on? My breath is so short that I can't speak, and I can't remember any words, even if I could. Zach takes the phone from me.

'Hey, Tom! It's Zach. Listen, me and your mum are going to come and pick you up, okay? But I don't have the address, so I need you to tell me if you can remember how you got to the house? Do you remember anything you saw on the way?'

I lean in so that I can hear my son's voice. He sniffs, and I can hear a muffled sound as he wipes his nose – probably on his sleeve.

'There was a pub,' he says. 'We drove for an hour and then stopped there for dinner. That's where Monica says Dad must have got ill. He had some dodgy fish, she says.'

'Do you remember what the pub was called?'

'No, but it had a rose on the sign. I remember because that's Mum's favourite flower and it made me sad that she wasn't here to see it.'

Zach and I exchange glances, and he grabs my hand and squeezes it.

'Okay, listen buddy, we're going to come and get you, okay? But do me a favour, don't mention this to Monica, because she might think it's a bit rude of you to leave before you've had time for any fun. Just carry on being yourself and reading your books and whatever, and we'll be there as soon as we can.'

Tom sniffs again, tells us he loves us, and then we hang up. My legs are shaking so much that I don't think they'll hold me up much longer. I slump down onto the chair, and clasp my hands together. I'm not a religious person, but dear God, please let my child be safe.

'What are you thinking?' Zach asks.

'I'm thinking that we need to do what we promised, and get Tom out of there as soon as we can.'

'I agree.' Zach sits next to me on the sofa, and he picks up his iPad. 'I'm going to search for pubs within driving distance that have a rose in their name. That will give us some clue about the direction they were travelling.'

I let my friend get on with his research, while I try to gather my thoughts. If Simon is ill, then who is taking care of my son? Monica does not come across as being a kid-friendly sort – no matter what she says – and the fact that Tom had to hide his phone from her, says everything I need to know. He's not happy in that house, and he needs to come home. But how do we find it? How do we know where he is?

'Right! Here's a start.' Zach passes me his iPad, open on Google Earth. He points at a tiny square, which I imagine must be a building. 'There's a pub called The Rose and Crown. It's on the road on the other side of Northampton. Only problem is, I can't imagine that they'd stop there for dinner, since it's not too far from here, and Tom says they drove for an hour.'

'Yes, but Tom is on his own time. Everything is an hour to him, regardless of how long it is. Is there a lake nearby?'

Zach runs his fingers across the screen, and the map shrinks.

'Nope. A little river, but no lake.'

'This is hopeless! I need to get to Tom. How can we do that when we don't even know where he is?'

As the words leave my mouth, a vision enters my mind. A glossy For Sale brochure... A huge, red-bricked house on the lake... An estate agent logo printed in bold across the top...

'Reid and Wright. Reid and Wright!'

My friend shakes his head.

'What are you talking about?'

'When we were having lunch with Simon and Monica, they spoke about his aunt's house, which they're now selling. It's on the lake and it's being sold by an estate agent called Reid and Wright!'

'Are you sure?'

'Positive. I remember the name because it's a play on words. Look...' I take the iPad and google the name. Sure enough, up pops an estate agent with the same name. I hand it back to Zach.

'Great. Now if they have the house in their database, we'll be able to get at least a rough idea of where it is.' He taps on the screen, and thirty seconds later we're both staring at the same photo as the one Simon showed me. 'Red Lake House, in Stoke-Welland. Is that it?'

I nod.

'It must be. I don't remember the name, but the house is the same, and so is the lake.'

'It's less than an hour away from where we are,' Zach says. He searches for it on Google Earth and nods. 'Look, it's about thirty minutes away from another Rose and Crown pub. We've found it. Come on, let's go.'

He springs out of the sofa and slips his shoes on. I follow his lead, grab my handbag and my coat, and then seconds later we're in his car.

~

'What do you make of Simon being ill?' I stare at Zach, and he shrugs.

'Like Tom says, he had the fish and it made him ill. It's not rare for that to happen. What bothers me more, is why are they at the lake house when they're supposed to be on the way to London?'

It's starting to rain, and Zach turns the windscreen wipers on. They screech across the glass, as though they can't make up their mind if they're needed or not.

'I already told you. They were going to London this morning and just staying at the house overnight.'

'It's just that Stoke-Welland is nowhere near a train station. Why would they go there, when Northampton has a direct line to London, and is just up the road from where we live? Okay, so they're no longer staying at Margaret's house, but they could have checked into a hotel for the night. It doesn't make sense to go all the way up here, when there's no public transport. You know what I mean?'

Zach takes a quick glance at me, as he drives. He's right. Why would they be in a tiny village, if the main aim was to make their journey to London quicker? They'd stay in Bromfield, or Northampton – like Zach said. The car heater is on full blast, but I'm freezing, and my brain has turned to mush. I try to call Tom, but his phone goes straight to voicemail, and the same happens with Simon.

I switch the radio on to calm my nerves, but the first song that blasts out is 'Firestarter' by The Prodigy. It's not relaxing, so I switch it off and stare out of the window. Tiny raindrops run down the glass, and remind me of the day Simon drove me to the clinic. I wanted to save my child then, and I want to save him now, but it seems to be taking hours to get there.

'How much longer?'

'According to the satnav, we'll be in Stoke-Welland in about twenty minutes. We then need to find the actual lake house, but that shouldn't be a problem. It's not a huge place.' He pats my leg. 'Don't worry, nothing is going to happen to Tom. He's just upset about his London trip, that's all.'

I thread my fingers together, and take a deep breath. I hope he's right. Yes, of course he's right. Tom is with his father, not a serial killer. He's fine. Disappointed, concerned for Simon's welfare perhaps, pissed off that he has to spend time with Monica no doubt, but not in danger.

Why would he be in danger?

I shake the words from my head and close my eyes. Fifteen minutes later, Zach shakes my arm.

'We're heading into Stoke-Welland now,' he says. 'Without a direct address, the satnav will take us to the centre of the village, so get up Google Earth on your phone, and follow the road.'

I load the app and find the road we're on.

'According to this, the lake house should be straight down here, on the right. It looks like a small entrance, so be careful you don't miss it.'

Zach slows down and we both stare at the trees and bushes on the other side of the road. Through them I can see lights in the distance, and then seconds later, the driveway appears.

'Shit, the gate is closed. We can't drive in.'

Zach pulls the car over onto the side of the road.

'I'll park here, while you see if it's locked.'

'If it is, shall I ring the bell? There's bound to be one.'

I open the door, and the cold air and rain pound down onto my coat and legs.

'I don't see why not,' Zach says. 'We're visitors, not intruders.'

I slam the door and sprint across the road. The rain splashes beneath my feet, as I make my way over wet, slimy leaves. The locked white gate stands proud at the foot of the driveway, with a postbox on one side, and an intercom on the other. A camera is pointed just above my head, and I wave at it as though my presence will inspire it to open the gate.

It doesn't.

I press the buzzer. Twice.

Nothing.

My hair sticks to my forehead, and the rain runs down my face as I look for a way into the property. Why aren't they answering? Why won't anyone let me in? Zach appears behind me, his clothes sticking to him already.

'Any luck?'

'No.'

He strides towards the gate, peers over the top and then hoists himself up onto a tiny ridge, halfway up.

'Come on, let's go.'

Normally I am a law-abiding citizen who would never think of jumping over somebody's gate without being asked, but today is different. Today I need to find my son, and if that means breaking my legs on a two-metre gate, then so be it. My friend gets to the top, and then offers his hand.

'It's okay, I've got it.'

I heave myself up to the top and together we drop down onto the gravel drive below. I lose my balance and stumble into the stones, ripping my jeans in the process. Zach reaches for my hand and helps me up.

'You okay?'

'Yes.'

The driveway is so huge it is almost a road, and we can't see the house even in the distance. The rain is lighter now, and although we're already soaked, I still welcome the brighter weather. I wipe my face on the back of my jacket, and continue the trek, until in front of us comes the now famous red-bricked house. We both stop and stare.

'Bloody hell, it's massive,' Zach says. 'No wonder Tom is homesick. I would be, too, rambling around in there.'

I can do nothing except nod.

24

Simon's inherited property is a mansion that the *Downton Abbey* characters would be proud of. Okay, it's a fraction of the size, but it is imposing enough, there's no doubt about that. As we walk closer, I can see the building in its full glory. There are three sections – the outer ones are four floors high, and the middle has three floors and imposing pillars on the ground floor. If I saw Miss Haversham standing in the top window, I wouldn't be at all surprised.

The windows on the outer sections are bowed, and it reminds me of a doll's house that my friend Sally had when we were little. Her dad built it for her one Christmas, and I was so jealous – especially when she refused to let me play with it. My dad decided to make me my own out of three shoeboxes, but it wasn't the same, and fell apart when my friend tried to force her Barbie doll in there. Now here I am, standing outside a real-life Victorian mansion, but to be honest, I'd rather be playing with the pretend one.

We arrive at the concrete steps leading up to the front door, which is flanked by the imposing pillars. I falter, as though out of my depth, but then I remember why we are here, and my feet rush up to the top step. The door knocker is in the shape of a lion, and reminds me of the one from *A Christmas Carol*. I use it and step back, waiting for somebody to walk down the hall, but nobody comes. Zach leans over and bangs it hard, but still nothing. We both stare through the window at the side of the door, but all we can see is a long, imposing hallway, and no sign of life.

'Monica! Simon! Tom! Where are you?'

I try to keep my voice light and calm, but it's hard, knowing that my son is somewhere in there, and he wants to come home. I take my phone out of my pocket and dial Tom's number. It goes straight to voicemail again, and when I try Simon's, it just rings and rings.

'There must be a back door, or some kind of tradesman's entrance,' Zach says, as he runs down the steps. I follow, and go straight to a ground-floor window and look inside. There is a sofa with gold legs, a glass coffee table and an old television sitting on a wall unit. It's the kind of ancient telly that has a huge back to it, and weighs a ton. There are also paintings on the walls, of men on horses, chasing foxes. Zach comes up behind me and puts his hands to the glass.

'This place is straight out of an episode of *The Crown*. Can you see Tom?'

'If I could, I wouldn't be standing here staring, would I?' Zach raises his eyebrows. 'Sorry. No, there's nobody in here that I can see. But then again, it's just one room in a house of dozens. Come on, we need to get inside.'

We traipse around to the back of the house, staring through each window as we go, and there's no sign of life anywhere. By the time we get to the plain green door at the back, our shoes are covered in wet leaves and mud. I suspect if Monica answers this time, she'll have a heart attack when she sees what we're bringing in with us. Zach knocks on the door with the side of his hand, and then tries it. It swings open, and our mouths fall open.

'Didn't expect that,' Zach says, and we both step into the kitchen, muddy shoes and all.

The kitchen is warm and smells of burnt toast and coffee. There is a half-drunk cup on the table, but it is cold to the touch, and has a skin on top of it. My stomach rumbles. I haven't had anything to eat for hours. I can't remember the last time I was hungry. Yesterday? The day before? I don't know. I cross the room, swing open the door, and we're into the long hall, covered in a thick, red-and-black runner carpet. There are doors on either side and we push each one open as we go.

'Tom! Tom!'

'Monica! Simon!'

Nothing.

'Where are they? Why can't they hear us shouting?'

'It's a big house,' Zach says. 'They could be anywhere.'

We reach a huge staircase at the front of the house, which wouldn't look out of place in an old black-and-white movie. The banister is polished and shiny, but the red carpet looks dull, as though covered with dust. There are black-and-white tiles leading from the staircase to the front door, and my shoes make a squeaking sound as I walk over them.

'Shall we go up?'

Zach bites his lip and then shouts for Tom once more. When there is no reply, my friend takes the stairs two at a time, and I'm right behind him. We get to the top and the landing extends round from one side to the other.

'Tom? Are you here?'

When Tom doesn't answer, Zach rubs his eyes, turns and stares over the top banister.

'Are you sure this is the house you saw in the picture?'

'Yes, definitely. Shit, Zach! What the hell is going on? Where's Tom?'

His name catches in the back of my throat, and tears spring to my eyes. What has happened to my son? I can't cope with the possible answers to that. Although I've got my phone on full volume, I still check to see if I've missed any calls, and then I try to call Simon again. There is no answer, but just as I'm about to hang up, Zach grabs my arm.

'What?'

'Can you hear that?'

We both hold our breath and sure enough, somewhere in the far reaches of the house, a phone is ringing.

'Where is that coming from? Simon? Simon?'

I rush down the hallway, opening one door after another, and the phone continues to call out, getting louder and louder with each step. I stop outside a white, wood-panelled door, and it is clear that the ringing is coming from inside the room. I hesitate – a moment of lucidity, wondering what Simon will think if he sees me waltzing around his house like I own the place. Zach has no such qualms, and springs the door open.

A horrendous stench hits us, and we both gag and put our hands up to our noses. I try to hold my breath, but it's no good, and as I inhale, I can feel the dank air invade my nose, my throat and my lungs.

'What is that?'

I stare at Zach, but he doesn't reply. Instead, he takes a tentative step inside the room, while I hover at the door, my shaking legs unable or unwilling to move.

'Oh my God!'

'What?'

Zach is motionless and mute, which prompts me to gather enough energy to follow him in.

Though I soon wish I hadn't.

Simon lies on the bed; his head pointed towards the door, eyes open, with a trail of vomit dried to his cheek, and gathered on the pillow beneath him. His face is grey, his hair stuck to his head, and his arms are ramrod straight on top of the covers.

Even from ten feet away, I can see that my ex-lover is dead, but that doesn't stop me from shouting his name at the top of my voice. I don't know why, but I half expect him to blink, rub his eyes and ask me what on earth's going on. Except he doesn't, and the realisation that he has gone makes everything worse. I run to his body and go to touch him, but Zach grabs me and pulls me away before I have the chance.

'Don't touch him,' he says. 'Don't go anywhere near him.'

The next few minutes is intense, and even though Zach and I share many words, everything is muted, surrounded in a cloud of sorrow and confusion. How am I supposed to react to this? Ten years ago, this man was my lover, but he was never really mine. He never really belonged to me. Since he's been back in my life, he's done his best to be good to Tom, but in spite of that, my biggest memory of him will always be that he didn't want his son in the first place. I have no right to mourn him, but his death gives me no joy. It just leaves me feeling numb.

'Shall I phone an ambulance?'

I stare at Zach, as though he has all the answers, but he doesn't reply. Instead, he flings the window open, gagging as he does so.

'No,' he gulps. 'Phone the police.'

I try to unlock my phone, but my shaking hands make it impossible. Three times I enter the passcode, and three times it says it's incorrect.

'Shit! I can't do this. My hands won't work.'

'Give it to me.'

Zach takes the phone from me, I tell him the code, and he

unlocks the handset. As he does so, I hear the roar of an engine, and I rush to the window.

'It's Margaret!'

Zach drops the phone onto the bottom of the bed, and stares down at the drive.

'Your principal? Monica's sister?'

'Yes. She must have known that they were here when I saw her last night. Lying bitch!'

I race out of the bedroom, and take the stairs two at a time, until I'm faced with the heavy front door. I can hear Margaret trudge up the stairs outside, and as she presses the bell, I look around for the key.

There isn't one.

Zach reaches me in the hallway; his own phone pressed to his ear. Just as he does so, Margaret stares in at us through the window at the side of the door. Her mouth falls open, and she throws her arms up in the air.

'Charlotte!'

The word rings in my ears, as I bound down the hallway, and into the kitchen. The door is still open from when we entered earlier, and I throw myself out into the cold, morning air, and sprint round the corner to face the principal. No matter what has gone on between us during the last few weeks, I still need her help. This is not the time to hold grudges.

'Margaret! You've got to help us. Simon is upstairs. He's gone... He's...'

My boss rushes down the steps towards me, her flared jeans wafting as she does so.

'What do you mean he's gone? Where has he gone?'

'He's dead! I mean that he's dead!'

My entire body shakes, and Margaret grabs my arms.

'Are you sure?'

'I'm positive. My friend is calling the police.'

Margaret wipes her mouth on the back of her hand, and exhales, just before Zach appears behind me. His breath is short and fast from the sprint around the building.

'The operator says they will send someone as soon as possible. There's been a pile-up on the dual carriageway, and they're down to limited resources.'

'Did you tell them it's an emergency?'

Zach nods his head.

'Yes, but there's nothing they can do for him, so...' He pushes his phone into his back pocket. 'They'll be here soon, I'm sure.'

'We need to find Tom. I can't have him seeing Simon like that.'

Margaret looks over my shoulder, and points towards a row of bushes that runs along the drive.

'Here he is now.'

We turn and sure enough, there is Tom with Monica. Both of them hold fishing rods, and I can hear Monica's voice, jabbering away like a demented seal. What is she doing? Doesn't she know that her husband is dead upstairs? It appears not.

'Tom!'

My son drops his fishing rod on the ground, and bounds towards me.

'Mum!!'

'Hello, baby,' I say, as he lunges into my arms. Zach ruffles his hair, and Tom smiles up at him.

'Good to see you, Champ,' he says. 'I told you we'd find you.'

My son stares at Margaret. He doesn't know why she's here, but he's so used to seeing her every day, that it doesn't occur to him to ask. Monica arrives beside us; a frown tattooed across her forehead.

'What are you doing here? We're supposed to have Tom for the entire weekend.' If she knows anything about Simon,

Monica doesn't show it. Instead, she scowls at Margaret. 'Did you tell her we were here?'

Margaret ignores the question, and I can't help but notice that Monica doesn't seem to be in any shock that her sister is on the property. These two are total opposites – Monica is obviously the power-dresser of the family, with her sleek bob and silky suits, while Margaret must surely be the family reject, with her flower-power style that's better suited to someone half her age. Still, they have a sisterly connection that goes beyond anything I've known. For Margaret to take revenge on me for something I did to her sister ten years ago, shows just how strong their bond is. Even if it makes no sense to me at all.

My eyes flit from one to the other, and water floods into my mouth as if I'm going to be sick. What is Monica going to say when she finds out Simon is dead? Or... Or does she know already? Oh God, did she do something to the father of my child? My stomach can take no more pain, and I run to the bushes, and throw up the few scraps of food I've managed to eat during the past twenty-four hours.

'Mum!! Are you okay?'

Tom and Zach appear behind me, as I wipe my mouth on an old tissue I find in the depths of my pocket.

'I'm okay,' I say. 'I'll be okay.'

'Did you eat some fish, too?' Tom asks, and I shake my head and try to get myself back together.

'No, I didn't have any fish. I've just got a bit of tummy trouble, that's all.'

Zach makes sure I've recovered, before heading back to Monica and Margaret. Monica's face is screwed up, as she stares over at the bushes. The idea of somebody being sick anywhere near her property must be frightful for her.

'I'll ask again,' she snaps. 'What are you doing here?'

'The question shouldn't be why we're here,' Zach says. 'The

question should be why did you tell Charlotte that you were going to London, when all the time you were coming to this house in the middle of nowhere? What's the deal with that?'

Monica glowers at him. The last time she saw Zach was the day we visited her house – Margaret's house – looking for Simon. There's no way she's going to answer any of his questions, but he keeps going.

'Did you have any intention of taking Tom to London? Or is this some kind of incident that we need to report to the police?'

'Zach!' I motion towards Tom, but he's too busy playing with a snail to notice our conversation.

'Mum, I'm going to put this snail on a bush, so that he doesn't get stood on.'

He holds the creepy-crawly an inch from my nose, and I try not to look repulsed.

'Okay,' I say, and Tom skips off towards the shrubbery at the other side of the road. Margaret steps forward.

'Monica, we need to talk…' Her voice trails off, as Tom reappears. 'We need to talk without Tom.'

My son looks from Margaret to Monica, and then Zach puts his hand around Tom's shoulder.

'Come on. Let's go and open the front gate, in case the postman needs to deliver some post. Then you can show me where you were fishing. Did you catch any big ones?'

As they walk away, I can hear Tom telling Zach all about a dead frog that he found washed up at the side of the lake. My heart breaks when I think about how that's not the only loss of life he'll have to contend with this weekend.

25

'W hat's going on?'

Monica's voice comes at us on a wave of suspicion and aggravation. Having started the conversation, Margaret now stares at the ground, which leaves me to deal with the fallout. I lick my lips, and they're dry and cracked against my tongue. How am I going to tell her that Simon is dead? Does she already know? How do I deal with this situation?

'Somebody needs to tell me what's going on,' she snaps. 'Or I swear...'

'Simon's dead!' Margaret throws her arms in the air, and eyeballs her sister. 'You wanted to know? There you go. Your husband is dead.'

Monica stumbles backwards, straight into one of the pillars that decorates the house. Her breathing is shallow, erratic, and she puts her hand to her throat, as though that will help her to get a breath.

'That's a lie! You know that's a lie!' Monica stumbles up the front stairs and rattles on the door, but it's still locked fast. She turns back towards Margaret, her face screwed into a ball of rage. 'How could you? How could you be so evil as to say that?

Simon is upstairs, sleeping off a bout of food poisoning. He was fine when I saw him earlier. He was asleep!'

If Monica had anything to do with Simon's death, she's hiding it well. I step forward and reach for her arm, but she pushes me away, and then sprints off towards the back of the house.

'Monica!'

Margaret and I follow her; together but apart. The woman who has made my working life a misery over the past weeks, is now on the same mission as myself, but I'd do anything to get away from her.

We reach Monica just as she pushes open the back door and rushes into the kitchen. I grab her arm, and she spins round, bouncing off the old wooden table as she does so. The cup and fruit bowl vibrate, and the table legs make a screeching sound against the tiles.

'What?'

Monica's face crumples, and she ages ten years before my eyes. Her long eyelashes are clotted with mascara, and there is a line of unblended concealer drawn across her left cheekbone. She grabs onto the side of the table, and her body deflates like a burst balloon. She knows what I'm going to say, but the words are still almost impossible to share.

'Monica, I'm afraid Margaret is telling the truth. I saw Simon ten minutes ago. He's gone. I'm so sorry.'

I expect her to burst into tears, or faint or have some kind of animated response, but instead, she slumps down into a chair, and says nothing at all. I lean towards her, but Margaret grabs me. I can feel her long fingernails digging in through my coat, and it takes all my energy not to push her off.

'Leave her,' Margaret says. 'It'll sink in soon enough. Where is he? I should go up and see him.'

'He's...'

My voice trails off, as Monica pounces out of the chair and points her finger into Margaret's face.

'You made this up, didn't you? You're doing it to spite me! Saying that Simon is dead, so that you can swing in and take him back. You're pathetic!!'

Monica's voice is so high-pitched, that my first reaction is to cringe and cover my ears, but then some of her words stick in my mind. 'Take him back.' What does she mean by that? I look over at Margaret, but her blank face reveals nothing at all.

'I need to see him,' Monica cries. 'I need to see my husband.'

She half stumbles, half falls down the hall, but by the time she reaches the stairs, she's out of breath and gasping for air.

'Monica! You've got to stop. Sit down and get your breath back.' She gawps at me, and then slides down onto the stairs, her hand clenched around the polished spindles. Her breathing is erratic, but I rub her back, and slowly she starts to calm down.

'I need to see my husband,' she says. Monica's eyes are wide and they glisten with tears, while her knuckles turn white as she grips onto the banister. Margaret offers no help whatsoever, and is quite happy to stand back and watch as I try to diffuse the situation. A bit like at school, really. She is always able to hand over an ill child, without any thought for their well-being – or mine. God forbid she should ever get her hands dirty.

'It's better if you don't go upstairs,' I say. 'The police won't want anyone to go into the room until they've checked Simon over, and besides – I'm sure you'd rather not see him that way.'

'What way?'

Margaret steps forward and slaps her hand against the banister.

'Oh, for God's sake! She means dead! You don't want to see him dead!'

Monica ignores her sister's words and before I can stop her, she heaves herself up, and stumbles her way up the stairs, calling Simon's name as she goes. Margaret and I follow her up to the first floor and along the corridor, and as Monica flings open the bedroom door, the wind from the open window whips in, freezes my body and stings my eyes. Simon's body stares at us from the bed, just as it did when I saw it before, only now the shock of finding him has been replaced with a flood of emotions that hit me right in the centre of my heart.

This man was a mystery to me, I cannot deny that. When I was nineteen years old, he made me feel beautiful, wanted, embarrassed, unloved, and discarded, all in the space of a couple of months. He spun a web of lies, and left me at my most vulnerable, but when he returned to my life, he did try to have a relationship with his son, which is something I suppose. Isn't it? I didn't want him in our lives, but he persisted, in spite of my wishes. Was that because he had Tom's best interests at heart? Or did he want me to suffer? I have no idea, and I'll never find the answers, standing here, in this doorway, with these two strange women.

We all stand statue-like. Nobody saying a word for what seems like hours, until out of nowhere, Monica howls, runs to the bed and throws herself at Simon's body.

'Don't you leave me!' she shouts, as she tries to lift him into her arms. He's too heavy though, and flops back onto the bed, his head now stuffed between two pillows. Monica collapses onto the duvet and sobs, while Margaret steps forward. Slowly. Cautiously.

'Monica,' she whispers, and touches her sister's shoulder. Monica doesn't flinch. It's as though all of her energy has drained from her body and sunk into the bed. Margaret tries again, and this time Monica lifts her head, her normally pristine hair stuck to her face with tears and snot.

'Leave... Me... Alone...' she snarls, and elbows Margaret in the ribs. She flinches, but it doesn't faze her. She's made of tougher stuff.

'You can't stay in here,' Margaret says. 'You don't want to see your husband this way...'

Monica turns on her sister, her teeth clenched and her nostrils flared.

'Unlike you!' she snaps.

Margaret steps back, and her bottom hits off the dressing table. A long, thin ceramic vase tumbles onto the floor, and comes to a standstill at her foot. She looks down and kicks it under the table, where I'm sure it will be lost forever.

'What do you mean by that?'

'You've wanted him dead for years.' Monica sniffs. 'Well, here he is! Dead! You must be thrilled!'

'Oh, yes of course!' Margaret snaps. 'Death always fills me with joy. Maybe you could drop dead too, and we'd all be happy!'

In the time we've been in this room, I haven't said a word, and see no reason to get involved now, but how do I handle this? My ex-lover lies in the bed, while his wife and sister-in-law go for each other's throats just inches away. This is all too weird; too horrifying. I came here to collect my son, and now I'm faced with death and a destructive sibling relationship.

I want to grab my son and take him home, but I have to wait for the police to come, so that I can tell them how we found Simon's body, and why it has now been moved. Does it count if it's been moved just a few feet? I have no idea, since I've never been in this situation, but the idea of talking to the police fills me with horror. How can I give a statement about such a terrible event? And afterwards, how am I supposed to tell Tom that the man he has just come to know after almost ten years, has now been taken from him? It's all too much, but I have to say something. I can't let this situation carry on.

'Your arguing isn't going to make things any better,' I say. 'I have a son who hasn't been told that his father has passed, and I can't have you two blurting it out in the middle of a fight. Tom deserves more. Simon deserved more!'

Monica purses her lips and scowls, while Margaret bursts out laughing.

'Oh, here she goes! The mother of his child has spoken!'

'What?'

'You! Little Miss Perfect! The woman who had Simon's child. Even if he didn't want the little runt, but that meant nothing to you, did it?'

I can't believe how full of vitriol Margaret is. I kind of understood her hating me on her sister's behalf, but she seems to hate Monica just as much. Nothing makes sense, but I try to remain calm.

'It was ten years ago,' I say. 'Time has moved on and it's pointless going back over old ground. Simon's dead, and I know you're pissed off that I had an affair with him behind your sister's back, but if she can forgive me, why can't you?'

Margaret launches forward, and her face is so close to mine that I can smell her cigarette breath. As she speaks, spit splatters onto my cheeks, and I close my eyes and pray that she'll disappear.

'You don't get it, do you?' she shouts. 'You didn't have an affair behind Monica's back, you did it behind mine! I was Simon's wife when he was with you! I was the woman he wanted to leave for you!'

26

Someone once said that there are three sides to a story – his, hers and the truth. The truth in the case of Simon, his wife and I, lies somewhere in the middle. As I stand in the same room as Monica and the first Mrs Travis, I realise that ten years ago I didn't have any clue what Simon's wife was called. Her name must have been Margaret, but he used to call her M or Her, or That Bitch, and that was good enough for me. Some may say I was stupid not to find out what her name was, but in my defence, I was just a teenager in love, with no interest whatsoever in my married lover's wife. Why would I want to know anything about her? He was going to leave her for me anyway, wasn't he? Besides, why should it be strange that he called her M? My Aunt Melanie was always known as M, so what was the difference? None that I could see.

Ten years later, when I saw Simon in Waterstones, I just presumed that Monica was the wife he had when he was with me. She was old enough, her personality seemed to match from what Simon had told me, her name began with M, so why would I think she wasn't the old Mrs Travis?

Maybe because I was stupid.

Brain-dead.

And now I'm paying the price.

Margaret – the first Mrs Travis – grins at me, like the cat who got the cream, as my old granny would have said. Monica remains mute; sitting on the bed, staring into space and alone in her thoughts. Perhaps she is completely innocent in all this, but if so, why did she want to involve herself in my pregnancy? What was the point of that?

'I can tell that your mind is whirring,' Margaret says.

'You could say that. Monica told me that she found out about me after hearing Simon on the phone to the clinic. She followed me there with the intention of asking me to give her the baby. How could that be the case, if you were married to him then? Was it all a lie?'

Monica's face flashes back into consciousness, and she jumps up from the bed.

'I wanted to keep him,' she says. 'Simon and I had been having an affair for years, but the bastard would never leave Margaret. What I told you was true – I thought that if you would give me the baby, it could force his hand into going further with our relationship... Then he would leave Margaret, and accept me and the child as his new family. But in the end, I couldn't do it. Asking you to give up your baby was too bizarre even for me, so in the end I kept quiet.'

My legs turn to string. Simon was seeing me and Monica behind Margaret's back? This is mental. It's all too much.

'You got him in the end though!' Margaret shouts. 'Child or no child, you wore him down and off he went. Goal achieved!'

'Ha! I may have got him, but you still insisted on being his friend, though, didn't you? You couldn't keep away!'

My blood feels as though it's pouring into my feet. Watching these two women argue over their relationship with Simon, when he lies dead right next to us, is freaky and disturbing. I don't even know what to think about his passing. I stare at his cold body, but it gives away no clues. Could food poisoning cause him to die? And so soon? Why am I thinking about this? Where are the police? I just want to go home.

'Oh, please!' Margaret snaps. 'I kept in touch with you because you're my sister, and our neurotic, coercive mother wouldn't let me break ties. "It'll be bad for family dynamics", blah, blah, blah. Besides, you were happy to be in touch with me when it suited you. If we had fallen out, you wouldn't have had a home to come to, when you came back to Northamptonshire. You'd have had to stay in this creepy dive, in the middle of nowhere.' She throws her arms in the air. 'Ugh! I'm done with this. I'm going home.'

Margaret pushes past me and heads back into the hall, but Monica is quick to follow. I take one last look at the father of my child crumpled on the bed, head hidden between the pillows, and arms splayed out at his sides. I have so much to say, and yet I have nothing. Except maybe goodbye.

I leave the room and quietly close the door behind me, as though slamming it might cause Simon to be disturbed. The fighting siblings stand at the top of the stairs now, still throwing barbs at each other; still trying to prove that they were the loves of Simon's life. I don't know which one would wear that crown, but I do know that it's not me. I have to get out of this house. I need to find my friend and my son, and run far away from this hellish place.

But first I have a question.

'If you knew I was Simon's ex-girlfriend, why did you even give me a job? And why has it taken this long for you to hate me?'

Margaret looks up and laughs, as I make my way towards them. It is a guttural snort that reaches the very centre of my brain.

'Charlotte, I had no idea that you – or your son – were associated with Simon when we first met. It's only been since Monica came back to town that I've known. Until then, I had no idea that Simon had a child with you or with anyone, but my sister was more than happy to give me that information. After that, it seemed sensible to bring Simon into school as a speaker. I wanted to see his reaction; throw some petrol onto the fire of his relationship with Monica.'

'So, I was just a pawn in your game with your sister?'

She lights a cigarette, takes a long drag and then exhales it into my face, causing my throat to dry to dust, and my eyes to burn.

'That was part of the plan, but as we have seen, Monica decided to reinvent herself as stepmother of the year, so that kind of backfired on me. But I also wanted to see the sickly smile wiped off your face, and that certainly worked. All those years of being this pretty little receptionist, ever smiling, ever helpful, ever friendly... And all that time you were yet another one who had screwed my husband, and his bastard child was walking the halls of my school. Don't you know how disgusting that is?'

I think back to the working relationship I had with Margaret over the years, and can't believe that I never knew who she was. But how could I have known? I may be many things, but a mind reader is not one of them.

'You wanted to take your revenge on me, by bringing Simon into our lives?'

'I wanted revenge on you all,' she snaps. 'Why should I live a dejected life, because you, Monica and Simon took what you wanted, without a thought for my feelings at all? I wanted to cause as much disruption for you, as you did for me.'

Margaret takes another drag on her cigarette, stubs it out on the polished banister, and then throws it into a gigantic pot plant at the side of the stairs.

'You've always been one for revenge, haven't you, Margaret?' Monica rubs her eyes, and leaves a stripe of mascara across her temples. 'You act like you're so damn innocent, but you made my life hell growing up. Always telling on me for some misdemeanour or another. You loved to see me upset. Well look at me now! Does this make you happy?'

Monica wipes her nose on the back of her hand, as more tears tumble down her cheeks. If Margaret feels any sympathy at all, she doesn't show it. Instead, she flings her head back and laughs, like some kind of baddie from a cartoon.

'Oh, I'm happy all right, but not in the way you think.'

'What do you mean?'

Margaret points down the corridor.

'You think that Simon died because he ate a bit of fish? Think again!'

'What do you mean?'

'I mean that when the police perform the post-mortem on him, they won't find any killer fish in his system. No, they'll find your sleeping pills. You left them on the counter while you were still in my house, so I dissolved them into Simon's bottle of whisky. You're so out of it most of the time that you didn't even notice they were gone! I must say, I had hoped they'd knock him off before now, but I guess he was keeping his Scotch for a special occasion, like this weekend. You know how our fabulous husband loves a good celebration!'

My blood runs cold. Did I hear this right? Margaret is admitting to the murder of Simon, but is happy to let her sister take the blame? Yes. Yes, I'm pretty sure that's what I just heard. I don't like Monica, but I can't let this happen to her. I need to get her away from this madhouse.

'Come on!'

I grab Monica by the arm, but she turns and slaps me across

the face. My ear buzzes from the contact, and I rub at my irritated skin.

'What the hell was that for?'

'You! If you hadn't come into our lives, none of this would have happened!'

I can't believe what I'm hearing. This is the woman who told her sister who I was, and then encouraged a relationship between Simon and Tom, when I was hesitant for them to even meet. How is that my fault? How is any of this my fault?

'I wanted nothing to do with either of you,' I say. 'I'd have happily gone through my life without any contact at all, but you and Simon were the ones who wanted Tom and I in your life. You were the ones who wanted him to spend the weekend with you!'

'You don't get it, do you?'

Monica scowls at me, as though I'm the stupidest person she has ever come across. Maybe I am, because I don't understand anything at all.

'I'm sure you'll enlighten me.'

'Simon didn't want you in his life, he just wanted Tom. That's why we said we were going to London this weekend, so that you wouldn't know what was going to happen. We were supposed to head to Dover this morning, so we could get Tom out of the country and away from you. Simon hated the way you were raising his son – drinking with strangers on weekdays, letting Tom walk down the river on his own, and throwing a fit when Simon bought him a little gift. We were going to give him a wonderful, safe life in Europe, but then Simon got ill overnight, and it all went to hell.'

The hairs on the back of my arms tingle, as I think about what could have been. What were they going to do? Hide Tom in the boot of their car while they boarded the train? Or were they planning on using the ferry? I have no idea, but I do know this...

I always knew I was right not to trust her and Simon, but everyone around me persuaded me otherwise; told me that I was a terrible mother if I didn't let my son have contact with his father, and like a fool I believed them. I should have listened to my instincts.

I know Monica is expecting a reaction from me, but I refuse to give her one. How dare they think I am an unfit mother? What gave them any right to decide that, based on a couple of weeks' contact with Tom? I can't be around Monica any longer. I need to phone the police to see where the hell they are. I slide my hand into my pocket, but my handset isn't there. Shit, I gave it to Zach, and he dropped it onto Simon's bed. It must be still there.

I leave the evil sisters on the steps, and sprint down the corridor towards the bedroom. I'll retrieve my phone as quickly as I can, and then find Zach and Tom and get the hell out of here. I reach the room, and I'm just about to push open the door, when I hear it.

A scream so raw, it's almost primal.

I run back up the corridor, and see Monica and Margaret arguing at the top of the stairs, exchanging insults that go back years, decades even. From the large window in front of me, I can see down into the garden, where Zach and Tom walk back towards the house. I cannot have these women fighting in front of my son, so I rush forward with the intention of breaking them up before Tom arrives on the scene. It is then that I notice Margaret is clutching a large knife, and the blade is pointed towards Monica's face.

'You were always jealous of me!' Margaret sneers, and the light from the window catches off the knife as she waggles it up and down. 'Ever since we were kids, you always wanted what I had. Every doll I owned, every book I read, every piece of plastic jewellery in my trinket box. Everything!! Then when we were older, you always had to dress up when you knew my boyfriends were coming over. Every other day, you'd be in your jeans and T-shirt, but the moment the doorbell rang, there'd you'd be, make-up plastered on your face, and the tightest skirt on your scrawny body!'

Margaret rages at Monica, but fear of the knife prevents her sister from retaliating. Instead, she cowers against the wall. All I can do is stand in silence and watch; my feet rooted to the floor.

'Please, Margaret,' she says. 'Please don't do this. I know we've had our differences, but at the end of the day, we're sisters.'

'You don't know the meaning of the word!' screams Margaret. 'If you did, you'd never have gone out to steal my husband. Two years you were with him behind my back! Two years! And even when I found out about you and took that overdose... Even then you carried on! You couldn't get him away quick enough! But I'll tell you something... The moment you came back to Bromfield, I started sleeping with Simon again. How does that make you feel?'

Monica's mouth falls open, and her chest rises and falls as the shock of Margaret's words hits her.

'You're lying. Simon would never do that. He would never cheat on me.'

It's probably inappropriate for me to even think about this subject, but I can't help remembering the times Monica told me she wanted Simon to settle down. It was clear she didn't trust him, but what did she expect? He was seeing me and her behind his wife's back, so what hope did Monica have of him being faithful to her? Margaret points the knife at me, as she talks to her sister. It catches the sun and sends shards of light across the stark, white wall.

'Your precious husband was seeing this one when he was married to me, and sleeping with you. What makes you think he'd ever change?'

The sisters stare at each other, and neither says a word. I wonder if this is the end of it, but before I have chance to back away, Margaret lunges at Monica with the knife. Both women scream – Monica out of sheer terror, and Margaret as she loses her balance, and falls backwards down the long, unforgiving staircase. Her body spirals and lurches, and the knife catches her stomach as she falls. Then finally, she lands at the bottom, her head cracking on the vicious hall tiles.

And then there is only silence.

Margaret lies at the bottom of the stairs, her neck appears broken, and a stream of blood cascades out of her ear. The knife lies next to her open hand, and Monica runs down the steps, shouting her sister's name, over and over again.

'Margaret! Margaret!' Monica stares up at me, her eyes full of water. 'I didn't touch her.'

'I know you didn't. But for God's sake, take the knife away from her… Just in case.'

Monica leans forward and takes the knife out of Margaret's hand, just as I look up and see Zach's face in the window next to the front door. I rush down the stairs, past the sisters and look for the key. It's sitting right there on the little oak table, next to the door. How did I not see that before? I slide the key into the lock and then manage to heave open the wooden door. The cold autumn air floods into the hallway, and the low sun catches my eyes. As I hold up my hand to protect me from the bright light, Zach stares past me towards Margaret's body, and then back to the concrete steps, where my son is climbing up with a huge stick in his hand.

'Fuck!'

Zach shouts at Tom to stay away, and as he does so, a police car crunches up the driveway, stops and a young constable gets out. I sprint out of the house, down the steps and over to meet him.

'Please! Come quickly!' I say, and we both run into the house, where Margaret's mangled body lies next to her shocked sister.

'What happened?' The policeman takes out his phone, but it is far too late to help. I point towards Monica.

'Please help us! This woman – Monica Travis – has attempted to kidnap my son, she's threatened me with a knife, and murdered two people, including my son's father.' Tears flood down my cheeks, and my breath bubbles at the back of my throat.

'She murdered your son's father?' The policeman is confused, as he should be.

'Yes! He's upstairs. Monica admitted that she'd poisoned him with her own pills, because she suspected he was having an affair with her sister.' I point to Margaret's body, crumpled in front of us. 'When Margaret admitted it was true, Monica went after her with the knife, and then threw her down the stairs.'

Monica gawps at me; her face white, her jaw slack and her nostrils flared. We all ogle the knife in her hand, and she drops it to the floor.

'I didn't do anything!' she cries. 'I didn't do anything at all!'

The policeman steps forward to restrain Monica, as she stares at me through wide, wounded eyes.

'Are you okay?' Zach asks, and I nod. As he takes me in his arms, I see Tom, cowering on the patch of grass, his face covered in tears. Despite my attempts to keep him from the drama, my son has heard every word of what I just said to the policeman. I run out of the house, down the steps and throw out my arms.

'Tom! Come here, baby!'

I scoop my son up, and give him a huge hug.

'Did Monica really kill my dad and Mrs Holmes?'

I wipe his tears with the back of my sleeve, and kiss his damp cheek.

'Yes, she did,' I say. 'I'm afraid she wasn't a very nice person after all.'

As another police car zooms up the drive, we move to the side of the lawn, and I look back through the open door, just in time to see Monica being handcuffed and read her rights. She stares at me, and I stare right back. I told her that if my son was ever upset in her care, I wouldn't be responsible for my actions, but maybe she didn't believe me. Well, now she knows. I might have given up my acting classes all those years ago, but I'm still one hell of an actress.

THE END

ACKNOWLEDGEMENTS

It has been such a joy to write my second novel, and I couldn't have done it without the love and support of my family, friends and readers. I thank you, each and every one...

Mum and Dad – Thank you so much for all of the encouragement you continue to give me, and for being excited about the projects that have come my way this year. Even when we're not together, I can always feel your love heading in my direction, and I'll always be grateful that you're mine.

Paul, Wendy and Angelina – Thank you for all of your love, support and encouragement. Look, Angelina – Silly Aunty Shell wrote another book!

Claire, Helen, Loraine, Sharon, Katharine and Jackie – Thank you for all the laughs, chatter and love in our WhatsApp group. I am so grateful for the support we give to each other, even when we're far away.

To my reader friends – Thank you so much for buying my books and making my dreams come true. Because of you, I am able to continue writing my stories, and sharing my love for books. I am tremendously grateful to each and every one of you, and hope that I can share my work with you for many years to come.

To Betsy, Fred, Ian, Tara and everyone at Bloodhound – Thank you for giving me a home for my stories, and for being a constant source of encouragement for me. I am grateful every day that I sent my first novel to you. It changed my career and my life. Thank you so much!

Finally, to my amazing husband, Richard, and beautiful daughter, Daisy – Thank you for everything you do for me every, single day. Your love is a constant source of joy for me, and I can't imagine my life without you. Daisy, never forget that all my dreams came true, because of you. I love you both. xx

A NOTE FROM THE PUBLISHER

Thank you for reading this book. If you enjoyed it please do consider leaving a review on Amazon to help others find it too.

We hate typos. All of our books have been rigorously edited and proofread, but sometimes mistakes do slip through. If you have spotted a typo, please do let us know and we can get it amended within hours.

info@bloodhoundbooks.com

Made in the USA
Monee, IL
15 August 2021